STINGERS

KENNETH PASSAN

SEVERED PRESS

HOBART TASMANIA

STINGERS

PROLOGUE

Over a short period of time the fertilized eggs developed into larval planulae. These settled onto firm surfaces located on the sea bed and gradually developed into polyps.

For several years, the polyps remained as such, feeding at will when their food floated by. When the time finally arrived, they began another transformation into a form that is a precursor to its final adult stage, called an ephyra.

Now they have begun to look like what they are. After further development, they matured once again into the final stage of their transformations, the medusa stage. For some species, the initial stage would be the most important one of all. For these hundreds, perhaps thousands, of maturing creatures, they may not gain much more in size, but their deadliness will precede their reputation.

At the ephyra stage they will already have become self-mobile. The medusa stage is the final and complete fulfillment of what they were meant to be and are. They've been around for millions of years, and may even outlive man when the time arrives. They are survivors which have always been and will always be. They neither elicit nor obtain any affection for anything, not even for themselves. They are things now that swim or float, uncaring about anything except eating; asexual, going wherever the elements take them, and doing what they are meant to do to anything that gets in their way. They are unstoppable and uncontrollable. And they will soon be on their way.

The currents and tides will have an effect on when and in which direction they will go. Although they can swim, it's slow going and uses up their energy. They prefer to save that energy and go with the flow.

As polyps, they weren't very mobile. But now having fulfilled all the requirements of full adulthood they're ready to tackle the world. Where they go and end up, nothing or no one knows until it's too late. They feel the current picking up and they're starting on the move. The time has arrived and they are now on their way.

CHAPTER 1

Pompano Beach, July 30

The summer could have been a typical Florida one of any year. It was July, hot and humid. How else could one describe such a sunny day in Pompano Beach? Palm trees, beautiful weather, white puffy clouds floating across the sky, leaving the sun alone to exhibit its full, bright glory. For someone visiting Florida, it would be just perfect except for the ninety-five plus degree heat which, by itself, would have been quite tolerable. Add the humidity to that and you have the feeling that you are being melted down into nothingness while water is pouring out of you.

The locals don't even bother going to the beaches, despite their overpowering welcoming sights. Under the hot summer sun, without sandals the feet can burn. Without lots of sunscreen, everywhere else on the body that's exposed can burn. Going into the ocean for a nice refreshing dip at this time of year will leave you feeling like you're swimming in sweat. For the uninitiated to Florida's outdoor activities such as swimming, during the summer one can very quickly realize that there is no such thing as a refreshing dip, whether it be in the ocean or any outdoor swimming pool without water temperature regulators. It's virtually an instant wakeup call that tells you that you're in the right place but at the wrong time.

The city with its beautiful beaches is in Broward county, about thirty one miles north of Miami on the state's Atlantic coast. Its average high temperature is ninety-one to ninety two degrees Fahrenheit. It has been known to reach a temperature of a hundred and seven degrees Fahrenheit, which set the record there for a high. Average yearly temperatures are about eighty three degrees.

As with most cities, populations can fluctuate from year to year. Annually the influxes of migrants from other states to move to Florida varies in their numbers while remaining a constant source of new residents to the state.

At the same time, tourism continues to flourish in almost every part of Florida, although more in some locations than others. Pompano Beach is one of those locations. But with Florida having the summer climate that it does, and although tourism is at its lowest during the summer months primarily because of the heat and humidity, there are always still a few who will brave the temperatures and even the regular thunderstorms that invade the area for whatever reasons they may have. The locals know who they are when they see them walking on the beach or going into the water. They may smirk at their foolhardiness but decide, well if that's what they want to do, more power to them.

It was one day at the end of July-the thirtieth to be exact, that two couples visiting Pompano Beach from Kansas City, Missouri decided to do just that.

Being from a home location that was landlocked, even this beach during the summer was a real treat for them. But even landlubbers can feel the heat of sand under an all-day burning sun. It didn't take them long to decide to keep wearing their sandals. As for laying on the sun to try and get a nice tan, well that kind of went by the wayside also. Renting a couple of umbrellas and chairs for the four of them appeared to be their only option, and they took advantage of that.

With only a few other brave souls on the beach, it was almost as if they had the beach to themselves.

Samuel Castrella, or Sam as he preferred to be called, was a twenty two year old, dark haired, dark-eyed six-footer who was just a tad on the heavyset side. As a beginning accountant back home, he was just starting out in his career and hadn't been too involved in any kind of athletic activities. He had always been more of a book and numbers worm than anything else. But he'd always enjoy an opportunity to swim in a friend's pool when he could.

His girlfriend, Julie Rondike, found him attractive and had been an item with him for about two years. She liked the fact that he was clean shaven because she didn't particularly care for facial hair. But she cared enough for Sam that she would have accepted that in him if he really wanted that. In fact, if he wanted to look like Magilla Gorilla, she would have gone along with that, provided he allowed her to trim and make neat his hairy appearance to keep him from looking like an orangutan which just got up in the morning. But she thanked God she didn't have to worry about that. He had no interest in becoming a walking ball of hair.

Julie, at twenty one, was educated, having graduated from the University of Missouri with a degree in economics. She enjoyed her job as a financial analyst for a national chain department store in Kansas City. Her long-blond hair, blue eyes and petite, five foot two frame was a stark contrast to Sam. When walking together, one could easily picture a giraffe and a mouse doing the same thing. But those who knew them didn't laugh because they were, in their minds, as compatible as any couple could be, and were happy for them.

Rob Steiner and Rosanne Wechler, were a bit more free-spirited. Although not as close as Sam and Julie, they still enjoyed each other's company and had been dating for about six months. They were both seniors at Kansas State and after graduation, planned to expand their horizons by setting off in their respective careers wherever it took them. While Rob planned on a career in teaching and had his sights set on particular locations to start off his career, Roseanne wasn't yet sure what she wanted. Although her Bachelor's degree would be in biology, she had yet to seriously research organizations for potential employment. She planned on doing that, however, but by her own schedule. That schedule she planned for after completing this visit and returning back home.

After finding a spot on the beach to plant themselves, Rob set up the two umbrellas while Sam and the girls set up the chairs.

"Man it *is* hot out here," said Sam. "I can feel the heat of the sand through my sandals."

"Yea, me too," replied Roseanne. "Not too many on the beach."

"Nope. Good for us, maybe." Julie looked around as she spoke, then started applying sunscreen..

"Hey, I'm going back to the car to get the cooler. I think we can use some cool ones right now." Sam turned around and started heading toward the car.

"Yea dude, sounds like a plan," yelled out Rob. He turned his head to look out at the water.

"Think I'll check that out," he told the girls.

They decided to do the same. While engaging in small talk about their time here so far, they watched the tranquility of the ocean. There was no breeze and the waves were fairly small. Overhead, they heard the chirps of a couple of seagulls flying.

Soon they all entered the water. For them, this was paradise, despite the heat. There was nothing back home like this and they intended to enjoy every minute of their ten day stay here before heading back to the dregs of inland city life.

Sam saw them going in as he approached their beach spot with the cooler. There was no way he was going to wait around here. His drink could wait. Soon he was halfway down to the water s his friends stood halfway submerged, laughing and having a good time at the feel of the water.

****

Three months earlier-off the coast of Australia

Unknown to most people, including scientists, the ocean current subtly began changing its normal running course. A portion of it started heading slightly west-northwest. As it slowly continued to change, there were entities in the water that depended on the running of the current to get around. Wherever the current went, they went. It had always been the natural order of things for this subtropical environment.

The entities floated, visible if you looked closely for them but invisible if you weren't looking for them or weren't expecting them or didn't know about them. To most other creatures, including humans, they were like ghosts which could appear or disappear in the blink of an eye, yet always still be there. They could be in one spot one minute and then another spot in the next minute; yet they did nothing significant to move themselves. Any propelling movements by them was either so subtle that it was barely noticeable, or vigorous enough to equate them to human Nascar racers for their species.

Very slowly, they headed further away from the Australian coast. They were mindless, yet intelligent in some strange, little understood way. They had no brain, yet knew what was around them and knew what there was they could feed on. They had no idea where they were going. They never would. But they also wouldn't care, for to care was to feel and *that* they could never do. Their only purpose was to float, eat, make babies and just survive. That's all. Whatever crossed their paths had to deal with them. Anything alive that confronted them would very quickly meet their end. And the entities would continue to float, eat, make babies and survive some more, as if nothing happened.

They could never know that their journey would be the longest they'd ever taken, but it wouldn't matter to them. They'd end up in another region, another area, another part of the world. To them, it'd all be the same. They were in the water and they floated. A simple life for a simple creature. They'd already proven how deadly they could be without ever knowing it. For them, surviving and defending themselves meant only one thing they were obligated to do: kill. It was their nature and always had been for millions of years.

Perhaps it was their destiny to expand their territory, or to find a new home. Whatever the reason, it would take a while to get there. But time was on their side and they had it all. Wherever the current took them would make no difference to them. That would not be the case to the inhabitants of where they ended up.

Days and then weeks passed. Their course had changed to a more southerly west and then increasingly southerly as the current took them where it didn't normally go. Chaotic currents seemed to crisscross each other at the Cape of Hope. For a while, they were tossed around until a current caught them in its clutches and maintained its hold on them as it coursed westward, far above over eastward flowing currents. As the current changed to a more northerly course along the western coast of Africa, it started heading out toward more open sea. As it spread out and sunk to deeper depths, it left the entities floating freely in the Atlantic. Now they were at the mercy of the wind, waves, and weather. It would only be a matter of time before they would reach their new home, which was their final destination. They couldn't have known that. They only did what they were meant to do and nothing more, nothing less.

****

Pompano Beach, Florida, July 30

The lifeguards came on duty, one hour after the two couples had arrived. At 9am, the air was already baking. There were three of them in that stretch of beach. During the summer months when the number of swimmers was down, there was only a minimal number of guards required and present. Up in their tower chairs (some called them lifeguard high chairs), they sat underneath the umbrella which attached to the back of the chair. Without it, they could burn quickly under the summer sun, even with sunscreen. So its protection of them was of paramount importance, especially with only a skeletal crew available.

Jimmy Mackson was from Fort Lauderdale who had moved here in his new found independence. His interest in helping people stemmed from the fact that his father was a firefighter and his mother was a nurse. His only difference from them was that he liked to set his own hours. Providing first aid and lifeguarding was considered a good way to start out until he established a more firm foundation of a life-saving career. Although his father was a little disappointed that he didn't follow in his footsteps and go into firefighting, he was grateful that at least Jimmy had chosen to help rather than harm, choosing the path of lawfulness rather than lawlessness. So despite his slight misgivings, he gave his son his blessings in how he wanted to start out a career. He'd always been a good son and he had no doubts he would remain the good person that he was.

On this day Jimmy happened to notice an occupied beach spot with two umbrellas and four chairs, about a hundred feet to his left. There was a cooler there, some clothing, and beach towels laying on the beach chairs. Their owners weren't there, so he figured they were in the water.

As he looked out at the water, he saw a few heads out there. Brave souls, he thought because he knew the water would be too warm to be refreshing. Wearing his sunglasses, he daydreamed as he kept watch over those heads. It could get pretty boring after a while just sitting there, so he oftentimes daydreamed as he kept watch. At the same time, he did his best

to maintain his alertness to anything happening out of the ordinary. Lifeguards weren't allowed to listen to radios because they had to be on the alert and able to hear any sounds of distress out there.

His walkie talkie radio issued to him by the beach emergency services department of which the lifeguards were a part was the only communications device allowed, in addition to their cell phone. Any lifeguards caught listening to music or audio outputs on their smart phones or other Android-type devices could be reprimanded or suspended for a day.

Jimmy had about an eighth of a mile stretch of beach he was responsible for. So with his head and sometimes with only his eyes, he would scan from side to side slowly looking for anyone who might need help or were showing definite signs of distress. He saw none so far. During the on-season, the beaches were packed and so was the water. It wasn't always easy to see someone among a huge throng of people who was in distress. Now, it was fairly easy to spot something like that. Even so, even with his binoculars that he used sporadically, this would be a day that he'd most likely never forget.

He thought he saw arms waving off to his right of someone in the water. There were only two people he saw out in that direction. One was close enough for him to see that he was coming out of the water fairly quickly. He picked up his binoculars and took a closer look. The one nearly running out of the water appeared to be panicking.

Jimmy stood up quickly. He couldn't hear well from the distance the swimmer was located, but he saw the fully open mouth, the man stumbling and then collapsing to the ground. He immediately got on the radio and called the base station who then contacted the First Responders EMTs. At the same time, the other person still in the water-he couldn't tell if it was a man or a woman-seemed to be thrashing around. The person seemed to be trying to swim toward shore but every attempt to do that was interrupted by more severe thrashings. Then Jimmy heard the sounds of screams cut through the air.

After he practically jumped off the high chair and started running toward the collapsed swimmer, he missed what was happening far off to his left. When he reached the swimmer he was looking at still partly in the water, the lifeguard from the other assigned spot arrived also and they both noticed what they'd never seen before.

The man looked to be in his forties, and he was having what appeared to be a seizure, a grand mal, to be more exact. They had assumed automatically that he had epilepsy until they saw the markings, which then gave them pause about that. There were black, string-like markings all over his face and on a couple of large areas of his body. The man was screaming in intense agony and arched his back as he screamed, alternating that with his seizure-type movements that appeared like the clonic-tonic movements of epileptic grand mals. The two lifeguards were horrified, not sure of what to do but trying to do *some*thing to help this man. They were unable to hold him down. When they tried, he screamed even louder and spittle came flying out of his mouth.

As he twisted and turned between his screams, his eyes started to roll back. EMTs and para-medics arrived with life-saving equipment and immediately were confronted with a situation they had somewhat experienced but still nothing like this. Yes, they confirmed, the man was having seizures. But they didn't believe they were epileptic.

"Yea, something's not right here," said Jimmy. "Even if he does have a seizure disorder, look at those damn marks all over him. What the hell are those?"

The two paramedics very quickly scanned and assessed the situation and came to an equally quick but unusual decision.

The lead paramedic yelled out. "Someone. Anyone. We need vinegar. Get some vinegar and get it here as fast as you can!"

The two lifeguards looked at each other and responded together. "Vinegar?"

One of the paramedics who was trying to inject the victim with a pain medication, said "Yea. Vinegar. This man has been stung by some kind of jellyfish. Vinegar will help quell the stinging effects of the stingers. We need that before he goes unconscious."

The two guards decided that one of them would run to the nearest convenience store, which was nearby. The other radioed to the base station to see if there was any there.

Lifeguards knew that at a certain time of the year, common jellyfish would sometimes come around. Although people now and then had been stung by them and it hurt, they never saw anyone stung who screamed like this, let alone had seizures. Those had never caused anything serious in anyone they stung and were considered more of a nuisance than anything else.

The victim continued to scream louder and more intensely, indicating to the paramedics that his pain was increasing. He continued to thrash and as he arched his back more frequently and more severely, the string-like markings became more pronounced and red-black in appearance. They looked angry and quite nasty. Whenever the paramedic tried to inject the pain med, the man's body moved violently from side to side and up, making it impossible to make the injection.

Meanwhile, another lifeguard from the base station arrived and saw the swimmer that had still been out in the water come running in. He, too, was screaming in pain, although not as intensely as the victim on the beach. One of the EMTs noticed the same string-like markings on his left lower arm. After checking him as fast as he could, he saw that was the only area where he was stung. But it was enough.

As seconds passed and then minutes, the second swimmer's screams also intensified and he subsequently collapsed to the ground. Now both men were screaming constantly. *Where the hell is that vinegar?* thought one of the paramedics.

Suddenly the first man started turning blue and gasping for breath. His mouth opened as wide as it could but he was unable to make a sound as he arched one more time in silence, then let out a loud rush of air and stopped breathing. By this time, fire personnel and police had arrived and were all over the surrounding area of the scene. All beachgoers in that area were asked to leave immediately. No one as yet knew what was happening there. But for now this area of the beach was closed off to the public until further notice.

Paramedics checked the first victim for vital signs but found none. EMTs then broke out the AED defibrillators and airbag. After making the proper connections on the man, the paramedic turned on the machine, waited for it to tell him that it was ready, yelled out, "Stay clear of the patient, setting off the charge now", waited for one second, and then pushed the button. The victim's torso bounced up and down once. The defibrillator detected no apical or heart pulse. While the paramedic checked for breathing, the machine was charging up again. Then it said, "no pulse detected. Prepare to defibrillate again. Set to 200 joules." This meant that the unit was setting for the maximum charge because the first lower setting wasn't enough to start the heart up.

The machine then spoke again. "Ready to defibrillate. Ready to defibrillate. Clear away from the patient and when ready push button." The paramedic looked around and again told everyone to stay clear, also making sure at the same time that he wasn't touching the patient.

"Clear. Clear. Setting the charge." He waited one second then pushed the button again. The man's torso bounced up slightly higher then settled down. They waited and the paramedic watched. The chest remained still. The man's color remained a bluish tinge. They checked for circulation but found no pulse. He was clinically dead.

"Let's get him to the hospital, stat." They picked him up, put him on the stretcher and without hesitation led him to and into the ambulance. Within two minutes, they left the scene. Meanwhile, the other EMT team was working on the other victim with a second ambulance standing by to transport. Although he didn't appear quite as injured as the first victim, he was clearly in not much better shape. Whatever had done this to these two men, it seemed that less injury didn't necessarily mean less suffering. He still screamed in intense pain and still twisted around. Then the vinegar arrived and they doused the now red-black angry protruding markings on his left arm with it. He screamed even louder as they prepared him for transport to the hospital.

Then his eyes rolled up in his head. When they tried to lift him to put him on the stretcher, he convulsed and arched his back as the other one had done. His screams were continuous now, with rictus grimacing and foamy spittle flying out of his open mouth. His thrashings became more violent as they saw and tried to help a man dying violently right before their eyes and in their hands.

With a lot of effort and multiple helping hands, he was finally managed onto the stretcher and then tied down firmly so he wouldn't fall off. His eyes stayed rolled up and his mouth stayed open but became suddenly silent. The markings on his left arm became redder and even more pronounced. As they put him on the ambulance, he stopped moving.

"Oh shit!", one of the EMTs cried out, "Looks like he's coded." The other EMT jumped inside and they connected him to life support equipment, oxygen, and did vital signs checks. The third EMT closed the doors, climbed behind the wheel and soon this ambulance was off to the ER.

Police approached the lifeguards at the scene still trying to process all that had happened in the last few minutes. The two officers were obviously concerned about what happened to the victims. When they asked, Jimmy spoke up and explained it all.

"Any idea what did this?" asked one of the officers.

"One of the paramedics said it was a jellyfish."

"Jellyfish? Really? Haven't heard about any around here for years. Last sting I heard was down in the Hollywood area. Someone on the beach down there accidently stepped on one of the tentacles of a dead Man O' War which he didn't see and it still hurt like hell. But he didn't die. They took him to the ER and after an hour or so, he was out of there on the way home."

"Well, I gotta tell ya, I don't think this was one of those," responded Tom, the other life-guard. "If it was, we would have, or someone would have spotted its blue sail sticking above the water and announced its presence. Even then, they don't usually kill, just hurt like the devil for a while."

"Allergic reaction maybe?" asked Jimmy.

"On *two* victims, one right after the other? I don't think so, dude." Tom seemed to be a little more medically attuned than Jimmy.

Then Tom happened to look over to the area that had been temporarily forgotten.

"Hey. No, no, hey, look, look over there, Jimmy." Jimmy turned to look. Off in the distance he thought he saw some heads in the water. Not moving except with the undulating movement of the water's surface. The two police officers also looked. "Oh my God." As if telecommunicating with each other, they all started running back to Jimmy's other area at the same time.

Jimmy looked at the beach spot with the umbrellas and chairs. The cooler was still there. The occupiers hadn't returned. Then he looked back out to where they saw the heads. Four chairs. Out there were four heads. It was only in an instant that he put two and two together.

CHAPTER 2

Miami Marine Institute, Miami, Fl., July 30

Monday always seemed to be a day when the sudden drop of the number of tourists was more obvious. Of course it really wasn't. It only seemed that way. Tourists were there every day to see and be awestruck by the beautiful aquarium and non-aquarium exhibits of all kinds of sea life that they might never see otherwise, except on television. What really made Monday seem not so busy were the crowds that packed in there during the weekends. Sometimes the main exhibit room looked like wall to wall people. People from all over the world who visited Miami always made sure they visited the institute.

It was no wonder. Some of the aquarium exhibits were the size of small cars, while others were the size of small to medium sized houses. They were so beautifully and expertly put together that one could have easily thought they were actually looking at the bottom of the ocean. Exotic creatures of all types, from small seahorses to crustaceans to large sharks-almost every type of sea creature-could be viewed and admired in one of the many aquariums of this world popular institute. There were even a few species of jellyfish that occupied one of the larger tanks.

A lot of people helped maintain and run this tourist attraction. From cashiers in the souvenir shops, to tank cleaners, to the scientists who helped collect and study all of the many species of sea animals that exist and were part of the exhibits, all were involved in some way keeping the institute and its occupants well-cared for and attractive to sightseers as well as to scientists from other parts of the country and the world.

In one of the laboratory sections of the institute where tourists were not allowed, the thirty-four year old woman was studying a specimen of a baby eel that was found floating in an area off the coast not far from the institute. It had been discovered by a small boy who had showed it to his parents when walking along the beach. Because his father had been a bit of a marine enthusiast, he had decided to bring it here to see if the scientists were interested in studying it. His decision, of course, had paid off and the institute took it gratefully from him. Her boss, Danny Worthington, a senior PhD and part time professor at the University of Miami, asked her if she would have a look at it and see what she could determine as to how it died, especially so young. Of course her fifty-six year old boss was a wonderful supervisor who treated her quite well and with the respect that she earned. He never showed a holier-than-thou attitude that some bosses tended to flaunt. Although at times he could be quite firm in his decisions, he was always fair, always listened to ideas or suggestions that his employees had, and took them into consideration before making a decision. Sometimes he agreed with them, sometimes not. But they respected him for who he was and the kind of person he was as well as his decision-making skills.

Rebecca Wares herself was a very well-educated woman who knew her marine creatures every bit as well as most PhDs in her field. Perhaps she knew even more when it came to certain creatures of special interest to her. Despite her parents hoping she'd go into nursing, she decided that wasn't what she really wanted. She loved biology but didn't want to use that for a nursing career. Instead, she preferred to advance her knowledge of it as much as possible and then use that knowledge in scientific studies, specifically of marine life.

Originally from Connecticut, she attended the University of Connecticut for her bachelors in biology, then the University of San Diego for her Masters in marine biology. Several years later, she graduated from that same school with a PhD in that field. After searching and finding out where she could go from there, it didn't take her long to land the job at the Miami Marine Institute where she'd been ever since. Even though her educational endeavors had taken her cross country, she didn't mind that. The programs she had entered and completed had the exact courses and requirements that she wanted, which was why she was so selective in her schools, no matter the location. And now she was where she truly enjoyed to be.

With her eight year tenure there, she was now pretty solid in her career and in addition to her studies, was already prepared for a new challenge.

As Rebecca turned the dead creature in her hands, her phone rang and she picked it up. It was Tony Abner, the marine assistant who sometimes asked for advice on something he found or was curious about.

"Rebecca Wares here," she answered.

"Hi Becky. Tony here. You probably already know that from your caller ID."

"Hey! What's up?"

"I found a little something yesterday that's kind of weird, but I'm not sure what it is."

"Oh? What do you mean by weird?"

"Well, I think it may be from some kind of jellyfish. It's just a small piece and I don't think it's all of it. It's very small, like the size of a large thimble and is kinda shaped like it too. I've never seen anything like this before. Thought you might want to have a look?"

She looked down at her eel, while thinking about this. "Where do you have it now?"

"Got it in a tank over in F one. I put it in there, cause I didn't know what else to do with it. In case you or someone else wanted to see it."

Rebecca thought for a minute and then decided. "Well I'm not a jellyfish expert if that's what it is. But you have my curiosity going here, so I'll be over. Are you there now?"

"Yea. That's where I'm calling from."

"Ok. I'll be over in a few and will check it out."

"Ok. See you in a few. Thanks."

After hanging up, her mind started going a mile a minute, trying to think of what it could be. Might not be a big deal or any deal at all. Might be nothing. But then again, what if it *is* something? Her scientific nature was not something that allowed her to put off a good mystery for later. She put down the eel and placed it into a pan of cold water to help preserve it and headed out of the lab. Why put off for later what can be done now?

****

Pompano Beach, Florida, July 30

The lifeguards and police officers looked out at the four people in the water who didn't seem to be moving, except for their heads bobbing in the water.

"Hey," yelled out Jimmy. "Hey, is everybody all right out there?" They were about a hundred or a hundred and fifty yards out from shore. There was no answer, but they thought they saw part of one arm raise a little out of the water.

Jimmy ran over to the special area off to the side to get his skidoo. After jumping on it, he started it up and quickly sped off toward the swimmers. It didn't take them long to see that something was very wrong. There were two men and two women. Three of them didn't respond to his talking to them. The fourth had her eyes open but could barely talk. When her arm lifted part way out of the water, he saw some angry black string-like marks which contrasted sharply against her milky white skin. They gave her arm a marbling effect. Then when he looked at her face again, he saw some of those same marks on one side.

He got on his radio. "Call 911 again. We have four more victims here. Three unconscious, one barely conscious." Immediately, he grabbed a hold of the woman and pulled her part way onto the back of the skidoo. There was a tiny platform on the back of it that he could fit just enough of a person to be able to take that person to shore.

The officers and Tom approached Jimmy to assist and they took the woman and laid her on the beach. The woman, who they estimated to be in her early twenties, started screaming in agony.

"Where are you hurting, maa'm?" asked Tom. He was dumbfounded as to what had happened to her and her comrades. "Jimmy, go get the others. I'll see what I can do here until the EMTs arrive."

While Jimmy rushed back out to bring in the others one by one, Tom tried to get information out of the woman. Although she tried to talk, something terrible was preventing her from speaking and she cried out again. Meanwhile, the officers looked at her in shock and seeing those angry black string-like marks all over her grow angrier and blacker, they felt helpless to do anything, but asked nevertheless if there was anything they could do.

"Vinegar. Can you get me some asap?"

The officers knew immediately why he asked and one of them scrambled off without saying anything. They didn't know what happened to the other bottle and figured it would be easier just to buy another bottle at the nearby convenience store than to look for the other one.

Within five minutes, the officer was back with the vinegar. When he returned, the first responders had also returned, this time with three ambulances and twice the number of medical personnel. Trucks and sirens were everywhere. Stretchers were brought down, an oxygen mask was placed on the victim still thrashing about, and CPR was being attempted on the three un- responsive victims. The masked woman was transported out first on the way to the ER, while defibrillating attempts were being made on the others. Crowds of people were gathered where the parking lot ended and the beach began. Police cordoned off the area to keep curiosity seekers out of and away from the scene.

Jimmy and Tom, as well as the two original police officers stood by to assist if needed as the first responders attempted to revive the unconscious victims. Soon all three were put on stretchers, placed inside the ambulances, and whisked off to the hospital. They didn't know if those unfortunate three had been revived, but hoped so for their sakes. One of them prayed out loud that they would make it. They had noticed the angry black markings all over them as well. Jimmy found that extremely disturbing. Six victims here at his section of the beach. Victims of what? Some kind of jellyfish, it looked like to him.

But how could that be? There hadn't been sightings of them around here for years. Why now? Why here? Where did they come from and what the hell kind of jellyfish were they? The ones they'd gotten around here in the years ago past had been the typical ones that frequent some of the warm, subtropical waters on the eastern coast. Sure they hurt if you ran into them. Especially the Portuguese Man O' War. But it didn't cause death to most victims or serious convulsions as in these people. And although it would leave angry red tentacle markings, none of them were black and red and raised like these. This was a mystery which was seriously endangering peoples' lives.

"Hey, Tom, c'mere a minute."

Tom walked over to Jimmy. "Got any ideas as to what this could be in the water?"

"Jellyfish, by the looks of it," Tom responded.

"No shit, Sherlock. Anybody report to you about seeing any of them out there?"

"No. Nobody reported seeing anything. What the hell is out there that we can't see?"

Jimmy looked out at the water, now devoid of all swimmers. It looked just as peaceful and inviting as ever. When once it had always been all of that, now its inviting tranquility held a deadly secret to anyone swimming in it. He watched the gentle waves lapping up onto the shore and shook his head.

"I don't know, Tom. Even with my binocs, I saw absolutely nothing. But we need to find out. I got an idea. Do me a favor. Notify home base and confirm their temporary closing of this area of the beach. Find out if they'll close this entire half mile area of beach or only this spot. I'm going to make a call and see if I can get the opinion of an expert on this."

"Who you going to call?"

"A place that might be able to provide some answers. Let's go."

While he walked away making his call on the cell phone, Jimmy walked over to his assigned spot. It was clear he was now off duty, but would stick around for a while anyway to make sure. A call came in for him and when he answered it was the beach emergency services supervisor. It was now official: the beach would stay open but there would be no swimming along the half mile stretch of beach until further notice. Each section would have signs posted with this order by its respective assigned guard. The signs would remain in place until the danger had passed and it was considered safe again to swim.

In the nearby shed where some things were kept for the lifeguards, Jimmy took out several NO SWIMMING signs and posted them along his stretch of beach near where beachgoers would step onto the sand. He wanted them to know right off the bat that the water was off limits to everyone until further notice, by order of the town of Pompano Beach.

After he completed this, he took out his smartphone and got on the internet to try and find what he was looking for. It didn't take him long to find it. He took out his pen, found a piece of paper and wrote down the phone number.

****

Miami South Beach, July 30

At eleven in the morning, beachgoers started to pile onto the beach. Despite the heat, humidity, and hot sand, there were still plenty of die-hards who came prepared for that. Carrying their chairs, umbrellas, and everything else that went with beach sunbathing, only the foolhardy braved the sand without sandals on. And only the uninitiated believed the ocean water would be refreshing, until they got in.

People were already patronizing the many concession stands for food and drink. In all, it was a typical day at the beach during a hot summer. Or so it seemed initially.

Many of the few people in the water were standing in waist-deep water, while a few others were just entering it. Some people were chatting about everything and nothing, while some children were laughing, giggling and splashing each other.

All the lifeguards were at their stations watching all that was going on, alert for anything that could occur at any time. Their skidoos were parked and ready, and their first aid kits were close by and ready to take on a moment's notice. Their walkie talkies occasionally broke through the beach air with the communications between other lifeguards and the main base station. For now all seemed to be fine, and that's the way most of them liked it.

Less than a quarter mile beyond the furthermost perimeter of the authorized swimming area, the current below the surface which was affected by the Gulf stream curved slightly inward for several hundred feet before curving back more northward and northeastward. The water was a little cooler where the current was and gradually warmed up nearer the surface. Out in the distance were sail boats and motorized craft taking full advantage of the beautiful calm weather and seas. They were seen and envied by a few of the swimmers who, in turn, were unseen by those on the boats.

Unseen to both the swimmers and the boaters was the large swarm which was slowly and gradually floating its way toward the shore, feeding along the way, and allowing the current and incoming tide to transport them wherever it took them. They neither knew where that was nor cared. They were not able to. They were only programmed to eat, float, make babies, and defend themselves. All were equipped to do all of that. Soon they would be involved in more than just floating around.

Miami Marine Institute, July 30

F-one was the building at the marine institute which housed special exotic creatures and had a lab for studying them. Specialists, such as Tony, were assigned there to study and care for the creatures which were housed there in large, seawater tanks. Creatures such as seahorses, rare species of starfish, and other creatures rarely seen were kept in one tank. In another tank were less common forms of jellyfish and bottom dwelling creatures such as moray eels, piglet squids, and marine fire worms which stayed near the surface. In a third tank were other rare finds of other smaller creatures for which little was known about them. Those who worked in F-one were focused on finding out all they could about each of them in their scientific quest to learn more about the sea and its inhabitants.

Rebecca entered the side door closest to the lab where Tony was waiting to meet her. After walking down the short hall, she found the lab door on her right and entered it. Her view instantly became filled with one small aquarium tank, long tables with all kinds of equipment and microscopes, and the sounds of water running continuously. She knew it was seawater, continuously pumped in to help prevent contamination and bacteria growth in the water where the creatures were kept. Tony was at a large desk behind a microscope at the far end. He heard her walk in and called out to her.

"Hey Becky, down here. C'mon over and take a look-see."

When she arrived, he showed her the small sample of some kind of gelatinous material, which was more translucent than transparent, and about the size of a quarter in diameter. When he picked it up, he suddenly screamed, instantly dropping the material. Becky jumped back in fright. What was going on here?

He covered his two fingers. "Oh My God. Oh my God, that hurts. Ahhh!!!"

"Tony, let me see your fingers!"

She looked at them as he did his best to stifle the screams he wanted to let out. She could see the tiniest of puncture marks, almost invisible. "What the hell caused that?"

"I, uh…I don't know. All I did was pick it up."

"That was the first time you picked it up with your bare fingers?"

He nodded. "Yeah".

Whatever it was, what he had found, was obviously not meant to be touched. Question was, what was it?

It looked like a harmless piece of rubbery, gelatinous material. Nothing could be seen protruding from its surface. Yet somehow it had stung him.

"Get to the sink and see if running water on it will help." Holding his fingers in his other hand, he made his way to the sink. "Cold water, Tony," she added.

Through his groans, he managed to place his fingers under the running tap. Despite that, it didn't seem to provide any relief and his groans began to intensify along with the pain. She began to suspect a toxic venom which may have been injected. But how? There were no tentacles as in a jellyfish or octopus. And the material looked as smooth as glass. Wracking her brain for answers, she noticed Tony's self-control begin to break down. She ran over to him and look at his fingertips. They were now red and inflamed. She picked up the phone and called 911. Had there been vinegar around, she would have tried that first. It would have been only a guess but maybe it would have helped. Unfortunately, the institute didn't keep any around. *Something* to put in the suggestion box, she told herself.

She told him she was sending him to the ER. He needed to have that checked out and treated. "What could that thing be?" he struggled to ask between waves of pain.

"Hmm, I don't know, Tony. Maybe some kind of jellyfish but I'm not a hundred per cent sure. There's no tentacles. If there were, then we'd know. Whatever it is, you just found out it can't be picked up with bare hands. Something's on it that got you. Where'd you find it?"

"On a small stretch of beach, just north of south beach that is more private than public. I was just walking and picked up a small stone to skip it on the water when I noticed it on the stone. It looked like it was hugging it and when I felt it, it felt like a small glob of goo that didn't come apart when I touched it. It caught my interest and now here it is."

"So how'd you pick it up there?"

He screamed out when a wave of pain hit him. "With a stick I found."

She could have asked him further why pick it up with a stick then and not now, but decided it was now a moot issue. He needed to get it taken care of as soon as possible.

She looked at it in the glass container. Floating, it had a cup-like shape and looked to be the size of a thumbnail. It looked like it could fit over the tip of her finger.

A few minutes later, she heard an ambulance pull up outside the building. Escorting Tony out, she explained to the EMTs what happened and showed them the fingers involved with the stinging. With the source of the stinging unidentified as yet, she couldn't tell them what it was that did it, but she would try to find out as soon as possible.

She reassured Tony that he'd be ok and she'd check on him later; she went back inside as he was transported away.

If it was from a jellyfish, it wasn't from any she was familiar with or encountered. Maybe it was a piece of one, she thought. But then she had some doubts. If it was a piece of a jellyfish, why were there no tentacles? And without those, how could it sting? Very strange.

Picking up the phone, she knew she had to find out fast. And she knew who to call.

CHAPTER 3

She didn't get an answer, so she left a voicemail message to call her back with an after note that it was important. Before she could put the phone in her pocket, it rang again. *Boy, that was fast,* she thought believing it was from Jim. To her surprise, it was the institute.

"Hi, Rebecca, this is Shirley." Shirley was the receptionist near the front entrance of the building. She'd been here forever and was a most welcoming sight and personality who greeted visitors coming in with the utmost enthusiasm. It was clear she loved people as much as she loved her job.

"I'm sorry to bother you on your cell. I tried your lab phone there but I kept getting a busy signal."

"Hi, Shirl. That's strange because I wasn't on it. Must be off the hook, I guess. I'll check it after. So what's up? What can I do for you?"

"Well, I have a young man on the other line. Have him on hold for now. He says he needs to speak to someone who's an expert in marine biology. And he said it's urgent."

This was unusual, definitely not a typical call. And what he said suggested that he was not involved in her field, therefore was not a colleague. Almost all calls she gets, which aren't that often, are from fellow scientists.

"Did he say what it's all about?"

"No, he wouldn't elaborate. He did say, though, that people have died and something in the water, he claims, had killed them. " That sent a chill up and down her spine. *Something in* the water killed them?

*"*Sharks?"

"I don't know, Becky. He didn't say. But if it was sharks, why would he be calling *here?"*

"Good question. Ok, Shirl, hold on a minute. Let me check the phone at the other desk and make sure it's on the hook. Then I'll tell you to patch him through. Hold on."

"Ok, I'm holding."

Becky went to the other desk and saw the slight tilted angle of the receiver and straightened it out. No wonder the busy signal. She put her cell back to her ear.

"Ok. Put him through. It's on the hook now."

A few seconds later, the desk phone rang and she picked it up as she hung up on her cell.

"Rebecca Wares, can I help you?"

"Uh I hope so." It sounded like a young man and he sounded like he was scared, or worried. She wasn't sure which it was.

"My name is Jimmy Mackson. I'm a lifeguard over in Pompano Beach. We've had some incidents here and a couple of fatalities which occurred in the water. Nothing was seen in the water. No sharks, nothing. Yet two or three of them died."

Becky was shocked. This was certainly not what she could have expected.

"When did this happen?"

"About a couple of hours ago, maybe a little more. There were about seven victims. Two were found dead at the scene here. The others were sent to the hospital by ambulance."

Her mind was now racing a mile a minute. What the hell could have caused that?

"You say nothing was seen in the water? No fins, or anything swimming around in there?"

"No ma'am. None of us saw anything and no one reported seeing anything. So it's a big mystery."

"Well did you notice any injuries on any of the victims?" she pressed for more information.

Jimmy briefly hesitated. "Yea. We did notice some strange markings on most of the victims."

"Oh? Describe them to me please."

He then started telling her about the mysterious small black whip-like markings on some areas of the skin. He noticed markings on most of the victims. As she listened to his further descriptions and locations where they were seen on the bodies, she

26

was at the same time thinking of what could be the possible sources of these markings and what these markings actually were. She knew of certain jellyfish that caused markings from their stings.

"Ok, listen Jimmy. I suggest you close the beach until this is investigated there. Can you do that?"

"That's been done already. The beach itself will stay open, but no one is allowed in the water for now."

"Good. I'm going to plan on coming up there to check it out. Can you let your bosses know that?"

"I will. But I also have to let them know I called you."

Becky looked up, surprised to hear that. "You called me on your own?"

"Yea, I did."

She let out a breath. "Ok. Better let them know right away. Tell them they can call me if they want to. Give them my cell phone number, because I expect to be leaving here soon. Here it is. Got a pencil and paper?"

"Hold on a sec." She heard him fumbling around on the other end. "Ok, go ahead."

After giving him the number and hanging up, she called Dan, her boss, to fill him in on what she found out and what she wanted to do. She requested an assistant to accompany her.

"Ok, listen," he told her. "If you see what it is up there in the water, do what you have to do. Pics and all. Get a hold of James down in the keys and see what his take on this is. Getting samples, if you can, would be a priority. We need to find out what that is. I'll arrange for immediate funding for you. Pick out who you want to go with you and let me know. Give me about an hour."

"Ok, thanks, Dan. By the way, Tony got stung by a sample here today that he found on a rock yesterday. We don't know what it is. Looks like a small, cuplike material. Nothing seen on it that could sting, yet when he picked it up he felt it immediately. Got so bad I had to call an ambulance for him."

She could hear him on the other end slightly gasp. He only did that when he was caught off guard or very surprised. This news was likely both.

"Oh man. Is he going to be alright?"

"I think so. It was just on the tip of his finger. But it hit him like the burning pain of a branding iron. Just that little area. Anyway, he's at the hospital being treated. I'll keep you posted if I find out anything later."

"Yea, please do. I'll give a call to the hospital. Where is he, Miami Memorial?"

"Yep. That's it."

After mutually agreeing on checking on Tony and then her arrangements to leave for Pompano Beach, she went over to Tony's desk and took another look at that sample. The more she looked at the material, the more it seemed remotely familiar to her. Not in the sense of first-hand experience, but from what she'd observed in past training and documentary observations. If this was from some kind of sea creature, could whatever it came from be the kind of culprit that sent a number of people to the hospital up in Pompano and killed three people?

She decided to have Julie Perkins assist her. She was a good lab assistant and had been there for only a few months but was reliable and a hard worker. After contacting her over at the other building which housed crustaceans and allowing her time to prepare for the trip, Becky started gathering the supplies and equipment she would and might need, including gloves and containers for catching and holding specimens. After making sure she gathered together everything she would and might need for anything she'd come across in the water, she started bringing the stuff out to her SUV. Julie caught her eye as she was walking over and offered to help load the stuff.

"What are we going to look for, Becky?" she asked.

"Not sure. Possible jellyfish but nothing was sighted that caused the attacks. We have to see what we can see there. The beach emergency services will provide us with a lifeguard to drive us around the water with one of their boats. I've got heavy rubber gloves for the both of us just in case. Just be sure that if I give the word, you put yours on right away."

"After hearing what happened, you won't get any argument from me on that."

It didn't take long for the on load. Closing up the rear door of the vehicle, Becky indicated that they go inside.

"Now we wait," she said, "for the big chief to give us the go. Take a load off for now. I'm going to make a call to a colleague."

Once they were both back inside, Becky called James again. She hadn't heard back from him which surprised her. It would be terrible if she couldn't get a hold of him again and hoped that he would answer. Leaving voicemail messages, as she discovered, didn't always result in a reply.

Key Largo, Florida, July 30

James Robertson had a PhD in marine biology and was a real go-getter when it came to particular crustaceans and phylum, also known as jellyfish. He'd been on Key Largo for a couple of weeks now on a grant from the University of South Florida to do research studies on the anatomical structures which had to do with their built-in navigational systems, especially in the jellyfish studies.

Ever since he was a young boy, he'd always been fascinated with animals, especially sea animals. He didn't know why they fascinated him so much; just that they did. As a result, he didn't hold back on resolving all his countless curiosities about them, always asking questions of his parents who, not being experts in marine science, couldn't give him half the answers he was looking for. Consequently, he'd go to the library or museum, obtain books about sea life, and ask around there to see if anyone knew anything about them.

During his adolescence and in high school, he earned top grades in general science and biology. In fact, he did well in nearly all of his subjects, which got him in the top quarter ranking of his senior class. That earned him a scholarship at several well-reputed universities. He chose Princeton.

His seemingly divine gift in academics and the sciences followed him through both the bachelors and masters programs there. Deciding he still wanted more, his hunger to learn seemed insatiable. It wasn't long before he began the doctorate program in marine biology at Florida State University, which gained him an internship at the Miami Marine Institute. That was eight years ago. For James, time seemed to be meaningless because he enjoyed the work so much he believed he could do it forever.

Although his social life seemed to take a back seat to his studies and work, he didn't seem to mind it so much. Dating was an infrequent activity for him, although he had his eyes on a couple of women whose eyes seemed to take him in as well along the way. At some point, he settled on one particular woman who he enjoyed very much being with. Her name was Loretta. She was well-educated but not with a PhD. That didn't bother him because as he well knew, most people didn't have such an advanced degree anyway. What was so wonderful about her was that she understood his commitment to his work and never pressured him to pay more attention to her. She had a Masters in Psychology, so she knew that kind of pressure with someone of his dedication and commitment often prevented a relationship from developing into a fruitful one. Despite his dedication and commitments, he rarely ignored her and chose his times when he could relax and enjoy her company while keeping his work out of the picture.

Loretta Newsome had been divorced once as a result of an abusive husband. She didn't have any kids, which may have contributed to her ex's resentment, blaming her for not bearing any and thus the subsequent verbal and physical abuse. In truth, he later found out that he had abnormally low sperm counts which didn't sit well with him. Still, he blamed her for their childlessness. After one year of his constant abuse, she finally got the nerve to call it quits and their separation led to their divorce. There would be no patching up this toxic relationship.

As with James, she was in no rush for another serious relationship just yet. But she found an attractiveness in him that included a number of good qualities in not only his appearance and the way he looked, but in his character and personality. It was a far cry from her previous relationship. This man was warm and gentle, and had a compassionate nature about him that she found irresistible.

Their relationship had been warm but brief. She was pursuing an advanced degree and decided that this was not the right time for her for a serious relationship, but they remained friends.

As she continued to see her patients at the Largo Family Therapy Center, James was along a stretch of rocky shore examining a specimen of a dead fish that had washed up. It was very small, only about two inches long. It was its silvery sheen with the sunrays bouncing off of it that had caught his eye. Fin fish weren't his forte, but he suspected it may be a common shiner. But if it weren't for those markings, he would have ignored it and continued to assess the medium size moon jellyfish that he saw floating near the shore. It was the only one he'd seen and thought it was a little odd, as normally he always saw them in swarms. They weren't deadly to humans. Their stings were usually mild and usually didn't last very long.

On the fish, he noticed strange markings that he knew didn't belong there. At first he wasn't quite sure what they were or what could have caused them. Only one side of the fish had the string-like markings.

Then he suspected what it was and realized what he was looking at were markings from the tentacles of a jellyfish. But it was not the moon jellyfish because they didn't leave marks like that after stinging. In fact, only a few species left markings that obvious and clear and they were the more venomous. Portuguese Man O' Wars, which were actually not a true jellyfish, could leave such types of markings. So could the box jellyfish and Lions Mane as well.

He eliminated the latter two because they weren't found anywhere near Florida waters. The Man O' Wars, however could certainly be the culprit because they were seen along the coasts, but primarily the east coast. He looked out over the water of the Gulf of Mexico but saw nothing that could attribute the marks. But then again, the Gulf was a huge body of water, so what happened to this fish could have happened anywhere out there.

If he were just a tourist or passerby, he'd throw it back in the water and say "the hell with it". Being the scientist that he was, he couldn't do that. Rather, he took out of his, what he called, bag of goodies, a small plastic baggie that was similar to a sandwich bag but thicker and stronger. After putting some seawater in it, he plopped the fish into it, sealed it, and placed it alongside his bag of research items that he brought along most of the time. Studying any kind of marine biology out in the field like this could reveal unexpected surprises and he liked to be prepared for anything or at least almost anything.

He put the bagged fish into the cooler from the lab and then looked out again over the water as if he were trying to see what he didn't see before. There was still nothing to suggest what had killed the fish. The sea was relatively calm, with only small waves pecking at the shore. In the distance, he could see several sailboats making their leisurely way across the open water, and a fast moving boat with a skier not too far off from the shoreline.

Behind him, he heard a car pull up at the top of the embankment and turned around. At the top, a man got out and walked to the edge, looking down at him.

"Well, it's about time I found you. Whatcha doing down there, fishing for shiner bait?" It was Bobby, the lab assistant from the USF lab. He tended to be a jokester at times and it sounded right now like he was in that kind of mood. Time to give it back to him.

"Well, well, well. Naw, just doing some studies on *Aurelia aurita*, although I'd prefer- if they were- around the Chrysaora. Then again, I might decide to go further south and east and look for Physalia physalis. Need your opinion: which do you think I'd have the best luck with? Your answer in ten seconds please." He knew that Bobby had no clue what those were. The first was the relatively harmless moon jellyfish, the second the venomous Sea Nettle and the third the notorious Portuguese Man O' War.

"Yea, right, there Bud. You expect me to answer something like that? What am I, a lab worker or something?" Bobby chuckled, taking it in his stride. "By the sounds of those names, I can only assume they are something dangerous. No thanks, pal, I'll pass on that question if you don't mind."

"So what brings you out to this neck of the woods?"

Bobby sifted around and carefully made his way down the seven foot slope until he stood next to the guy who he admired and respected more than anyone else back at the school. He looked around and then out over the water to the lazily moving sailboats.

"Nice day for a sail, or swim," he responded. "Any significant discoveries yet?"

"Nothing significant as yet," James told him. He didn't want to say anything to the sometimes-zealous marine intern who also sometimes took things a little too seriously. He could be a bit of an alarmist at times. So he concluded that withholding the information about the killed fish was a wise decision. In case it was nothing, nothing was gained or lost.

"You on a break from the school?" he asked Bobby.

"Naw. Actually, they sent me to look for you."

"Who's *they?*"

"Dr. Henson's secretary. She apparently got a call from a woman down in Miami, a marine biologist at the institute who was trying to get a hold of you. They gave her your cell phone number after she told them the reason for her call. Later she called them back telling them she couldn't get through." Dr. Henson was the Dean of the Marine Science school. "Your phone ring at all?"

James took his cell out of his pocket and checked it. It was turned on but there was no indication that it had received an incoming call.

"No, didn't ring at all. In fact, it's telling me there was no incoming call at all. Let me check the voicemail, hold on. That call must have been mighty important for them to send you all the way here looking for me," he said looking at Bobby while he dialed for the voice mail connection.

"They said it was. Urgent, they called it."

James listened to the automated recording for voicemails and then pushed the button to listen. Apparently there *was* a call on it after all. He didn't know why it didn't ring, but the connection had been made to his voicemail.

"Hi, Dr. Robertson. James. This is Rebecca Wares down at Miami Institute. Can you call me as soon as you can? There's an urgent matter that's been brought to my attention. In fact, I have a sample of something that could be in your professional realm of expertise, although I'm not sure. The sample has hurt one of my workers and I had to call for medical help. Please call me as soon as you can." Then she left her number.

"Hmm!" He looked at his phone as he hung up. He wondered what that was all about. The fact that Bobby had been sent twenty five miles to his location from the school to tell him to call this woman, and the fact that her voice had the sense of urgency to it told him this was nothing he should ignore. *Somebody got hurt from her sample?* What the hell kind of sample could that be?

He had known Rebecca for a few years. Although they were professional colleagues, they were also friends. Problem is, he was also attracted to her. In the back of his mind, he had told himself he wouldn't mind dating her, although he was hesitant about doing that. To him, any female who was that pretty was guaranteed to already have a boyfriend. He left the back of his mind to return to the forefront that was the present.

"Looks like she got through after all," he told Bobby. "To my voicemail. Don't ask me why it didn't ring. These high-tech things aren't always as high-tech working as they should be. Anyway I better call her back. Stick around for a few. Want a soda? Got some cans in the other cooler over there," he added, pointing to it.

"Yea, thanks. I can use one. But, I'll have to take it with me. Gotta get back and collect some data on my desktop." He opened the cooler and took a can out. "Thanks. Jimmy. See ya later back at campus. Good luck on that call."

James waved. "Ok, thanks for coming out here to let me know. I'll see ya back at the school. If he asks, tell John I should be back around four thirty or five." John was his scientist partner, although senior to him in tenure there at the lab. Bobby acknowledged he would and soon was gone.

Typing the numbers on his phone, James put the phone to his ear and waited for her to answer.

CHAPTER 4

Pompano Beach, Florida, July 30

They were all gathered around their boss and waited for the inevitable announcement. Rich Munson had been around for a number of years instructing and training new lifeguards until eventually he became the Director of Lifeguard Security in the beach division of emergency Services. He had worked hard and earned his way up the difficult ladder to reach where he was now. Through his stamina and perseverance, along with his desire to succeed, he had finally made the grade and the top position. Although it was a lonelier position than he had realized, it nevertheless made him realize that for him it was well worth the effort.

Dan was neither a laissez-faire leader nor a dictator. He ran a tight ship and expected no less than by-the-book protocols at all times when on the job. This helped save lives and prevent any collateral mishaps or worse. Deviations from this he wouldn't tolerate.

At the same time, he realized that every emergency situation was different. Sometimes things, unexpected things, happened that no one was or could truly be prepared for. These were things that no training manual covered. In these cases, good common sense and general preparedness for any emergency as well as keeping a cool head could mean the difference for someone between life and death. Those he picked for the job not only had to have all the state's qualifications and be certified as lifeguards and first-aid lifesavers, they had to have the basic personality characteristics of good self-control, intellectual reasoning, and a lot of common sense. He tolerated no bad attitudes in his squadron.

Now circling around him outside the beach headquarters of the EMS division, he knew that it was a good time for this meeting. The beach all along this area of the city had been temporarily shut down until the cause of these injuries and deaths was determined. Devastating to the tourist trade, the city had made it clear that it wanted this problem taken care of and solved as quickly as possible. It would employ any means or use anyone to get the job done, including hiring someone professional from the outside who would do it. As it was, the city director of emergency services in coordination with the beach director of EMS informed Dan that his staff would be immediately assigned to beach security and preventing anyone from going in the water.

"Ok, people, I hope we're all here. Let's get started. Can you all hear me?"

He looked around and saw heads nodding all around him. All in all there were about thirty five lifeguards.

"Ok. Here's the deal. We all know what's happened. The city has shut down the beach. Hopefully for only a day or two. We don't know yet how long for sure."

As he spoke, he turned around slowly to ensure that all could hear what he was saying.

"The city is conducting an investigation right now. Something in the water did something to those people. Right now we don't have a clue as to what it is. A certain person was contacted about this. Jimmy Mackson, where are you?"

"Over here." Dan turned around to the voice in the circle behind him.

"Jimmy, I appreciate you contacting the institute about that scientist. Gotta remember to go through me first next time, ok? I know it was an emergency and all. But call me first next time."

Dan didn't want to berate Jimmy or anybody else in front of everybody else, so he left it at that and made just a general related announcement.

"In any emergency situation, you need to make any or all requests or recommendations through my office. Especially when it comes to contacting professionals or experts on the outside. I know this wasn't in the rule book so I need to clarify here. If everyone called out to someone on their own for help here, it would be a real mess. This office wouldn't know what was going on. So please remember to let this office do the finger walking in the yellow pages for outside help finding. Everybody got that?"

Everyone nodded and "yeps" were heard throughout the group.

"Good. Now there will be a couple of people coming up from the Miami Marine Institute tomorrow. Couple of marine biologists who are going to inspect the waters around the beaches here. They'll need your complete cooperation in helping them. Two boats will be provided to them with a lifeguard on each one. I'll decide who goes on the boats with them. The rest of you will patrol the beaches and make sure no one goes in the water. You'll also make sure those No Swimming signs are all up everywhere so no one can miss seeing them.

"We have a lot of beach to cover. Those of you from the northernmost end of the beach I know had to come by car to get here. You're the ones farthest from base here. Please be sure your radios are in proper working order and that they are fully charged when you come on duty. If any of your radios are not working properly at all, despite the full charges, contact me immediately and I'll get you a replacement. Any questions so far?"

He looked around. Everyone seemed to be understanding the situation a little more fully. One hand was raised to his left. It was a young woman named Lily.

"Yes Lily?"

"Are we allowed to go out on the skidoos in our area?"

"Good question. Everybody hear the question?"

He didn't hear any "nos" so he continued. "The answer is yes. Only one of you in each area can go out on the skidoo if you spot something since you're all well-qualified drivers. Take your radio with you if you go out, and for God's sake, please don't get it wet. But--and I can't emphasize this enough--you are NOT to pick anything out of the water or even touch the water. Nothing seen in the water is to be touched. Not even if you recognize it. I'm saying this because I've spoken with the scientist on the phone from Miami. From what she tells me, there's a killer in the water. She doesn't know what it is, but what she DOES know is that it won't jump out of the water and bite you or knock you off the skidoo. If it were something like that, then obviously there would be no small boats going out there, let alone skidoos. Best not to take any chances."

Another hand went up. Dirk, the bodybuilder from Area 3, about half a mile down the beach from home base.

"We spot something, we don't touch but radio in to you?"

"Yep. You got it."

"Are these people going to check all the beach areas?"

"Yes. Of course, it's impossible to check every square inch of the water. They'll be doing a relatively brief but thorough survey of each swimming area. After all the swimming areas have been checked, they'll check the borders just outside the swimming areas to see if anything is coming in from the ocean and possibly from what direction. Once they come into your area, there will be no skidoos out there, unless they specifically request one of you to be out there with it. That's up to them. If they request it, you need to let me know. And if anyone goes out in a skidoo at any time for any reason, you need to let me know beforehand. Don't go out there without telling me first. Other than that, stay clear of those areas until they're finished."

"How long are they going to be here?" A voice from the other side this time. It was Sandy, the young teacher assistant who worked here during school summer vacation.

"Probably for a couple of days. Depends on what they find. But as long as they're out there, the beaches will remain closed. The city doesn't want people panicking if they see people picking stuff out of the water and they know they are not tourists. On the other hand, the city also hopes they won't be here long and the beach shutdown will be only brief. We'll have to see.

"Any other questions?"

That seemed to be it for questions. No one else raised their hand, which suggested to Dan that they got his message and understood.

He now had to announce his two selections for the two boats that would carry each scientist. After telling Tim and Sue, there was no feeling of elation in having been chosen. Rather, a feeling of apprehension permeated the atmosphere around the group. Although the two selectees felt no sense of real danger in the mission, still, dealing with the unknown in this situation gave them no measure of comfort. They were trained to do a job and they would do it.

They were told when and where to report the next morning. The boats would need to be prepared before the two scientists arrived.

****

"Hi, Jim," she said almost immediately after he identified himself. "Thanks for calling me back. Got a couple of minutes to talk?"

"Yea, Becky. Just finishing up here. They told me this was urgent. What's happening down there?"

She then told him about what was discovered, what happened to Tony, and described the sample, stating the thing had stung Tony even though it didn't look like it had anything to sting with. She couldn't understand it and had never seen anything like it before.

"Strange. Where did he find it?"

"Somewhere on a non-public isolated beach not far from here."

"How did he obtain it in the first place without getting stung?"

She explained what Tony had told her. Apparently he had forgotten to wear protection or use a tool to pick it up in the lab. He had when he first found it, which explained why he hadn't gotten stung on its discovery.

"Got a pic you can send me now?"

"Sure. Give me a sec," she said.

James could hear her fumbling with her smartphone and knew she was looking for the picture of the sample she had taken, to send to him. Wonderful devices these camera smart-phones, he thought to himself.

"Ok, I'm sending now." A few seconds later, his phone sounded a notification ring and he opened up the text with the picture attached. And there it was.

He looked at it carefully. "Got it, Becky. Give me a minute or two to take a look at this thing."

It was very unassuming. Looked almost invisible. Only the translucent slight coloration distinguished it from the relative clearness of the water. It was very small. Smaller than he imagined. But he knew that smallness sometimes meant greater danger, depending on what that creature was, if it was in fact a living organism. In the world of marine science, smallness didn't necessarily equate with harmlessness.

As he looked at it, his mind was flipping through the "pages" of his memory banks in his attempt to find a match or potential match with all that he knew. He noticed what looked like the top of what could have been a bell, with its arching curve. The water somewhat distorted its shape so he had to take that into consideration.

Toward the opposite end of the curve, he couldn't really see anything. In his mind, his thoughts started narrowing down the possibilities with its collected data from his observation. Yet there still wasn't quite enough he could see in the picture to determine what it could be. The fact that it had harmed someone told him two things: it was dangerous, and it was, what had been, a living organism. Some kind of sea creature. But he couldn't tell for sure by the picture alone. He put the phone back to his ear.

"Well I've looked at it, but can't tell for sure what it is. It seems to be missing something that it should have, but again that's an unknown."

"Any idea at all what it could have been? Any potential suspects?" she asked.

James shook his head. "I don't know, Becky. I can't tell for sure."

"Jim, are you aware of a serious problem in the waters at Pompano Beach that has made the city close down the beaches?"

James snapped his head up. This was news to him.

"No," he said loudly. "No, I've been out here on the keys and hadn't heard any news. What happened?"

She then told him what had been told to her, from the first injuries discovered to the fatalities, to the beach shutdown. "Julie and I are going up there tomorrow to investigate."

"Wait a minute. When are you leaving tomorrow?"

"In the morning. Probably around nine or nine-thirty the latest. It's about an hour and a half ride from here."

"I need to see that sample. I'm getting some ideas but I need to see it to clarify them in my mind."

"Oh? Anything you can tell me?"

"Not right now, Beck. I don't want to say anything right now because I don't know for sure, and I need to see and examine the sample before you go up. How late are you going to be there today?"

"Well I usually leave by five. It's twelve forty five now, so I have a few more hours here."

James looked at his watch, mostly by habit. She had already told him the time.

"Ok, listen. I'm coming up there. Let me gather up my stuff here and I'll be there before you leave. Should take me a couple of hours to get there. Three the most."

"Ok. I'll wait for you. Any problems on the way, give me a buzz."

"Sure thing. Oh, and Becky?"

"Yea?"

"Better keep that sample secure so anyone else going in there won't get too curious. Last thing you need is another injury. Until we know what it is, I highly recommend keeping it under lock and key."

"Point well taken. Will do. See you when you get here and do drive carefully, will you?"

James smiled at that. Rebecca was always the one to recommend careful driving, despite the fact that she herself sometimes drove like a bat out of hell. Women, he thought. After a few minutes, he was packed up and after throwing the three equipment and tool bags in the car, he started the car, quickly called the school to tell them the situation that he was going to investigate something mysterious and dangerous and he would keep them posted. After leaving the voicemail, he hung up and took off heading north up the keys. He had to go that way anyway because the university was in that direction, but he would still be a distance from it.

As he drove, he was thinking about that thing. One thing came into his mind and it was not something he really wanted to think about. In fact, it scared him. Despite that, it could possibly fit the bill for what and where that thing came from. He was hoping it was a far-fetched possibility and tried to make himself believe that it was. His thoughts about it deepened, and he found himself almost not stopping in time for a car which had suddenly put on the brakes in front of him. Realizing he better not have an accident now, he decided to let up on his thoughts and concentrate more on driving. He needed to get there in one piece and it had to be today. There were no other options.

CHAPTER 5

Miami Marine Institute, July 31

It was about 3pm when James reached Miami. He had been just north of the central part of the keys. Had he been down in or near Key West, his chances of making it to the Institute before Rebecca left would have been slim to none. It would have been, at the very least, an eight to ten hour drive.

He never really liked driving through Miami, or any large city, for that matter. For him, there were always too many people, too much traffic, and too much noise. Actually, too much of everything. He was certainly not an anti-people person, coming from a large family and having numerous friends. It's just that he considered city driving a hazard in and of itself, even with all the safety measures.

He knew where the institute was and it was only five minutes away from where he was. After making his way through all the traffic lights, the drivers who drove like they wanted to get somewhere yesterday, and those who didn't seem to have a clue as to where they were or where they were going, he finally reached the entrance to the grounds of the Institute. It was a very welcome sight, even after only three hours of driving.

He pulled around the main building where tourists entered and went to the back of the grounds where the research and lab facilities were. After finding the right building, he parked and went inside where he found Rebecca at her desk studying what looked like a small crustacean. She looked up and smiled.

"Well he's finally here." She got up and gave him a hug. "Glad you could make it. Must have been a good trip. You made good time."

"It was ok," he replied smiling back. "Everything was fine until I got to the city here, then I had to put on the brakes every second or two. At least in the keys you're more on the gas pedal than the brakes."

They laughed. "That's the price you pay for living and working in civilization. Anyway, wanna see it?"

"Sure! That's why I'm here. Lead on, fearless leader."

Rebecca led him toward the back of the lab and to Tony's desk, which looked more like a lab counter than a desk. She pulled the jar from the locked cooler and showed it to him. Picking it up, he looked closely at it, trying to see whatever he could that he couldn't see in the picture.

"So this is the thing we're all wondering about, eh?"

"Yep. That is it."

He kept looking at it, turning the jar to see if he could get better vantage points.

"I'd like to examine this outside the jar."

Rebecca turned. "Oh here, have a seat." She pulled up the chair and gave him a pair of gloves which were thicker than latex while staying just as flexible, yet thinner than thicker rubber gloves while having its more protective qualities. She also provided him with a pair of tweezers.

Taking a glass plate, he pulled it to in front of him, then took the specimen out of the jar with the tweezers and placed it on the plate. There it was. The shape suddenly appeared as it lay flat. It was only about the size of a thumbnail and translucent. He suspected what it might be. He knew what it definitely was.

"What do you think, Jim?" Rebecca looked at him examining it and waited for his answer.

"Well, I think, um, it is some kind of jellyfish. Or was. The question I'm wondering about is, is it a baby or something else?"

The question seemed more rhetorical than direct, so she didn't answer. "Let me look at it through the microscope here."

She retrieved the instrument at the other end of the desk, allowing him to pull it close to him. Checking that it was plugged in for the light source, he then carefully put the specimen on an examining plate, put the plate under the down-pointing four lenses, and then looked through the ocular lens at the top of the scope. Adjusting for size and clarity, he found the correct setting and started his examination.

He was looking for something specific.

Rebecca's voice broke the silent air. "Want something to drink, Jim? Coffee, tea, soda?"

"Uh, yea sure. Coffee if you have it," James replied as he continued to make adjustments and look through the eyepiece.

"We sure have it. Cream, sugar?"

"A little of each, thank you."

After she returned with it and placed it beside him, he was looking straight ahead of him, as if in deep thought.

"See something?"

"Well," he started to say clearing his throat. "Did you have a chance to look at it through the microscope?" When he looked at her, she could see a definite look of concern on his face.

"Yes. After Tony showed it to me, I had taken a quick look, then had to take a call from someone. Didn't have a chance to really examine it until after Tony had gone to the ER."

"What did you see?" he asked her.

"I saw what looked like tiny, miniscule barbs on the body. I believe these are what stung him. Originally I had thought jellyfish, but then I thought, what jellyfish stings from its body? And why no tentacles if it *is* a jellyfish? I thought it was pretty strange."

"Yea, it is strange, alright. It is a jellyfish. I looked for where there should be tentacles, and I did find areas where they were. Why they aren't there now is a big mystery."

He turned to look at her. "Better sit down." His eyes directed her to the seat behind her and she sat.

Rebecca began to feel worried. "What? What is it James? What kind of jellyfish is it? Is it a baby?"

He took a deep breath, looked down and then looked at her.

"Becky, when you go to Pompano Beach, I want to go with you. You're going to need the help. And I suggest you bring three diver wetsuits. Not for diving."

Her eyes widened just a bit, which was enough for anyone knowing her that she was taken completely by surprise.

"Wetsuits? Are you serious? Why?"

He picked up his coffee cup and took a sip of the drink. "Well, I can tell you this. It's a jellyfish, but not a baby one. I did find one small piece of a tentacle sticking out from a part of the bell. It's barely visible to the naked eye, but I saw it under the microscope. Looks like it had been torn off. Probably happened to all the others too. By what or why, we may never know. It doesn't seem to fit any species from these waters, or any waters around Florida. I have a strong suspicion and it's not one that anyone would want to hear. If I confirm it, this area's in trouble."

Now Rebecca's concern was all too obvious. "I did suspect it's venomous, after seeing what happened to Tony. Do you think this may somehow be connected with what happened up at Pompano?"

"Hmm, maybe. Only way to know is if any of these are found in the waters around there. But, if this is not a baby as I don't believe it is, then there's only one species of jellyfish I can think of that this could be."

"Can't be a baby anyway. It looks like it's beyond the polyp stage."

"Right," James agreed. "It is." He looked at it again.

Then he looked up at her. "You know what I'm thinking, don't you?" Although he was the jellyfish expert, she, too was a marine biologist and had knowledge of these creatures. At that very moment, their minds seemed to connect.

Her hand went to her mouth but her eyes said it all. "Oh, my God. Irukandji. No way. How the hell could that be? Aren't they from the waters around Australia or Hawaii?"

"Yes, they are. Or were. Originally they were thought to be only from those waters. Now they've been known to be as far away as Japan and even the British Isles. Incredible. They've been known to migrate with the currents under the sea surface. But in the past, they were never thought to be this far from there, and especially in these waters. If this is what it is, which I believe it is, then I'm afraid we've got a serious problem on our hands. An invasion of these things could send a lot of people to the hospital in a relatively short span of time."

She stared at the seemingly harmless thing on the glass plate. "I don't know a lot about these things. I know that they are, uh, from the box jellyfish family which are pretty nasty to people and everything else. Tell me something else I should know. We could be running into these things tomorrow."

"Let's go on the computer and I'll show you some colorful pictures of what they look like in the water. I think you will need to see for yourself. I'll first give you a brief rundown. I don't know what you don't know so if I say something and you already know it, just say, 'I know'."

"Ok. Agreed."

"Basically, there are five species of Irukandji. This is the one I believe is *Carukia barnesi*, a common one. It was first seen off the coast of northern Australia by the Irukandji people who lived there, hence its name. I don't think I need to name the others for you. Just know that this is the one we're dealing with here.

"You probably also know that it's one of the most venomous animals on earth. Its venom is roughly one hundred times more powerful than a Cobra's. Believe it or not, it's not always fatal. However, for it to be non-fatal to someone, the appropriate treatment must be given almost right away. When that's not possible, the person could die in a relatively short period of time."

"Jim, you said this thing has stingers in its bell. I thought they were only in tentacles."

He picked up his coffee and took a swig, then put the cup down.

"Normally they are, in all jellyfish. Except this one. This is the only species that has them in its bell as well as tentacles. That's why Tony got stung when he touched it."

"I need to get some coffee myself. I'll be right back. Want another one?"

"No thanks. This will do. Go get yours. It's good, really," he replied. Rebecca got up and disappeared to the other side. In a couple of minutes she was back.

"If I were a drinker, this would probably be a whiskey. I sure need a drink after finding out what this is. In my case, coffee is just perfect."

"Ok. There were casualties and injuries at the Pompano Beach waters. At least two or three people have died, from what I was told. Others I don't know about, except they were stung and were in agony. What can be expected if one of us got stung?"

She wanted to hear it from an expert. Not that she didn't believe what Jimmy the lifeguard had told her. But to hear it from someone who had the necessary knowledge would make their investigation and preparing how to deal with the problem all the more urgent. Not to mention the fact that if anyone on the mission got stung, she needed to know what to expect and how to deal with it.

"Now keep in mind that being stung is not an automatic death sentence. So panicking, if stung, will get you nowhere. This particular species causes what's called the Irukandji syndrome. There would be severe, excruciating muscle cramping. Feels like your muscles are trying to rip right out of you. You'll also have severe pain in the lower back, a burning sensation of your skin and face. There might be vomiting, severe headache. Your heart will race so fast you might believe it's going to burst. And often surviving victims have complained of having felt a sense of impending doom. Not a good feeling at all. People who are elderly, or very young as children are more likely to die. As well as people allergic to the venom or others who are immunocompromised would almost surely die. There would likely be scars left on the victim's skin, which would be permanent. Their tentacles, which can be over three feet long, despite their tiny 5mm bell, can leave these ugly marks. If the person survives, he or she is lucky to have only those. For those who die, sometimes fatal brain hemorrhages can result from the stings which of course would be the cause of their deaths."

There was silence for a few moments as Rebecca was processing in her mind this terrifying information. It was hard to imagine something this small causing so much damage and pain. What really made it so dangerous was its small size. Entering swimming areas with lots of people, it could remain invisible while each of its long thread-thin tentacles shot out thousands of nematocysts, needle-like darts filled with toxic venom, on contact with the surface of another sea creature. Or the skin of a person. No one would be able to see any of these creatures in the water, unless they were looking specifically for it.

The more she thought of it, the more she dreaded the mission tomorrow. But it had to be done and she was bound and determined that they would get to the bottom of this. If they did find any of these creatures in the water, she really didn't know what they could do about it. But first they had to determine if there was a solution at all to the problem. As a marine biologist, even though not a specialist in the jellyfish species of sea creatures, she knew that little could be done to keep the area free of these creatures once they infiltrated an area. Just like any other species, it would be next to impossible. Because they didn't swim only on the water surface.

"Jim, I think I better arrange for some wetsuits and diving equipment also. You scuba certified?"

"Yes I am."

"Ok. Did you bring any personal belongings with you?"

"No. But I'm only an hour away from here. What time you leaving in the morning?"

"I'd like to leave here by seven thirty. Get there around eight fifteen or so."

James got up and went to the desktop computer nearby. "I'll plan on meeting you there. I'm going to bring my camera and try to take some close up pictures if we spot them in the water. Maybe take a couple of samples."

Finding a marine website, he came to the screen showing color pictures of the various toxic jellyfish out there. As he scrolled down, Rebecca saw color photos of the Lions Mane jellyfish which was reported to be as large as eight feet across, then the Portuguese Man O' War with its blue sail, the Sea Nettle found in the Chesapeake Bay which was as large as one foot across and tentacles greater than six feet long, and then the notorious box jellyfish of Australia and other Pacific islands which had been known to kill hundreds of people.

Finally, he honed in on the Irukandji. "Here it is with its tentacles. Notice the similarities of its bell with our sample here."

Rebecca looked closely at it and agreed. "Yes, it does look nearly the same. It's difficult to see the tentacles but there they are." She saw them, looking thinner than threads and almost completely invisible.

James slowly scrolled down the screen for more information and pictures, while trying to ignore the delicious perfume scent of Rebecca as she bent her face down close to his to look at the screen. She was a very attractive woman. Despite the fact that she was his colleague, he wasn't above building up the nerve to ask her out. But this was not the time for that. He did enjoy that perfume. Looking at a bunch of jellyfish before a dangerous mission was not the time or place to let the mind start wandering.

He sat back and released the mouse from his grip. "Well, I guess we've seen what we need to. I think I'll hit the road and head back. Got to contact my boss back at the school and let him know what I'll be up to tomorrow. He'll probably ok my going and will want me to keep him in the loop and let him know what's happening."

Rebecca stood back up, brushing back her long brown hair. "As long as it won't be a problem for you, we certainly can use your help, Jim. Thank you for that."

He stood up. "Hey, what are friends for? Thanks for the coffee. See you tomorrow morning then?"

She nodded with a smile. "You know where the beach is?"

"Yea, I've been there a couple of times in the past. Been a while but I remember how to get there," he said halfway to the door.

"I'll have all the gear, suits and equipment ready. We'll be in parking lot C, near the main shower room building. Drive carefully."

"I will," he said with a wave, and was then out the door.

She sighed as she walked back to the front of the lab and to her desk. Before she left for the day, all the wet suits and scuba gear would be added to the equipment already in the two vehicles that they'd be taking up to Pompano. There was no reason to wait until morning to get this done. At seven thirty, she wanted to pull out for the hour and a half trip up there. Julie would be expected to meet her here at that time and they'd start out together. Rather than wait, she went to the gear closet and pulled them out. Tomorrow would be a long day.

CHAPTER 6

Atlantic Ocean, thirty five miles east of Key West, July 31

Sam Weston had been looking forward to this trip all year. His two week vacation from his accounting job in New Jersey was always used for his pleasure sailing and these areas around the keys were his favorite haunts.

Divorced at thirty-seven, he had been married for only ten years. It was fortunate that it was an amicable divorce because she had obtained custody of the children. And *because* it was amicable, she had allowed liberal visitations for the two children, Amy and Josh. She had allowed them to go on the two weeks with him to the Keys and enjoy pleasures of sailing on his thirty foot sail boat. Although they hadn't gotten along too well in their marriage, they were the type of couple that got along better *not* being married.

With him now on the boat, he made sure they wore lifejackets and were sitting down. They were still young, at ages ten and eight so he had to ensure that they were seated and well away from the edge of the boat. He was a good father to them and loved them more than anything. There was nothing he wouldn't do to protect them from harm.

It was a beautiful day for sailing. It was sunny and a balmy eighty degrees, a little breezy but just enough to keep the boat moving at a reasonable pace. The kids were really enjoying it and having a good time.

They also enjoyed staying in Key West where they could enjoy an entirely different world from theirs in Trenton. The streets in Key West were narrow with apartment buildings, homes from the days of Ernest Hemingway which were old, refurbished and had an attractive quaintness about them that would make one wonder what it was like living here back in the early 1900s.

Here out in the waters off the coast was still another world from the touristy business of Old Key West. The sea was calm and in the distant horizon they could see large vessels slowly making their way toward wherever they were going.

"Daddy, do you think we'll see any dolphins out here?" asked ten year old Amy.

As Sam steered the boat, he looked out over the water. "We might, honey. They're around. We just have to keep looking. Let me know if you spot any."

"Ok. Hey," she pointed out toward the west in the direction of the coast. "I thought I saw something jump out of the water."

"Where?" yelled little Josh.

"There, see?" She pointed to lead Josh's and their father's eyes out to where she was looking.

"Oh yea. You're right. There they are. Wow." Sam was excited about seeing them, although not as much as the kids.

"Wow. Cool," exclaimed Josh, giggling at the sight. "Wish I were a dolphin so I could do that too."

Sam laughed. There were a lot of things little Josh wished he could be. Later on as he grew up, he'd be glad he was still who he was.

Steering the boat more toward starboard, he began to make his way back toward the coast. They'd been out here for about two hours and he didn't want the kids to become sunburned. Two hours out on the open water was plenty of time to get their enjoyment. Even with the sunscreen on them, their sensitive skins could take only so much sun. He was not immune to sunburn himself.

He had to keep maneuvering the main sail according to the wind which seemed to be in their favor. Should the wind change direction, which it could at any time, he could run the inboard engine and make their way back to the marina that way. It was a good backup which he not only appreciated having, but considered it an absolutely necessity, along with the containers of fuel in case he ran short of gas.

There were also the Gulf stream currents he had to remember. They had to be considered when sailing this boat out here, so if he found himself making little headway despite the winds, he would rev up the engines for the extra boost to counter those currents. Didn't happen very often, but he was prepared whenever it was necessary.

They were a little too far off the coast to see land. Sam started thinking that maybe he'd sailed out a little farther than he should have. By sailors' knowledge, the horizon was about twenty miles distant. Once he did see land, he'd know about how much farther they had to go. To himself he had decided that the next time, he would keep the coast in sight. There was no reason for them to go this far out. Knowledge gained, lesson learned. That was his decision and he would stick to it.

Then he saw the boat making little headway and decided to bring down the sail and rev up the engine.

"Alright kids, fasten your seatbelts. Sail's coming down and engines coming up. We're going to head on back, ok?"

They didn't say anything, but he saw them nod their heads. He knew they didn't want to go back just yet, but quietly had accepted the fact that their fun trip today had to end. At least they had a good time. Maybe tomorrow they could do it again, Josh was thinking.

The breeze seemed to pick up a bit. The skies were still sunny with the number of white puffy clouds increasing. As Sam began changing his method of propulsion of the boat, he realized that he'd brought the sails down before revving up the engine. Just the opposite of what he'd wanted to do. *Shit,* he thought to himself. Oh well, too late now. He turned the key and pushed the button to start the engine. Surprisingly, it didn't start right away as it usually did. He checked the key to make sure it was turned all the way to allow the charge from the battery to flow through, then pushed the button again to light up the engine. It turned over repeatedly but didn't start.

Son of a bitch, he again said to himself. This was the first time this had happened. He did the same thing he would have done if this had happened in a car. He kept turning the key and pushing the button. All he could hear was the engine turning over, but it didn't catch. Now he realized that this time he was fortunate to have brought the sails down first. Right now they were dead in the water and he needed to look at the engine and try to see what was amiss in there. He wasn't a mechanic by any stretch of the imagination. For him to try and dabble with the engine was like a bicycle repairman trying to fix an aircraft engine.

"Amy, can you come over here for a minute?" He decided to use his older child to man the helm while he checked the engine. "Josh, stay there. I have to check the engine for a minute. Don't get out of your seat, ok?"

"Ok, Daddy. I'll stay. Can I help?"

Sam smiled at the offer. Leave it to his little boy to want to help him.

"No buddy, there's nothing you can do to help, but I appreciate your offer. What you can do for me is stay there safe and sound. I'm having your big sister steer while I check the motor, ok?"

"Ok."

With Amy at the helm, he gave her brief instructions.

"Honey, just hold the helm as steady as you can. I'm only going to be a couple of minutes. If I can't get the engine working, I'll put the sail back up and we'll get back with that."

"Ok," she replied.

Fortunately he had a radio on board, although he had never used it yet. He realized after thinking about it that he'd made another novice mistake. He hadn't checked it before they left the dock to make sure it was working. After calling himself an idiot-to himself-he made another decision not to make *that* mistake again also.

While he checked within the engine compartment behind his daughter, Amy held the helm firmly in her little hands and looked around. There were continuous dark gray clouds all along the horizon. If she had noticed them, she didn't seem to think too much of that. The breeze had picked up a bit. She didn't notice that the clouds were moving in faster than it looked. She heard the clanging sounds of her father hitting something, as if trying to get it to work. But the sounds didn't last long because soon after that, he closed the compartment door. He was still clueless as to what was wrong.

Wiping his hands, he looked out in frustration and approached Amy.

"Ok, Amy. I need you to still hold the helm. I'll have to put the sail back up. We're going to have to sail back in. Once I take the helm back, I'll need you to go back to your seat, buckle yourself back in and keep an eye on your brother for me. Can you do that?"

Amy nodded. "Yea, Daddy, I can do that. Everything ok?"

Although he wasn't sure yet, he wasn't about to tell her *that.*

"Everything will be fine. Ok, I'm going to do it now."

Back to the mast he went and started pulling up the sail once again. He hadn't noticed the dark cloud bank becoming darker, heavier, and closer to them. It was now covering a quarter of the sky. The strong breeze was now increasing into a mild wind.

Back in his seat, eight year old Josh was being quiet as he was starting to feel the beginnings of fright. The boat began to roll just a little more and pitch just a little more, as waves started forming in the previously calm seas. He watched his father pull up the sail and his sister holding the helm. He looked up and saw the clouds become thicker and darker as they neared the sky overhead them, and saw a brief flash of lightning off in the distant clouds.

Once Sam got the sail up, he struggled back to the helm as the boat began to roll and pitch more. It was getting harder to maintain balance as the waves began to increase along with the wind. He didn't want to scare the kids by informing them of a sudden, unexpected storm or squall. He knew they were already scared and could see what was happening for themselves. His job was to remain as calm as possible and reassure them that they would all be ok and get them back to land as soon as possible.

After making sure Amy was secure in her seat, Sam was working the sails and the jib, attempting to tack leeward toward the coast. Unfortunately, he was unknowingly ignoring his compass and concentrating more on keeping the boat sailing, believing still that the coast was off to his right. What he wasn't aware of was that with the increasing prevailing winds, the boat had changed direction. If the coast had been off to his right initially, it was no longer. With no land in sight, all around him everything looked the same.

As the clouds now increased to cover three fourths of the sky, the winds picked up even more. Sam knew they were in desperate trouble now. Going to the radio, he turned it on and called out a Mayday on the distress frequency. The return was only static. He repeated the mayday several times with his position that he last knew of, but no one answered. The static remained. He could kick himself for not checking before they left the dock.

The children were now terrified and were starting to cry. The boat was rolling and pitching at the same time, and a few of the waves starting cresting over into the boat. Rain started falling on them as the squall grew in its intensity. Gusts of wind now moderate to heavy started racking the boat and bending the sails to almost the bursting point. The storm was unexpected, had approached them quickly, and they were now under full attack by Mother Nature in the middle of nowhere. Sam had no clue now as to where they were. He looked at the compass and realized that the boat was pointing east instead of west, the opposite direction to where he wanted to go. Although the windward direction was now southeast, he had to try and turn the boat around to head the other way. It was more difficult than he realized. All their lives were now in his hands as he struggled to maneuver the boat. He prayed silently that he could get them out of this but his prayer was interrupted by a violent gust of wind that nearly capsized the boat. The kids were now crying and yelling, barely audible above the screaming winds.

A huge wave crashed into the boat, knocking it sideways but the boat remained upright and afloat for now. Sam continued to try and call for help as the boat ever so slightly started turning westward the way he wanted it to go. The situation had become desperate now and he was doing all he could to save them. They were in a worst case scenario in the middle of the ocean. He'd never experienced anything like this before. Their very lives were threatened and there was no help in sight.

Again another wave. Another near roll-over. This time he heard a loud crack from above. When he looked up, he saw the sail rip apart from the mast. The main mast had cracked and was now bending downward. It looked like a bent broken bone that almost separated from the rest of it.

"Oh dear mother of God," Sam exclaimed out loud, without being able to hear himself in the screaming wind. Once again he tried the radio, yelling repeatedly 'Mayday Mayday', and his position. He didn't know if anyone was hearing him because there was no response. But he had to try, just in case there *was* only a one-way communication and he was the transmitting end. He looked over the wheel and saw his terrified children trying to deal with what could only be described as unimaginable horror. He blamed himself for this situation and promised God that if only He would help them, he'd never put them in this situation again. He'd never been a believer and it was certainly unknown as to whether this one-time prayer of desperation would be answered.

Suddenly the most violent gust of wind hit them. Sam was knocked off his feet by something hitting him on the back of his head. The lower broken half of the mast had come around and violently hit the man who was struggling so hard to keep the boat afloat and for their survival.

At the same time, what could have been described as a rogue wave hit the side of the boat. The boat started to roll further to the side than it had ever been before. It was now at a forty five degree angle. Normally in calmer seas on the sailboat, with the proper crew and handling of the boat, it could be brought back up to its ninety degree position to the horizontal angle of the sea. In addition, the engines would start. But now, it was if the sailboat and its three person crew were doomed from the start. Sam was silent and still on the deck. The kids didn't know that their father was dead. The boat was continuing to roll into a fatal angle and when they didn't see him appear from behind the wheel, Josh nearly panicked. Amy released her seat belt and struggled to walk forward in the violently pitching and rolling boat. As she saw his body on the deck and noticed he wasn't moving, she screamed out his name.

The boat slowly continued to roll past the forty-five degrees, bringing the children closer to the water. Slowly but determinedly the winds and waves pushed the boat over until its contents and crew were in the water.

It wasn't long before the kids, alive when they went into the water, felt the incredible pain and burning all over their bodies. They screamed as loud as they could, as the twenty five foot waves picked them up and dropped them. No one could or would hear them, including themselves, their voices drowned out by the screaming winds and pummeling rain. Only the silence and blackness that overtook them gave them the relief they needed that allowed them to move on to something and somewhere far better than what they'd been going through.

****

At the US Coast Station in Key West, a petty officer second class radioman heard a faint distress call on the radio unit. Turning knobs to try and decrease the static and increase the volume on the call, he was trying to determine if the call was coming from their district area and if anywhere near the waters of Key West or any of the other keys. He heard faint screaming sounds as if from high winds but wasn't sure if they were winds and thought he heard a voice, possibly male, yelling Mayday. He heard numbers but couldn't quite make out what they were. It was possible that the caller was saying latitude and longitude numbers but he wasn't sure. Then the call went dead.

Trying to pinpoint the position of the call was next to impossible. Then he had the presence of mind to ask his supervisor, First Class Petty Officer Ray Bowman if there was any significant weather in their district area. When Bowman informed him of a reported squall about thirty miles out, east-northeast of Key West, that's when he told Bowman about the call. Bowman took it seriously and contacted the lieutenant in charge of the station. Knowing the area affected by the squall, he notified the Coast Guard Air Station at Miami of the faint, received distress call by someone suspected of being in that squall area and in serious trouble. Immediately, personnel were alerted. Within minutes, pilots and aircrew were onboard the MHC Dolphin helicopter and preparing for takeoff to the coordinates of the reported squall area. Because there were no exact coordinates of the distress caller, they would have to search the entire area where the storm was reported if they had any chance of finding him at all. It was a dangerous mission which could very well put the helicopter and its crew in serious jeopardy.

But the Coast Guard was not a service to back down from dangerous situations, including that of weather. Other lives were at stake which might depend on them and if they were out there, this crew was determined to find and save them. It was basically a roll of the dice. Five minutes later they were airborne.

CHAPTER 7

Miami South Beach, August 1

Although it was the off season, there were still some die-hard beachgoers, who wouldn't, or couldn't, stay away from the beaches. Not surprisingly, they were tourists who, for whatever reason, chose to come to Florida during the hot mid-summer instead of the less brutal warm periods during the early to mid Spring or mid to late fall seasons. The locals, of course, knew better. So did the snowbirds, those residents of the north who would come down to their vacation homes in Florida during the cooler, less humid months. While Florida enjoyed the cooler fall and winter seasons with no snow but still comfortable temperatures, the north-as in New England- would suffer the onslaught of cold temperatures, icy weather, and snowfalls that only children or avid snow skiers could really appreciate.

Those on the beach had to wear sandals and sit on beach chairs because the sand was too hot from the beating sun to even walk on barefoot, let alone lie on. One could get burned from above as well as below, which is why most people never bothered going there where cool relief, even from the water, could never really be truly attained.

The few in the water just stood waist deep but didn't bother swimming. They were likely finding out that going swimming in very warm water with the humidity and heat of Miami during the summer was nearly the same as swimming in sweat. Yet if they were from a distant state, they were determined to enjoy Florida as much as they could while they were here. Those who came here for the first time at this time of year realized their mistake and many likely vowed to choose a better time of year the next time they came down.

South Beach was a very large, long beach that seemed to stretch for miles. Lifeguard high chair stations were located about every three hundred feet and all had umbrellas attached to them to protect the guards from the burning rays of the sun. The sand was white and palm trees dotted the beach as far as the eye could see in various locations. It looked like the kind of beach one might see in the Hollywood beach movies of the fifties and sixties. Perfect and inviting in every way. The water appeared so inviting that even a non-swimmer would be tempted to enter.

With the sun beating down on it every day, it's no wonder the water temperature was in the eighties. It was perfect for the creatures that were floating in unseen from further out, not far outside the reasonable swimming areas for people. They weren't in any hurry. The current and incoming tide would take them into where they neither had a clue of or cared. They were what they are and they would do what they do.

Some of the waders decided to become swimmers and that's what *they* did. Kids played catch with beach balls in the water while their parents stood close by and watched them, at the same time making sure their children didn't wander out too far. A few teens threw Frisbees on the wet, hard-packed sand along the water's edge. There was even a volleyball game with a few brave souls on the hot sand, as if they were daring their sandals or beach shoes to come off. In fact, one sandal came off one of the kids' feet and he yelled in pain and ran to the water quickly for relief, while his buddies laughed their butts off. Despite their amusement at the expense of their friend, they did throw his sandal to him so he wouldn't have to repeat the experience. Not surprisingly, he decided to stop playing and vowed to wear beach sneakers next time he wanted to play.

About a hundred feet from them, a couple in their mid sixties visiting from Michigan, were strolling in the water a few feet from its edge. Up and down in both directions of the beach people dotted the sand. If this was an in-season time, the beach would be packed and the water would be filled with swimmers, body surfers in the sometimes moderate to large waves, and those just having plain old fun in the water. It would be cooler then and just as refreshing as its coolness.

Seagulls flew everywhere above and you could hear their cries for food which, even at this time of year, they expected and knew would be around the relatively few beach goers. Some of them landed on the beach, walked around, and would peck at the sand as they seemed to discover little tidbits or morsels of food scraps that were invisible to human eyes.

The weather seemed to be perfect, with no signs of bad weather, let alone a squall which had been battering a portion of the ocean to the northeast. It was about one thirty in the afternoon- a typical summer day in Miami and one of its fine beaches. A whistle blew in the distance, which didn't appear to alarm anyone initially. Unlike most other whistlings, primarily by lifeguards when they wanted to restrict someone in the water from doing something foolish and against the rules, this one didn't stop. The fact that it continued and repeated over and over, soon caused other whistlings further and closer by to start up as well, did catch people's attention and most people, both in and out of the water, were looking in the direction from where they were coming from.

The group of teens playing volleyball stopped playing. People in the water stood up trying to see what they could see. The two Frisbee players suddenly lost interest in their playing and looked down the beach in the direction where everyone else was looking.

About a fifth of a mile southward down the beach, lifeguards took a lifeboat and skidoo and went out as fast as they could to what appeared to be someone in distress. Beach witnesses were viewing what was appearing to be a rescue. Was someone having a heart attack in the water, or a stroke? Was someone drowning or having a seizure? Did someone get bitten by something in the water? No doubt witnesses were asking each other those questions. Those in the water not far from the site came out and stood on the beach until they could find out what exactly happened.

When the rescuers reached the victim, they found an eighteen year old boy yelling in pain. He was trying to tell them, in-between screams, that the back of his leg was killing him and now the pain was starting to spread all over. The rescuers were seeing that he was trying to keep from screaming through his mouth closing it and grimacing, but it was all he could do from opening his mouth and letting it all out. After pulling him out of the water quickly and into the lifeboat, the guards assessed him and then saw the black, evil-looking tentacle scars running the full length of the back of his left leg, from buttock to the Achilles tendon.

"My God, what the hell is that?" exclaimed one of the guards. The thread-thin snake-like markings looked like black varicose veins and looked as painful as they actually were to the victim.

"Holy shit," mumbled the other guard under his breath. He didn't want to forget the fact that the victim could still hear. The last thing they needed was for the suffering victim to panic from what he was hearing.

After reassuring him that he was going to be alright, the second lifeguard radioed in for EMTs and paramedics. One of the lifeguards looked in the water but didn't see anything that could cause such a horrendous injury. There was no bleeding, just those scarring marks. But they couldn't imagine the amount of pain the victim was enduring. As the guard was motoring back to the beach on the boat, the victim went into a sudden seizure. He stopped yelling, arched his back so much that the guard thought he was going to break it. The foaming at the mouth became an additional focal evidence of intense agony. He'd never seen anything like it in his life.

He'd seen seizures before, of course, being in public service. But he never saw arching of the back like this in anyone having an epileptic seizure.

After reaching the beach, both lifeguards jumped out of their watercrafts and did their best to keep the victim safe from self-harm during the seizure activity. Soon police vehicles arrived and then the cops came onto the beach, followed quickly by ambulance personnel who had just pulled up and then exited their vehicles. When the EMTs and paramedics arrived at the boat, the young victim's seizure had stopped, and he appeared unconscious.

The stretcher was ready for him. The medics then pulled the victim carefully out of the boat and gently laid him on the wet sand, away from the water's edge but not on the dry, hot sand. Their assessment was exact and swift. His blood pressure was decreased to a dangerous low of 88/50 but his heart rate was at a life-threatening 185 and was thready. They turned him to examine the marks on the back of his left leg and were taken aback by the severity of their appearance. Without saying, they knew he was stung by something dangerous and life-threatening that was apparently in the water. They asked if anyone had seen anything in the water, but no one admitted to seeing anything.

The young man was in shock, and he did not respond when they talked to him or from any physical stimulation they tried. He had to be rushed to the emergency room as fast as possible. Within seconds, they had him on the stretcher and quickly picked it up to carry him to the waiting ambulance. They couldn't roll the stretcher on the sand.

A man came running up to them and was frantic.

"Hey, what happened? What happened to my son?"

The lifeguard he ran up to assumed, correctly, that he was a family member.

"Uh, who are you sir?"

"I'm his father. My name is Ronald Westcoat. That's my son, Danny. What happened? Where are they taking him?"

The guard then explained what happened and which hospital he was going to.

"He's going to Miami Dade General, sir. It looks like something nasty stung him in the water, but we don't know what as yet. He's breathing and is being treated right now as we speak and as he's being transported. You can find out at the ER any updates as to his condition. By the way, is he allergic to anything?"

"Just penicillin. Oh my Lord. Damn. What the hell could have done that to him?"

The lifeguard repeated himself. "We don't know, sir. Does he have a history of seizures or have epilepsy?" He was quickly taking notes to pass on this information to the medics as they couldn't find any of this out from the victim. At this point in time, speed was of the essence.

"No. No, absolutely not. He doesn't have epilepsy. Never had a seizure in his life."

"Is he on any medications?"

The father was thinking as he looked down. "No, I don't think so. He's been living at the dorm at his university and spending the weekend with me here. As far as I know, the only med he takes is Benadryl for allergies."

"Hold on a sec, sir."

The lifeguard got on the radio and passed this information to his dispatch back at home base. They in turn radioed that to the ambulance dispatch for the transporting ambulance. The hospital would have all that information before the ambulance arrived.

The guard looked at the man and suggested he go to the ER where he could give them any other information that they'd need on his son, in addition for him to get updated on the progress of his son's condition and treatment.

"Dispatch to Charlie One."

The lifeguard responded to his call sign. "Dispatch, Charlie One. Go."

"Be advised sector one and two are to be closed for the rest of the day. Later we will determine regarding tomorrow. All water activity shut down. All lifeguards to remain on duty to keep people out of the water. Please ensure all persons in the water have been evacuated out."

"Roger, dispatch. Copy that. Will commence evac now."

And so it began. For about a quarter mile of the beach area, which included Charlie One's, the water was left devoid of all human swimmers. Not that there were that many to begin with. Had this been the in-season, evacuation would have been a virtual nightmare. As it was, it didn't take long for the evacuation to begin and end. As Charlie One took care of this in his area, so did Charlies Two and Six. Soon, everyone was on the beach.

Unbeknownst to the lifeguards in the affected areas, all the other, unaffected areas received the latest news which spread like wildfire. There were people coming out of the water in those areas despite those not being affected. Apparently the scariness of something in the water hurting people was enough for many people to want to get and stay dry. In some people's minds, this was reminiscent of the movie "Jaws". Except that this was real, and what was in the water apparently was no shark. Other people did think this was a shark that attacked the victim, although they had hardly any facts about the victim or his injuries. Assumptions were being made by people who heard about it, without any real basis to their assumptions. Although the media had gotten word of the incident and the scar marks left on the victim, all was hush-hush regarding what caused the injuries-for good reason.

People left the beach, while a hardy few stayed. The beach areas looked empty and the few concession stands that were open felt the brunt of the financial loss of business. Still, as there were people on the beach, whether a few or many, they'd remain open until closing time. For as far as they knew, maybe tomorrow the entire beach areas would be closed.

The areas were quieter. Only the birds interrupted the sounds of the water washing up on shore. It was a serene, lonely scene that seemed befitting of an incident that had destroyed, at least temporarily, the atmosphere of joy and pleasure that this beach always instilled in most visitors. As it now was, until closing time the lifeguards walked the lonely beat of the beaches. Not to be potential rescuers, but to keep people out of the water. Once *they* left at the end of the day, there would be no one there to perform that duty. Anyone foolish enough to go into these now-endangered waters without lifeguards around, especially at night, was asking for trouble and would very likely get it.

CHAPTER 8

Thirty five miles northeast of Key West, August 1

The US Coast Guard's Lockheed HD 130 aircraft flew over a pre-determined area of one hundred square miles in a search pattern called a parallel, which is one that covers large areas. Because it didn't have the information to focus on a more confined area, thereby expanding the search grid, the plane was used first to see if the crew could spot any signs of survivors of the vessel which they believed was reported to have capsized. Although the communications had been broken and barely intelligible, they realized that it *would* be if the captain and crew were caught in the middle of the squall. The storm had abated somewhat, but the winds were still heavy at times and the rain was still significant albeit diminished from when the first report came in.

The plane could cover a larger area in a shorter expanse of time than a chopper, and time was not on the side of the victims below. The pilot struggled to keep the plane flying as smoothly as possible as the co-pilot and crew looked out for any signs, no matter how small or remote, of any survivors. Even so, it was like looking for a needle in a haystack. With the heavy seas below displaying the white tops of the crashing waves, the chances of survival in the water were quite slim. Still, they had to try. If they spotted something and believed it to be a survivor or a body, the chopper would be called out.

Despite their experience, flying in this kind of weather was always very risky business. Out over the open ocean, anything could happen and their lives were always on the line. Yet they knew the dangers and were always willing to risk their lives to save someone in need of help.

As they flew the search pattern, they covered a lot of miles in a short period of time. Flying back and forth, they used whatever optical tools they could to visualize better what was already difficult. With powerful binoculars, one of the crew members searched out a window looking for that needle. The pilots also scanned the waters below as best as they could while keeping the aircraft flying.

Suddenly the crew member behind the cockpit thought he saw something and said so over the microphone he was wearing. This microphone was necessary for pilot-crew communications because of the noise of the plane.

"I think I see something, about two o'clock. Possible overturned vessel. Every so often it pops up, likely between the waves."

"Roger," replied the pilot. "Andy, you get that?"

The co-pilot responded with a yes. "Looking down there now."

With his binoculars and the pilot in full control of the aircraft, the co-pilot, Lieutenant Andy Craig scanned the sea down below.

"I'm coming around," said the pilot, Lieutenant Commander Tom Overly.

Meanwhile, the crew member in the back went to the starboard side of the plane to the window and searched down there as well. When the plane positioned itself in the air where the object was first seen, the pilot had descended as much as he safely could without further endangering them.

There it was. What appeared to be the bottom of a boat.

"Oh boy," said Andy. He confirmed it to the pilot. "Spotting for bodies in the water."

That would be even more difficult. But now, they would need backup.

"Coast Guard Airbase seven, Coast Guard Airbase seven, this is Coast Guard Bluehawk, over."

"Bluehawk, this is seven, go ahead, over"

"Seven, Bluehawk. Overturned vessel spotted, appears to be possible sailboat." Then he gave the exact coordinates.

"Searching for survivors or bodies now, but extremely difficult. Suggest sending a chopper with rescue swimmer, over."

The request was acknowledged. Immediately after that, a chopper and crew with swimmer were dispatched to the coordinates, having also been told of the squall which was in its diminishing throes.

Once the chopper was spotted by the fixed-wing aircraft, communications between them indicated the departure of the plane as the chopper took over. It hovered over the boat looking for the crew, and it spotted a small body. It was right up against the upright keel but the crew did not see the face. The arms looked like they were from a small person. Immediately the rescue swimmer prepared to descend as the side hatch door was opened. Already fully suited, the pilot brought the craft down low enough for the swimmer to jump into the water.

Being fully trained and certified to swim in these heavy seas, the swimmer made his way to the upturned boat and toward the body. When he checked it, he saw it was that of a young boy. He had a strap attached to him that caught on something on the boat, preventing the current from carrying him away. But there was no doubt the boy was deceased. He could only be sure by having the boy lifted up into the chopper where they could more accurately assess his condition. Right now it didn't look good. With his arm, he waved for the other crew member to lower the line with the on-board crane. With the basket attached at the end of it and reaching the swimmer's level, he placed the boy's body inside the basket and gave the signal to raise it up. He never noticed the snakelike markings on the boy's back.

As the basket lifted back up, the swimmer checked around the boat and underneath the keel for signs of anyone else. He knew there had to have been others because there was no way he could have been out here alone. Not spotting anyone else around the boat, he looked out as far as he could see as the line lowered back down to bring him back up. He saw nothing but fifteen foot rolling waves with no bodies surfacing between them. It was possible that sea predators may have gotten them or they were carried off by the current. If either was the case, the chances of them being found were slim to none.

The chopper made a final go-round the area, while it still had enough fuel, as a last attempt to find whoever the boy had been with. After about a half hour of searching the area around the boat for about a mile to two miles in each direction, the fuel gauge indicated they should start heading back to base. The pilots hated that because they wanted to spend more time searching, in the hopes of finding the rest of the crew. It was a feeling of abandonment that always haunted a flight crew when it believed a job wasn't finished and had to be left behind, even for reasons beyond its control.

As they headed back, the enlisted flight crew checked the boy for any vital signs and other signs of life. They were all certified in advanced first aid and life support; their training, unfortunately couldn't help them revive the boy. The skin was cold and bluish and the pupils were fixed and dilated. There was no response whatsoever to any kind of physical stimulation. It was clear the boy was gone.

As they assessed the body, they were shocked to also discover the strange, whip-like markings on the boy's back. Initial thoughts that maybe they were birthmarks were quickly dispelled when they realized that such marks didn't look like these. Even though they weren't actual medics or medical personnel, still, they knew enough to realize that they were challenged by something currently unexplainable.

The crew member who discovered the marks told the pilot. The co-pilot, hearing the same communications from the crew member radioed into the base station, which then initiated a call to the ambulance personnel. Upon arrival, the body would be officially assessed by medical personnel and it would ultimately end up in the medical examiner's office. The most difficult part would be to determine who the boy was.

****

Miami-Dade General Hospital, Miami, Florida, August 1
The only thing that really saved the eighteen year old from a death that would almost certainly have occurred in an elderly person, young child, or a person with an already immuno-compromised immune system, was his youth, strength and good health. Even so, it was a struggle to save him from the havoc created by the powerful deadly toxins that had been injected into

him. The treatment was the standard for venomous jellyfish stings, which included prolific applications of vinegar to the sting sites.

After an hour in the ER, the boy had come to, but was just as emotionally traumatized as he was physically. His father was there to provide support and comfort. Being that his mother was sick at home from cold symptoms, she couldn't be there. But after being reassured he would survive, that brought a tremendous measure of relief that seemed to make his still on-going overall pain a tad more tolerable.

Little did anyone know that the fact that there were so few people at the beach and fewer still in the water was what prevented an overwhelming inflow of patients from there. By this time the tide and current had brought in unwelcome visitors to the area. In fact, there were at least thousands of what could only be described as a deadly invasion, which was yet to be discovered. And no one would know, until later, that this was only the beginning.

****

Pompano Beach, Florida, August 2
The early morning started off cloudy and gray with on and off again rain showers. Forecasters predicted that cloudiness would turn into sunshine later in the morning. Temperatures would be in the mid-eighties to lower nineties, and the humidity would be right up there with the temperatures.

As she pulled into the beach parking lot, Rebecca noticed only one or two parked cars. Business would certainly not be booming, neither today nor any other day, until this problem was identified and resolved.

Out of one of the parked vehicles she noticed the man getting out as he looked in her direction. It was James.

"Well well, our friend is here already," she said to Julie who looked out the window.

"Boy, I haven't seen him in a while. Looks like he's got a permanent tan there."

"Yea, well, if you spent as much time outdoors as he does, you'd probably have one too."

Julie had to concede to that. "Yea, probably."

Rebecca parked in a space close to his and got out, each giving a brief hug to the other in a friendly spirit of camaraderie. She'd known him for a number of years and, as far as she was concerned, he was one of the best in his field when it came to jellyfish.

"So what do we have going here?" James asked her.

Rebecca looked around the empty beach area and out to the water.

"Well, first we have to find the nearest lifeguard and let them know we're here. Once they provide us the boats, we'll bring whatever we need or can and head on out there to see what we can find. Julie, can you do me a favor and find one for us? Let them know where we are and where they have the boats. We need to know where to start from."

"Sure thing." As her assistant headed onto the beach, she turned to James.

"Ya know I'm worried about this. I hope this problem is isolated only to this area. If it spreads, it could spell disaster for a lot of the beaches along the coast."

James coughed, with hands on hips and looking around to assess the area, he had the same thoughts. "Yea, that's what I'm afraid of. But first, we have to officially confirm the identity of the culprits and locate where they are. If there's an invasion involved here, then these beaches might become ground zero. Especially if they are, in fact, Irukandji. This area has, to my knowledge, never seen any of these before. And the typical jellyfish that do appear here occasionally, are not the threats that these guys are."

"Did you bring all you needed?" she asked him.

"Yep. All that I would or might need, including special nets for taking out specimens and plastic transparent jars."

"Good. I brought the wetsuits just in case any of us have to go in the water. Fully head to toe, including facial coverings and masks. And of course the rubber gloves. They'll be a little awkward to work with but, hey, better that than to endure something far worse."

James nodded. "You got that right."

They saw Julie walking toward them with a lifeguard she found. He was on his walkie talkie and radioing to someone, apparently to let them know the scientists were here.

"Hey guys, this is Frank. He's our liaison with the beach EMS base."

After their introductory greetings and handshakes, they didn't waste time getting down to business.

Frank was a burly man who obviously worked out and seemed to be in shape to tackle just about almost anything. With curly blonde hair coming down to cover the tops of his ears, he looked like a dream to any woman who fancied a young, muscular, good looking blonde guy. Rebecca thought to herself if she had been younger, then maybe…Quickly putting those thoughts aside, she was the first to speak up. This mission was her baby and she needed to maintain control if they were to gather any headway for a solution.

"Ok, Frank, so which areas were reported to be affected?"

He pointed them out to her. "We'll be having a guard escorting you in each of the areas in the boat. You can be the navigator and direct where you want each boat to go. We'll "drive" so you can concentrate on what you need to. As we speak, there'll be three boats being put out there."

The three scientists saw those boats being pulled to the edge of the water in the area where they were, so they wouldn't have to walk far. The beach was actually miles long, but they would be concentrating mostly on the three northernmost sections, which comprised roughly a half a mile. From the beginning of the beach sand where the parking lot was to the edge of the water, it was roughly a hundred foot walk.

"Before you go out to the boats," Frank added, "better make sure you're wearing shoes or sandals. The sand is burning hot. Not fun to walk on this time of year."

"I believe you," replied Rebecca. She quickly looked at her assistant.

"Julie, I'm glad to see you're not wearing your high heels today." She was smiling and knew that Julie would know she was joking. Sometimes Julie liked to feed it right back to her. She looked down at her boss's feet. "I see you forgot to wear your ballet shoes today. You're slipping, Becky!"

After their brief stint of laughter and the levity settled down, Rebecca got them started. "Ok, let's get this show on the road, shall we?"

They all headed down to the boats and the three lifeguard coxswains that waited for them. The boats were about twenty feet long. Each had a large, Yamaha V6 outboard engine with horsepower of three hundred. They were equipped to get somewhere fast. Rebecca wanted to assess them first to see how much equipment they could safely bring on board. For now, she didn't think they'd need the wetsuits and their gear. But that could change later. She decided that the nets, rubber gloves, and jars would be required.

The three of them returned to the vehicles and got their respective equipment to bring with them. When they returned to the boats, James gave a quick briefing to the lifeguard coxswains.

"Are there lifejackets for us to wear?" he asked them.

"Absolutely. We won't bring you out unless you're wearing them."

"Good. I have to advise you not to put any part of you in the water. In other words, don't stick your hand or arm in it."

"After what happened, are you kidding me? Just don't fall overboard or I *will* have to go in."

James chuckled. "Let's not plan on that. Ok. I'm ready. Ladies?"

After they loaded the equipment and supplies on each of the boats, each scientist boarded. Soon they were sailing off to three different areas. Apparently, each lifeguard was assigned to a specific beach area already. Each scientist had nets, jars, and gloves for collection of specimens. Fortunately, the water was calm and the waves were small and subtle. They would be brought out to three hundred feet from shore. The plan was to slowly scan each sector of the water and gradually work their way in. If they found what they were looking for, they needed to note about how far out they discovered it before collecting and putting it into the jar.

Slowly and surely they scanned each sector, directing the guard where to go. They looked at the water for anything floating either on or just below the surface. Every so often, they had to reapply the suntan lotions they had applied in their vehicles. None of them were indifferent to sunburn.

Every once in a while they'd spot a piece of seaweed floating by. Their backs would straighten out immediately until they recognized it for what it was. Every time they saw something floating, it was instantly suspect until otherwise identified.

In her area, Julie scanned as the others. Even as an assistant, she was very good at what she did, being well experienced in the handling of certain sea creatures. Despite this type of creature being an exception from her experience, Rebecca had enough confidence in her to trust her in knowing what to do and the extreme precautions she had to take. Julie had a lot of common sense, so making foolish mistakes or decisions were not her forte.

Suddenly Julie spotted something, which kept her eyes intensely focused. She told the lifeguard to stop moving the boat and went to the edge, careful not to lose the presence of mind to keep her hand out of the water.

The object was white and just below the surface. It was small and seemed to be moving forward, although so subtly that she couldn't tell for sure if it was moving itself or if the water was moving it. She wanted to be sure of what it could be before reporting it. As she continued to stare at the object, which was, in her estimation, about as small as the end of a thumb, she looked for signs of anything attached to the object. From the shape of it, it looked somewhat like a cup or bell. As the water moved, the glare of the sun seemed to catch it just right. It was at that very brief, exact moment that she saw what looked like numerous threads sticking out from behind it. It looked like they were here.

" Oh, *Rebecca!*"

CHAPTER 9

Monroe County Medical Examiner's Office, Key West, Florida

It was fortunate that the Coast Guard rescue swimmer had the presence of mind to see and remember what the boat's registration numbers were on the bow end of the upturned vessel. Every vessel, no matter how small, was required by the state to have registration numbering and lettering on it, as with most other states. It was important, not only for tax reasons but also for identification reasons, that a record was kept on which boat or ship was whose and where it was home based.

Turns out during the investigation by not only the Coast Guard but also by the Florida Department Of Law Enforcement that the sailboat was registered to a Samuel Weston of Abbington, New Jersey, just northwest of Atlantic City. He was divorced and his ex-wife, Trudy, was at home not feeling well but able to get around. For that reason, she decided to not go with the family to Florida for the seven days of vacation that had already been booked. The airfares were non-refundable. Despite her ex-husband's protests, she had insisted they go, and that she'd be fine.

She reminded Sam that a significant amount of money would be lost forever with nothing to show for it if they *didn't* go. With a promise she'd contact her sister who didn't live far from them if there was a problem, Sam willingly but reluctantly left with the two children.

After discovering the names and ages of the two children and receiving the proper identification, the ME began the autopsy on the eight year old boy. He started with the external, examining the clothes. Nothing significant, of course was found. It was clear that death was contributed to by the capsizing of the boat. Although at this point he didn't expect foul play, he had to rule it out before he could consider other manners of death.

Unlike autopsies of victims or suspects of crimes or other suspicious deaths, he wasted no time in having the clothes removed by his morgue assistants and then performing an external exam of the body itself. This was important because he had to determine if there was any external cause of death. Were there wounds or other injuries present? If so, what could have caused them--human or animal? Not noticing anything on the front from face to the feet, they turned the body over and he saw what had been reported to him--long, ugly black threadlike marks down his entire back and down a portion of his buttocks.

He had seen markings something similar to this from certain jellyfish attacks on a few people who were highly allergic to animal venom. They had been marks left by the tentacles of Portuguese Man O' Wars which are not usually deadly to humans contrary to popular belief. Those scarring marks usually faded over time before disappearing completely.

These marks on the body were very angry and considerably more nasty looking. Could the sting, whatever kind of jellyfish it was-and he was certain it was from a jellyfish-have killed him? Possibly. But it was too soon to tell. Drowning and any other possible causes had to be ruled out first before he could consider the stings as a cause of death.

Disturbing as it was, even to him, to perform an autopsy on a child, he had to restrain all his emotions and concentrate on finding the answer for the boy. His mother, in New Jersey, had already been contacted by the authorities there when they had been contacted by the FDLE. She had been told that the sailboat with her ex-husband and two children had capsized in a severe storm. Help had arrived too late to save them; but the boy was found and was in the ME's office in Key West. He'd been found deceased at the scene. She immediately had gone down there to identify the body before the autopsy and collapsed in indescribable grief. It was bad enough to look at the body of her dead son, but to have to also endure the realization that her daughter and ex-husband were forever lost at sea was nearly too much to bear. For them, there would never be any closure.

He examined the marks closely which looked like thin, dark, spidery veins against the death-white skin. These, he decided, were *not* from a Portuguese Man O' War or any other jellyfish from around here that he knew of. He'd been a Florida resident all his life, and been a physician for thirty years, with twenty of them in pathology but had never seen marks this vicious looking before. At least not from any jellyfish he was familiar with.

As he examined each area of front and back, he made audio recordings on the speaker above the morgue table, noting each anomaly or suspicious marking; and emphasizing the tentacle marks. He checked the head for any injuries there, but saw only a small cut on the top, which in and of itself didn't look significant.

He had x-rays taken of the head, which showed negative brain injuries. No brain swelling, no internal bleeding there, no skull fractures, and no other anomalies. He opened the chest cavity with the Y-incision and examined the heart and lungs, finding and expecting no evidence of heart problems, and no evidence of drowning, which was what he *had* expected. He took blood and tissue samples and sent them off to toxicology, noting on the toxicology request form to assess for possible animal/jellyfish toxins in the blood or tissue. As a precaution, he also requested toxicology to assess for any medications or other drugs in his system. He had to make sure everything was ruled out in order to narrow it down to one possible then certain cause of death.

Once the autopsy was completed, he had all the information he could get to make his ruling and diagnosis for the death certificate, except for the toxicology report. He could not make out the certificate until he received that report, after which he would make his medical and legal diagnosis on the cause, mechanism, and manner of death. After the body was sewn up, his assistants covered it up and put it on a table which slid it into a cooler enclosure with a door that closed, to retard the process of further decomposition. He returned to his office and started filling out the paperwork on the autopsy, leaving the death certificate for last.

It was two days later when the report was faxed over to him from the state lab. He examined it as he did with any other report, but his eyes widened slightly with eyebrows raised as he noticed one of the findings. It was a positive and it was caused by something that he never would have expected. Not here in Florida, or anywhere else he'd been to before. Dr. Murray Brenin picked up the phone and immediately called the lab to confirm what he had just read. He'd never done this before. Although the report didn't say at what level the toxin became deadly, he wanted to find out. If the lab didn't know, they could find out for him. He wanted to make sure that they did.

****

With rubber gloves on and the wide-mouthed jar with its cover off and sea water inside, she carefully took the net and picked up the object in the water. Once it came out of the water, the cup-like shape became slightly less visible. Long, string-thin tentacles were lifted up with it. She estimated them to be about five or six feet--abnormally long for such a small bell. Although they looked harmless, she knew that they were likely as deadly to the touch as they were harmless-looking. It was the perfect example of how much looks could be deceiving. Because it was difficult to maneuver the entire thing into the jar, she needed a large metal pole with a hook to move it safely into the container without any of those tentacles touching anything.

The lifeguard started to move forward to help.

"No, no. Stay back. You come in contact with these things and you'll be in big trouble. Medically, that is."

"What is it?" he asked. "Is this the thing that's been hurting people?"

She finally and painstakingly got it all into the jar and closed the lid, making sure it was tight.

"I can't tell you officially what it is. That has to come from higher authority. What I *can* tell you is that it can probably hurt you pretty bad."

"Is it, what, some kind of jellyfish?"

"I believe so." Julie knew for sure what it was but because of the situation and her status as an assistant, she was forbidden by her job description to publicly announce, even to one public servant or anyone else, what she knew for sure. That was the job of the marine biologist and director of the Marine Institute.

"Can't tell you what kind. What I need to do right now is contact the others. Can you contact your colleagues and let them know I have a specimen?"

"Oh absolutely." He quickly picked up the radio and contacted each of the other life-guards. It was then that one of them told him several specimens suddenly appeared in the water around their boat. One specimen was collected from that boat.

Then the other boat said they just spotted a few also. The jellyfish were suddenly appearing all around them, coming seemingly from nowhere and everywhere. Hundreds, then thousands of them.

Julie got a hold of Rebecca on her radio using a different channel than the guards.

"I have one I took as a sample. It's an Irukandji. This is incredible. I also saw a regular box jelly nearby in the water. I think this area's being hit with both of them."

" Looks like we've got both here-you're right, Julie. Might as well bring it in."

After they signed off, she gathered the pole and hook and the plastic container, made sure it was as secure as it was going to be, and informed the guard that they should start heading back. Before they could move, the sudden sight nearly took their breaths away.

What they saw in the water would be anyone's worst nightmare. Surrounding them in all directions were hundreds, if not thousands, of the creatures. It was like something out of a horror movie. *Where the hell did they come from?* Julie wondered.

Radio communications were now constant and they were all instructed to vacate the area and head back in immediately. Without hesitation, all three boats aimed quickly back to shore and got up as far onto the beach with the boats as they could. For them, even just merely touching the water could be deadly. These things were now everywhere.

Once they were well onto the beach, they gathered together for a debriefing. Their task out on the water was completed before they realized it. There was no doubt in any of their minds now. The two scientists and assistant knew what was confronting them and this entire area. It was an invasion and a close sea encounter of one of the worst kinds.

Rebecca spoke up first. "I don't have to be a jellyfish expert to know what we have here. Can you confirm?"

James nodded. "Yes." Then he turned to the three lifeguards. "Who's your commander, chief, head honcho?"

One of them answered. "Paul Lambach. He's the director of all beach operations."

"Is he the head of lifeguards?"

"He's the head of the entire beach, responsible for all beach ops, which include patrol, lifeguards, and vendor operations."

"Get him here. He needs to know this and see this now." The lifeguard knew the urgency and with his radio called for Lambach to report to this area. He couldn't recall this ever happening before.

For Lambach to be called out, it would have to be a matter of catastrophic urgency. It was because of this rarity that he arrived only a few minutes later. He was not happy about it but realized this had to be pretty serious.

After they introduced themselves, Rebecca spoke up to fill him in on what was occurring and its current and potential impact on beach operations. She made it plain and quite clear that all water activities, including boating in this area, had to be shut down indefinitely or until the creatures disappeared. Seeing the shock on Lambach's face, she showed him one of the jars which had two specimens in it to make her point.

"What is it?" he asked.

"It's an Irukandji jellyfish, one of the deadliest known to mankind. It's a member of the box jellyfish family which are usually located in the Pacific, near Australia and off the coast of Hawaii also. The box jellyfish are considered the worst and deadliest of the jellyfish family.

"These Irukandji are much smaller than their cousins but their stings are even worse and more painful. Their venom packs a more powerful punch, more powerful than a cobra's, and are most likely responsible for the injuries which have occurred here a few days ago and a couple of deaths, from what I understand."

Lambach looked at it in awe, finding it hard to understand how something this small with strings attached could be so deadly.

"We have to close the entire beach area because of this thing? Why, how, where did they come from and how come they're here?"

James spoke up. "Mr. Lambach, we don't yet understand how they've come from the other side of the world, except by currents. Although there's a few that have been seen in this part of the world, most of them are over there, down under or in Hawaii. Why they are here in Florida no one knows. All I can tell you is that if anyone goes in the water, they are likely not to come out alive, or at the very least seriously injured and in excruciating pain. We have an invasion. And until they go away, no one can go in without immediately risking their lives. It's the water that has to be closed off to humans, not the beach itself."

"How much of the swimming area has to be closed?" he asked while still looking at the thing in the jar.

"Well," Rebecca started to say, "because we don't know how far these things are spread, we can't say for sure how much *should* be closed. I would say as much as safely possible. Have any reports come in recently about any other attacks or sightings further away from the areas of the latest injuries?"

The lifeguard shook his head. "I haven't heard about any more people being attacked since the last ones. That was in zone three, I believe. But since no one has been in the water since then, there wouldn't be any more reports."

"Which means the creatures could be in the water for, God knows how far down or up the coast," said James.

"Jim, could these jellyfish actually propel themselves through the water? I would think they could the same as their larger cousins." Rebecca thought that they could, and she was right.

"Yes, they can. Although they usually ride the currents, they can swim."

"Then we have a possible widespread problem. Mr. Lambach, I strongly recommend closing down the swimming areas up and down the entire Pompano beach area. No one should go near the water. Not even where it laps up onto the beach." Rebecca was now adamant about that.

"Oh for heaven's sake, not even to cool their feet on the wet sand?" Lambach said in a bit of frustration.

"Nope. Not even that. It's been known for any kind of jellyfish to float up onto the beach, including the Man O' Wars. Irukandji would be no different and it would be worse because they are much harder to see than the larger ones. Step on one of these without knowing it and you might feel the awful effects for days, including not being able to walk for a while, if you survive. Right Jim?"

"She's right, Mr. Lambach. I also recommend shutting down. Doesn't have to be permanent, But however long it takes before opening up again, it's still better than the city being on the receiving end of a whole slew of lawsuits."

Lambach took a deep breath and realized they were right. Already too many people were injured. Having a death among them was not something the beach authorities or the city itself would get over any time soon.

"Alright. I'll get on the horn now to the city and the mayor. Get in touch with me from time to time and keep me posted. As soon as you believe it's safe to re-open I need to know. The city's tourist economy, as well as the tourists themselves, are going to take a heavy hit on this. Tim there will provide you with my official phone number to contact me," he said pointing to the lifeguard.

With Lambach's departure back to his office at beach headquarters, the scientists and Julie discussed their next plan of action. What they all agreed on was that they needed to find out just how far this infestation went. Did it go to the northernmost and southernmost ends of the Pompano beach area? Or did it go beyond?

"Tim, can you stay with us a bit longer?" she asked him.

"Sure. Got all the time in the world."

Rebecca's cell phone rang. The others watched and wondered who was calling her and if it was something else that was going on. They could see the expression on her face change from apprehension to shock and then dismay. They perceived it to be less than good news.

"Oh no," she said softly looking down at the ground. "Oh no. That poor woman. I can't imagine…." The others could hear the voice of the person on the other end, but could not make out the words.

"That was the ruling on the boy? How far out was he found?"

After she had been told all the latest information, she thanked the person and hung up. The news was devastating on two fronts. She looked up at the others who stared at her, waiting for her to speak.

She told them the news about the overturned boat thirty miles out at sea, the discovery of the boy's body and the missing bodies of his sister and father. Even though they never knew them, it was still terrible news. But then she gave them the second punch which put them into shock mode.

"The medical examiner's office down in Monroe County said that the boy's death was ruled an accident. But the cause of death was the first they had ever seen. The boy's blood and tissues were filled with Irukandji venom. He was killed by Irukandji, not drowning or the elements as would have been expected. Had this not happened, then that might have occurred anyway. But the creatures got him first."

She looked out at the sea's horizon.

"They were out there. Thirty miles out. And there's nothing to stop them." They all looked at her in silence, then also out to sea.

"Houston, we've got a problem," she mumbled softly to no one in particular.

CHAPTER 10

Pompano Beach, Florida, August 2

Once the mayor of Pompano Beach was contacted, the decision was made to go public with the news as soon as possible. The media were contacted and soon the news spread, not only throughout the county, but throughout the entire state as well. Once the networks got word of what had occurred and was still occurring, the news went nationwide. It was a media frenzy with an almost unstoppable momentum. Something like this was unprecedented, not only in Florida but anywhere in the US.

Soon the governor's office and state EPA became involved. The state's Department of Fish and Game stepped in with the Bureau of Fisheries and everyone who had anything to do with the sea that worked for the government seemed to pounce on the Pompano Beach community. It was if a Pandora's box had been opened up. In fact, the investigations and the number of people involved in fighting this invasion problem became so intense and overwhelmed the normally quiet community so much that even the entire beach areas were now officially closed off to the public until further notice. In effect, it was a nightmare for the city.

For Rebecca and her crew, it didn't take long for reports to come into her from other areas. Some of them were funneled to her cell phone by the Institute. She heard about the eighteen year old boy in Miami who'd been stung, brought to the ER unconscious but fortunately survived.

So far she had marked down, as areas affected, the entire Pompano Beach area then as far out as thirty nautical miles northeast of Key West, and Miami. That was a fairly large area for a species which hadn't been known to invade before, at least not in the US. But was that the entire area, or was that just the beginning?

She decided that they needed to regroup and think what they would do next. They were the core of all these sudden other investigations, and she believed they had to maintain their status as first responders to what had become a public crisis situation. With the beaches now closed and no other place nearby to swim, who's to say that no one at night would try to sneak into the water when no one was around? Police had been notified to be on the alert at night for anyone trying to do that.

It was just after one in the afternoon. The group decided to find a place to eat lunch. It would give them a chance to plan and do what they could until the end of the day. They knew that other boats were in the water now looking for more of these jellyfish and already they were starting to feel crowded out. They got their specimens. What else could they do? They would use this time to research and determine ways, if any could be figured out, to resolve the problem. They chose to, temporarily at least, ignore the possibility that only Mother Nature could resolve this crisis. Remembering what they'd seen earlier on the way in, they left in their two vehicles, agreeing to meet up at the local Burger King just a quarter of a mile down the road.

At the restaurant, Rebecca thought of Tony and decided to call him to find out how he was doing. She knew he wouldn't have been kept overnight. From what the hospital told her earlier, he'd been treated and released.

She called him at home and he picked up.

"Hey, Tony, how are you? It's me."

"Becky, hi. I'm ok."

"When did they cut you loose?"

"Ah, roughly about five pm yesterday. The sting wasn't as severe as it could have been. Gave me pain shots and doused it with vinegar to help lessen the effects. The finger might be a little sore for a few days, but not enough to keep me out of business, know what I mean?"

"Well, that's good to hear. I'm so glad you're going to be ok. Just don't go into work until you feel you're ready."

"What are you up to?" he asked.

She told him all that had occurred and what they were doing right now.

"Holy Mackerel, are you kidding me? That news is pretty bad, but I sure would've liked to have gone up there with you guys."

"I know you would have, Tony. But get better first. I have a feeling that this will not be our only trip. There are reports starting to come in from other areas as well. We will definitely be able to use your help on an upcoming one, wherever that may be. They're spreading and this could very easily and very quickly turn into a statewide problem."

"Any reports of them seen in the Gulf?"

"So far, no. But one of the things we're going to do is check with the people over there, probably Pinellas and Sarasota counties, see if they've seen anything."

"Well good luck with what you're doing now. Keep me posted, will ya? And let me know when you get back. I might go back into the lab tomorrow to do some work. I can't see myself sitting around at home with my thumb up my ass wondering what to do. That'll drive me crazy."

"Just be careful if you go in tomorrow. That thing is no longer there, but just don't get stung again by anything else."

After assuring her that he wouldn't, they said their goodbyes and Rebecca went back to eating her burger, letting the others know the status of her other assistant. Then they began their discussion of options for the immediate future.

****

Gulf of Mexico, 12 Miles west of Key Largo, August 3

The six men on the US Special Forces team prepared for the dive. This was a training dive that was required of them periodically and regularly to help them maintain some of their highly advanced skills and technical expertise. The goal of this particular mission was to search for something which had been previously planted somewhere on the sea bed and retrieve it, within a specified amount of time.

They were based in North Carolina and had been flown down to the US Naval Air Station at Key West. That was the closest base to Key Largo. It wasn't clear to most of them why the dive wasn't near Key West instead of all the way up in the northernmost part of the keys. From what was told to them by their commanding officer, the sea topography and currents were more ideal up here for the purposes of the mission than down there. As always, some of them were skeptical about that explanation and thought it was pure BS, but who were they to question that? Part of the reasons they were chosen for the forces was to accept their orders and not question them, unless it was absolutely clear to all that it would be certain death to all of them with no chance for a successful mission. This was not that one exception. And so the mission went forward as always.

They were, of course, not to identify themselves to any curious civilians who might inquire out of curiosity as to who they really were, but rather who they were *portraying* themselves to be: marine environment students who were practicing the rudiments of their diving and research skills. It would serve to be a very plausible and worthy explanation.

Each man had a water buddy or partner, as they would call it, making up the three teams. The mission for them, although a training exercise, was to be taken every bit as seriously as if it were a real mission in an actual combat zone. The slightest lapse in any of them during the exercise, if it were a real mission, could mean death to one or both or all of the team. They had to treat it as if it would mean death to all if something was forgotten or a mistake were made. In the Special Forces, mistakes were likely to be fatal. In nearly all cases, there were no second chances. If you got a second chance, then you weren't in Special Forces. Everything was a one-shot deal. Period. Get it right the first time, or pay the piper for good.

On the thirty foot boat which looked like a civilian yacht but actually belonged to the US Navy, the men all donned their wetsuits and strapped on all their scuba gear. Their lead officer, Lt. Commander Earl Wrightly, would be supervising and monitoring his Seal Team from the boat, watching on camera monitors the movements of each of the teams. Another Seal team member, not part of the training exercise, would film below.

This mission was actually quite easy for them, although they didn't know it. Had it been an actual combat zone, they'd have to be wary of underwater mines, or enemy divers lurking around them. That part they knew because those possibilities had been ingrained in them from the beginning. In addition, there were dangerous sea creatures in every part of the oceans and seas and they had to be aware just as much and at all times of them as well as human predators. They were trained to become familiar with some of the bottom dwelling creatures dangerous to humans, as well as those which swam about freely. This training included bottom dwellers, such as the venomous cone snail and the blue-ringed octopus; and of the free swimmers such as sharks, barracuda, and the giant Humboldt squid. Those were easy to identify. The bottom dwellers not so much, and would be less clearly visible. It was at the sea floor where they really had to watch themselves.

Once fully suited and ready, Wrightly had them gather around him for a briefing on the mission. They weren't told exactly what to look for. Rather, they were to search for anything that didn't seem to fit with the surroundings. Whatever it was could be anything and could be camouflaged so well with everything around it that it could be easily missed.

"You'll have twenty minutes to find it, gentlemen," said Wrightly. "And that's pretty generous. The next exercise you'll have only half or less of that time to find it. Work well together and use your time wisely. Our second boat is out there to mark the surface boundary of this exercise. We have heavy lines extending down from the boat. We have sonar to mark where you are. With the radios connected to your masks, we will let you know if you are swimming outside of the designated zone and if so, will direct you back in.

"You'll have your spear guns. Does anyone not have his ready right now?"

No one admitted to it. They were trained to always have everything ready in the specified amount of time. If anyone had lapsed on that, that person AND his partner would be scrubbed from this particular exercise. So if someone goofed, his partner would also have to pay the price. No Seal could accept that. They were all fully ready.

"Good. Petty Officer Clark here will be monitoring the radios and passing information down to you when necessary. If any of you get in trouble, you know what to do. And if you *don't* know what to do, then you better figure something out fast. Your life could depend on it. Any questions?"

There were none. Each team wore a number which had been adhered to their suits, designating which team they were: one, two, or three. It was already recorded on the boat who was on what team.

"Ok. The clock doesn't start ticking until the third dive team is in the water. Check your radios now. Make sure you can hear Petty Officer Clark."

With that, they all put the attached radio devices near their ear. All heard his voice, and all acknowledged with the transmission click of the attached button to the radio. For the moment, they were pretty much set.

"Let's saddle up, then. Team One, are you ready?" asked the Lt. Commander.

"Ready," they both answered simultaneously while sitting on the boat's edge.

"Go."

Without hesitation, both leaned backwards over the edge and were in. Wrightly did the same with the other teams until all three were in the water, looking up at him in the boat. "On the count of three, the clock starts ticking. You got twenty minutes. You'll be given warnings of time left before that. When twenty minutes is up, you will immediately cease and desist your operations and return to the surface. Ignore the camera guy as if he weren't there. He's there for training purposes for our debriefing later. Ok. The clock starts……..now!"

All were immediately under and heading toward the bottom. They weren't told how deep it was. There would be time on real missions when they would not know the depth of the water they were in. They had wrist devices which told them their depth, so they were responsible for checking them frequently.

Team One consisted of Petty Officer 2nd Class Brad Hartley and Lieutenant Junior Grade Steve Coomley. Team Two was Petty Officer Third Class Raynaldo Gueverra and Petty Officer First

Class Lavon Charles; and Team Three was Chief Warrant Officer Ronald Davidson and Petty Officer First Class Timothy Wentworth. All were trained, certified, and prepared for whatever they would confront. Or so everyone thought.

Under the surface, the seas were clear. Barracuda were thought to be in these waters, which made them keep their knives in their ankle attached sheaths. These fish were notorious for being attracted to shiny objects which could and had been triggers for attacks by them on humans. So the knives stayed covered, unless it became absolutely necessary to remove them.

It turned out that the sea floor in their location was only fifty feet deep. There they saw a few splotches of coral taking hold on the mainly sandy floor, with seaweed slowly waving back and forth and small fish swimming in and around their undulating leaves. In their immediate area, they saw nothing that could be perceived as out of the ordinary.

Each team went in a different direction. The idea was to find the object, whatever it was, communicate that to everyone and everyone would return to the surface. It wasn't a matter of competition because competition had nothing to do with it. They were all part of one team; whether Team One found it, or either of the other two, the result would be that it was found by the whole team. Mission accomplished.

It was difficult to determine when or if they left the designated zone they were restricted to by themselves. They had to rely on the sonar up above and the communications to warn them of their positions. Down here it was a far different world than the air-breathing one they knew. Down here, *they* were the aliens, out of their natural element.

As each team searched the floor for any anomaly, none of them were aware of mobile anomalies moving into the area.

There were a few large rocks down there dotting the sand and patches of seaweed. In the distance, team one found a large mound of coral which turned out to be the end of a large reef. It was beautiful and rainbow colored, but they didn't have time to stop and admire God's creation. As far as they were concerned, the reef was a part of Mother Nature. There was a large hole or cavity near the bottom at one side of it. The members knew it could harbor hidden dangers, such as moral eels or other dangerous creatures. Or, it could be hiding their mission object.

If anything was in there, the blackness hid it well. As a result, they were extremely cautious when approaching it. Unlike impatient or foolish amateurs, they knew better than to stick their arms inside of it. In addition, the coral itself was razor sharp and could easily tear open their suits and slash into their skin as well. But they knew they needed to check it out before pressing forward.

One of them took out his flashlight while the other got the spear gun ready and aimed toward the black hole. As "lightman" cautiously moved closer to it, "spearman" stayed with him. Lightman didn't want to get too close, so when he believed he was at a safe distance, he shone the flashlight into the cavity. He did see something in there after about a minute, but it didn't look like any object out of its element. In fact, it wasn't. It was a crab trying to slink away from the light.

As he continued to shine the light further inside looking and searching with his eyes, he was unaware of spearman no longer working with him. As lightman continued his search in and around the cavity, spearman was thrashing around. He had dropped the spear. Unseen to anyone at the moment, the marks on his hands and face began to appear. His movements were chaotic, violent, and silent in the fifty foot deep ocean water. Beneath the mask and unseen to anyone who might have been near him, his eyes were widened as if in a frozen state of horror. He was unable to press the button to talk and no one knew what was happening to him.

When lightman finally took his attention off the coral cave and spoke to his partner, he looked over to see him a little further away, spearless and convulsing. *What the hell?*

Spearman was now trying to hold his hands and face at the same time, which looked like the impossible feat that it would be. He started swimming upward as best as he could. Lightman immediately called for help and told the boat he was bringing him up. Something serious had happened to him but he didn't know what. As he swam toward his partner, he stopped dead in his tracks. The swarm of what looked like thousands of small to medium-sized jellyfish reached the thrashing man. The swarm wall now enveloped him and quickly covered his exposed face, head, and hands with hundreds of long tentacles. With a look of terror that he had never felt before, lightman swam away from the oncoming wall, while notifying the boat.

"What? Say again, team one."

"I said, jellyfish. Thousands of them down here. They got Lieutenant Coomley. I can't get him because he's enveloped completely within the swarm. Right now I'm trying to swim away from them and to the surface."

"Ok, roger that. We see you on radar and are following you now. Be ready to climb on board immediately. Team two, your status?"

"This is two. We are ok. See something or a lot of things off in the distance to our starboard side. Don't know what they are."

"Team two, cease and desist your ops and get out of there now! Swim away from whatever you're seeing. We'll follow you on sonar. Get to the surface now and be ready for immediate extraction. Team three, status?"

There was no immediate reply.

"Team three, status? Respond please."

Only silence once again met Clark's call.

"Team three, if you hear me, we're not hearing you. Get to the surface now. Cease and desist all ops immediately. We'll follow you on sonar. Get topside now."

Lt. Commander Earl Wrightly was hearing it all and knew something serious had happened that was in none of their training manuals or in the Seal Time Manual of Operations. This was one for the books. Only he didn't know what it was yet, but knew it hadn't been written yet for *their* books. What the hell happened below?

"Sir, I see Hartley coming through the surface now, to our eight o'clock position. Looks like he's holding on to Coomley who appears unconscious."

"Let's get them out of there and onboard before something happens to him. Then team two. They should be coming up momentarily. Let's hope team three heard me."

They did. First they pulled Coomley on board, then Hartley, who looked like he'd seen the worst horror movie of his life. Then they went for team two. Both men were there, but one of them had been stung. And he was in no shape to talk very well. So far, two men had been injured by something below.

Not all the men had been stung. But those who were had snakelike angry red welts all over their exposed skin. They were doing their best to stifle their screams but the pain was so intense and agonizing that it would be almost impossible even for the most die-hard tough guy. Despite their toughness and undeniable expertise in the arts of searching, destroying, rescuing and killing, they were still human beings who would feel the same level of pain as everyone else in the world. Each had no choice but to let it out, and it was just as painful to hear them for the others as it was for the victims to feel it.

The commander immediately got on the radio for naval rescue and immediate medivac to the nearest hospital. For all he knew, these men could die right here and now. Little did he know how right he was. He hoped they could get to the hospital in time. After giving their coordinates, he maintained their boat's position so the medivac chopper could find them. He'd send up a flare as soon as they spotted the chopper.

"Chief," Wrightly said to his chief petty officer coxswain, "have a couple of your men search around with binoculars. Team three seems to be missing. We can move around this exact spot for a bit, but not too far. Two men are missing."

"Yes sir," he replied. There was no doubt that the chief was likely much more concerned than he sounded. Those were men he helped train months ago in Navy Seals Basic Training Camp. He helped mold them into two of the toughest fighting men in the world. Now they were missing-over what? Possible fish? *Fucking crazy* he swore to himself. *What the fuck is happening here?* Although he didn't know it for sure, he strongly suspected that all the others were thinking the exact same thing. Something, or some*things,* was down there and it had brutalized a number of their men. Two were missing. Were they dead or too injured and possibly drowning?

He slowly steered the boat in a large circular pattern so they could scan in all directions, yelling out to the boat crew to scan everywhere for sightings of team three.

"We're looking for CWO Davidson and PO1 Wentworth. Look real good guys. We gotta find them."

There was no sign of the two men. Repeatedly they called them on the radio, but no answer ever came back. They didn't have sonar on this boat, which was the only bad thing about it. Wrightly was tempted to send down a couple of divers that were uninjured, but thought twice about that. The situation now had become far more serious than he realized.

"Williams, call home base. Tell them there are two missing divers. They need to send search and rescue asap. Here are the coordinates."

The officer gave the radioman the numbers which were then broadcast over the radio. It was virtually a Mayday, which would alert all vessels with a reasonable range to the distress presently occurring.

"Navy 1051, Navy 1051, this is US Coast Guard vessel Condor, over."

The commander was surprised to hear a response so quickly but wasted no time in answering the response.

"Coast Guard vessel Condor, this is US Navy 1051, go ahead."

"Uh, Navy 1051, Condor. We are about three nautical miles to the northwest of your position. Do you require our assistance, over?"

"Condor, Navy 1051, that's affirmative. Please go to channel 51, over."

"Roger, 1051, switching to 51. Out."

When the Coast Guard came back onto the tightly secured channel, Wrightly was able to speak again. "We would appreciate any and all help we can get right now. We currently have two men missing in the water, one is seriously injured by serious stings. Be advised one of our medivac choppers is en route here to pick him up. Our search is limited to only the area within the coordinates given to the air station until after the extraction is complete, over."

"Roger, 1051. We are now en route and expect ETA in about seven minutes, over."

"Roger that, Condor. Are you a ship or small boat, over?"

"Forty foot SAR boat, over."

"Roger, Condor, thank you. We are a thirty foot white boat with naval ensign. Special Ops. One of our small vessels I anticipate to arrive, but don't know when. Much later than you, I expect. See you then. Out."

While men scanned the horizon for any sign of the missing team and for the Coast Guard boat, two of the boat crew that were also hospital corpsmen, were attending to the injured officer. They had never seen anything like it before. The angry, dark red welts over the officer's face and arms looked like they went through all the layers of the skin. Coomley was screaming and thrashing about uncontrollably, and they had to struggle as hard as they could to keep him from injuring himself, and them as well. As much as they could do for him with the basic and even the advanced first aid equipment they had on board, it wasn't the treatment that would help in his situation. He needed a hospital, and fast.

A few minutes later, they heard the faint chopping sounds. When a dot appeared in the sky, Wrightly called for the flares. When the chopper got close enough to where the pilot could see the flares from a distance, the crewman shot it into the air.

Within thirty minutes, the injured officer was on board and was en route to the hospital that would save his life if he arrived on time. Wrightly said a prayer under his breath that his colleague and brother-in-arms as well as friend would make it. Now the search would really begin.

CHAPTER 11

Miami Marine Institute, August 4

"We need to go out there to assess the area."

Rebecca was adamant about that. In speaking to her boss, Dan Worthington, and having filled him in completely of all the findings so far, including the numbers of victims and which areas of beaches they were attacked, she emphasized the urgency of the matter. It could very easily and just as quickly turn into a major crisis, which would make it more difficult to bring it under control. More people could be hurt or killed by these things.

Worthington had to make a decision whether or not to allow her to go out there. It was costly and she, at the same time, would be ignoring or sloughing off on some of her other projects, some of which were no less important in their research value to the Institute than the one she was investigating now. He made it a point to bring that to her attention.

"I know, Dan, I know. But we have a serious problem here. I know you can see it. The whole damn public is seeing it. Do you realize that no one is showing up at the beaches now? Or very few? The vendors are having to shut down because there's no business. Even boating activities are almost nil in comparison to before these incidents. We have to do something."

"Yea, I know, Becky, I know." Although he didn't really want to admit it, he knew she was right. He rubbed his chin and looked at her.

"Alright. Get out there. See what you can find."

The secretary then knocked and entered. "Doctor, you might want to turn on the TV. There's a special report you might want to see. CNN."

He got up and turned on the small TV on the other side of the room and changed the channel to CNN. Their eyes became glued to the screen. The picture opened up with the reporter.

"He'd been in the Navy for about four years and was on special assignment when the incident occurred. Lieutenant Steven Coomley was only twenty four years old. He leaves behind a wife and a young daughter. In the meantime, the cooperative searching between the Coast Guard and the Navy for the two missing divers came up empty. After four days of painstaking and relentless searching, it was finally called off and the two men were considered deceased. They are Chief Warrant Officer Ronald Davidson, who leaves behind a wife and three children, and Petty Officer Timothy Wentworth, a single man who left behind his fiancée.

" In the meantime, investigators from the Florida Department of Environmental Protection, Dept. of Fish and Game, and oceanographers and marine biologists from the Woodshole Institute in Massachusetts are looking into this invasion of jellyfish."

"Holy Shit!" Dan exclaimed, slamming his open hand down on his desk. "'Scuse my French." Becky nearly jumped out of her skirt at the sudden unexpected outburst. She put her hand on her chest and closed her eyes for a moment, without saying anything.

"You were right, Becky. And now the state and Woodshole are in on it. Next thing you know, the feds are going to want to jump into the picture."

He looked back at the screen and the reporters were talking about these deaths from jellyfish. They were apparently not the usual common kind that aren't life-threatening that people always see at beaches during certain times of the year.

"Investigators are looking into the kinds of jellyfish they are, and are expected to focus on those species that are dangerous to humans. These are some of the biggest swarms ever seen and are the biggest in the Atlantic Ocean." The network report started talking details about the most likely possibilities. The name *Chironex fleckeri* followed immediately by box jellyfish sent chills up and down their spines. Worthington turned off the TV, turned and looked at Rebecca.

"I know they've spread from Australia and some have been seen in the Atlantic. But never to this extent or anything close to it. This is definitely unprecedented."

Worthington walked back to his desk, then to the aquarium of small fish he kept in his office.

"Dan, if this is the case, then we might have double trouble. Don't forget the possibility of Irukandji as well."

He went back to his desk and leaned against it with his arms crossed. "Yea. There's that, too." His voice had lowered, as it always did when he realized serious situations they had to deal with. This one was far greater than any previous one.

He shook his head. "What do they say? Trouble comes in threes? Here, number one is what we think are Irukandji, then the box jellyfish, and all the deaths and injuries. There are your three."

"So we should get out there as soon as possible," she told him.

"Yes. Absolutely. Alright, Make your preparations. I'll call in the ship captain, crew and you'll go out in the institute's vessel. Take whoever you need to assist. I'll also assign someone to photograph everything, so that'll leave you free to do whatever you have to. We need to find out how far out this swarm is, from which direction they're coming and to where they are going. Get a sample or two to confirm the identity of the species and, for God's sake, don't get stung. Last thing we need is another funeral."

Rebecca smirked slightly, because the last thing she wanted was to get stung or for anyone else on board to get attacked either.

"When can the ship be ready to go?"

"Well, it's late afternoon now. It'll take a day for prep, which means most of tomorrow. I'll call everybody now. Figure on day after tomorrow in the morning. Get your people and your equipment ready tomorrow. What time did you want to leave?"

"I think seven am would be a good time. I'll get Julie to come along and I'll call James. I'm sure he'll want to come. This swarm would be his baby."

"Ok. Good. Then seven am it is, day after tomorrow. Thursday."

With her request being blessed twice over, she headed back to her office to start making the necessary arrangements, the same as when she went up to Pompano. Only this time they'd be going out on the Institute's one hundred fifty foot research ship, the Argonaut. On it was all the state of the art equipment that scientists would need. On this mission, she wouldn't need much of it, except the tank for holding specimens and special nets for extracting them from the water. If the swarm was as large as they said it was, it would take hardly any time to pick out a couple of each.

She knew, from some of her studies and working with James, that the *box jellyfish*—which includes the subspecies, *Irukandji*, are considered the most toxic jellyfish in the world, thus the deadliest. This makes the Portuguese Man O' War seem like a walk in the park when it came to the pain level from stings and the venom toxicity.

Called the Sea Wasp by some, it is considered a creature that should be given a wide berth by all which might encounter it. With their large, transparent bell, they can have as many as fifteen tentacles, each of which could be up to ten feet long. Each tentacle is known to have as many as half a million venom-filled darts, which are just like very sharp syringes and are called nematocysts.

Although they have no brain, they are the only jellyfish species which have eyes. Four clusters, to be exact, with one cluster in each corner of the bell. It's still unclear to most scientists why they have eyes when there's no brain. Yet they can swim quite proficiently, and can avoid objects that are in their paths.

Rebecca was also aware that each jellyfish, which are not true fish at all, can kill sixty adult humans. The venom acts fast and kills within minutes, causing cardiovascular collapse. It also attacks the nervous system, and can cause paralysis. It destroys skin cells as well as other anatomical structures. A victim who suffers a sting from just one tentacle can feel the same level of pain and agony as being branded with a red-hot iron. The pain can be so severe and the systems destruction so overwhelming that if the victim is in the water long enough, the venom can kill the heart's pumping ability. If the victim doesn't die from that, then drowning is likely to be the other cause of death. If a victim survives, the pain can last for weeks and the terrible looking whip-like scars left by the tentacles would be permanent.

Although Rebecca found this species fascinating, she was glad she chose not to specialize in this kind of sea creature. For some reason, jellyfish kind of gave her the creeps, although not enough to not want to learn more about them. For research and studying up close, however, she preferred to leave that to others who had more of a passion for them.

****

University of South Florida, Tampa, August 4
James made it clear he was elated to be going on the expedition. Because of the high profile of the situation and huge impact on tourism, the economy, and even the environment around the coastline and even out to sea, there was never a doubt in his mind that his boss would give his blessing. His expertise was needed along with Rebecca's. At the same time, they would be practically rubbing shoulders with the Woodshole Oceanographic Institute and possibly NOAA.

The plan was to meet them at the ship at six in the morning on Thursday, day after tomorrow. By that time, all the equipment would be ready, the crew would be on board, the investigative site would be plotted out regarding the coordinates of the search area, and all would be ready to tackle whatever confronted them out there. He expected that they would have to search for the area of the jellyfish where the navy injuries and deaths had occurred, as well as the area where the capsized sailboat was found weeks earlier, with two of the three on board forever missing. Those were a lot of areas on the open ocean to search. But he knew what they were *really* looking for. And *that's* what he hoped they would not find. Because if they did, it could spell trouble for a large section of the US eastern seaboard, depending on the current. Swarms of box jellyfish could certainly devastate or at the very least, seriously damage, the area's ecosystem and the tourist industry. These would include the notorious Irukandji as well.

He let his supervisor at the lab know that he'd be gone probably for at least two or three days, depending on what they found. Could be longer, he told him, if it was an emergency situation.

The next day he set out for Miami, having to travel southeast across the state from the Gulf coast to the east coast. It was roughly a six to seven hour drive and fortunately there were no hurricanes in the forecast. He had his hotel reservation for the eve of embarkation the next morning. He was excited, yet apprehensive. The unexplainable feelings he was experiencing were not good ones.

These were more of a combination of gut feelings and a sixth sense that told him what would be discovered out there would be far more than would ever be anticipated. These feelings also were, in a sense, based on the reality of climate change. For with global warming comes changes in weather patterns, sea current patterns, sea creature migrations, ocean level patterns, deterioration or disintegration of ecosystems and possible eventual extinction of various types of animals that depend ultimately on a consistent climate pattern for their survival. Those animals that cannot adapt to climate changes and don't migrate may very well succumb to the oblivions of extinction.

Then there are those creatures which thrive on climate changes and even global warming; creatures that truly don't serve much of a purpose or positively contribute to the ecosystems, especially in the oceans and seas of planet earth. Not only do they thrive with global warming, they multiply exponentially. These are the creatures that pose the greatest danger to mankind. If they multiply and spread enough, they become dangerous to most other sea creatures as well. They've been around for about six hundred million years. Jellyfish have been hated by humans for as long as they'd been around--except for scientists.

This is what worried James. Box jellyfish swarms are basically floating/swimming creatures that one could easily see as representing death. Look at just one of them and you see something that could take you out in a flash and with just a flick of a barest touch. Put hundreds or thousands of them together, and you see creatures of death that could take out tens of thousands of humans. Doesn't matter if they are the Chironex fleckeri, the common box, or the Irukandji.

It was a long drive but he'd get his rest tonight. He'd need it. Flicking on the radio, he just kept on driving and rested his mind a bit. Tomorrow would be a busy day and he wanted to be ready for it.

CHAPTER 12

Over the open sea, the skies were cloudy but rainless. The water was choppy but navigable. It was an area devoid of shipping and boats at that time--a virtual desert of water. Distance from land was about twenty five miles, so nothing as yet could be seen on the horizon.

The Gulf stream is a powerful deep current that maintains its strong influence of both its underwater world and the weather above, bringing with it whatever is caught in its control. While the jet stream in the atmosphere influences the direction of strong storms, including hurricanes when they come along, the Gulf stream also affects their direction as well. It's a two-pronged effect that influences our weather in general. It's something that man has never been able to, nor will ever, control. Because of both these factors, man would soon find still another problem they'd find difficult to control.

They came a very long distance and took a long time to get where they were. There would never be any way they could possibly know where they were in any point of time. But it would never matter, because they would never care. Slowly, gradually ever nearing the US coast, some of the lower currents branched out from the main stream and started heading toward land, which geographically would be the northern part of Florida and southern Georgia. As they made their unstoppable journey, others of their kind were already close to the rest of the east coast of Florida.

The swarm had arrived. Not hundreds or thousands, but hundreds of thousands and millions. Along the way, they had killed countless other sea creatures. Except for sharks, all fish were susceptible to their onslaught. Most of these creatures of the swarm were known by scientists as *Chironex fleckeri,* the *box jellyfish.* Others were *Irukandji*-a smaller subspecies. It was if they conspired together in a unified invasion of areas and shores where they didn't originate from or belong to.

It wouldn't be long before they were seen. They had no brains but the boxes had eyes to see, and the ability to detect direction and propel themselves forward while avoiding obstacles. It was almost a unique miracle of evolution that these box jellyfish could do all this with only their gelatinous bodies to act as if they were minds.

Above the water's surface, the breeze increased to a mild wind. Darker clouds started rolling in from the horizon to overtake and replace the rainless clouds. As they came closer, the wind slowly increased just a bit. Nothing was affected by this just below the surface. The wall of jellyfish also increased and remained indifferent to anything happening in the air. Soon they were nineteen miles from land.

If one were able to see the swarm from the air, it would be not only a spectacular sight, but also an equally horrific one. It extended for miles, with now countless numbers making up its members. It was a seemingly unstoppable force that could only be described as the face of death. Already, tens of thousands of fish were being killed by their flagellating tentacles, having minuscule darts of venom one hundred times more potent than a cobra's. They floated and swam, with the wall extending down to fifty feet and sixty in some spots. There were no obstacles in their way to impede their journey. Even if there were, they would have no effect on their forward motion.

A lone Portuguese Man O' War floated on the surface, with its tentacles snagged by the invasive numbers of the swarm. It was caught up involuntarily and was dragged beneath the surface by the relentless wall of jelly and tentacles. It would never surface again. And the march continued forward without the slightest hesitation or pause.

****

Fort Lauderdale, Florida, August 4
Although clouds clustered in various areas of the sky, the sun still had plenty of room to shine. There was only a slight warm

breeze, and the temperature was ninety six Fahrenheit, with the humidity up there at uncomfortable levels. It was late August. The beaches were not packed because it was still the off-season for swimming. But there would always be those who chose to go in the water anyway-just for something fun to do if not for any other reason.

Some kids were playing in the water. Those sunbathing on the beach were wearing sandals and sitting on beach chairs under umbrellas. It was the perfect weather and time to get badly burned if no precautions were adhered to.

Two young boys were playing catch with a beach ball in the water. Others were trying to body surf in the three foot waves rolling in and breaking on the shore. A father had his toddler daughter sitting on his shoulders as he walked around waist deep and every so often he dipped down to have her get wet. He made sure she had plenty of sunscreen on before she was exposed to the sun. An elderly couple swam slowly in the water, frequently stopping to look back at the beach.

All seemed normal. If it were the tourist season, the weather would be perfect, as well as the temperature. But the beaches and water would be filled with people. Those that braved the beaches this time of year enjoyed the lack of crowds, despite the burning sand and scorching sun.

Just beyond the authorized swimming area perimeter of two hundred feet from shore, a wall was closing in. Unseen and unexpected, its unified movement marched forward like an ancient Roman army force or the ancient Greek phalanx, unstoppable, seemingly invincible, and protected on all sides by an invisible armor, with long deadly weapons that extended downward and rearward at the same time.

The combination of a coastward breeze and mild currents brought them soon to the perimeter line of the human swimming area. The crossover was swift and as effortless as riding with the current. Those in their way, non-alert, would never see them coming. If anyone did see them, they had a little time- but not much- to get out of the water.

The lifeguard on the elevated beach chair looked out nonchalantly but routinely, scanning for anyone in trouble. He saw none. Before he relaxed for the next few minutes, he took his binoculars for one more, magnified scan. He always believed in checking twice to make sure he hadn't missed anything.

Starting from his left, he slowly made his way toward the right. He stopped his scanning suddenly, focusing on something that caught his attention but not sure of what he was seeing. It was to his one o'clock position. There was a father in the water with his young daughter on his shoulders, and an elderly couple relaxed and talking to each other, apparently keeping themselves lowered enough for only their heads and necks to be exposed to the sun.

Making an adjustment on his binoculars, he noticed something just below the surface of the water, just beyond the elderly couple. It looked like a large white mass of something, which seemed to be inching itself forward. He had to stay focused on it for a while to be sure he was actually seeing it and not being tricked by the light rays of the sun.

The white mass did not go away but instead seemed to be looming larger. He didn't have a clue as to what it was yet felt the hairs on the back of his neck stand up. Gut instinct inaudibly screamed danger at him. Jumping off the chair without thinking about it, he ran down to the water area and, trying to stay as calm as he could although with difficulty, he was trying to get the attention of the elderly couple who were looking the other way.

He yelled at them. "Sir, Ma'am, please come out of the water now. Someone needs to speak to you!" The lifeguard had the presence of mind to not say anything that would cause a panic. The elderly couple didn't seem to hear him. *Damn, just my luck they'd be hard of hearing.* He yelled at them again to come out of the water. Then he asked the father to come out with his daughter. He blew his whistle and waved frantically for them to come out.

The elderly couple, for some reason, thought he was signaling to someone else behind them. They turned but didn't see anyone, then looked back at him. Just when they realized it was *them* he was waving in, the mass was on them. Both of them opened their mouths to emit blood-curdling screams. He immediately ran into the water, telling the young father who was walking back to the beach to get out of the water now and go well onto the beach. The young man looked scared and walked swiftly to the beach, holding his daughter securely and carrying her in his arms now until they were safely back on the beach.

The lifeguard swam quickly to the couple, before stopping suddenly. They were now surrounded by what appeared to be hundreds of thumb-sized to large size jellyfish. Screaming continuously, they thrashed about then stiffened, as seizures now wracked their bodies. As the woman dipped below the water's surface, the man reached out to her in a vain attempt to save her, but then was stricken by something invisible, just below the surface. The lifeguard watched as the man screamed and began to convulse and foam at the mouth. His wife came up briefly to get air. The lifeguard's jaw dropped when he saw her face literally covered with what looked like   tentacles. Angry red-black track marks were being left all over the skin of her face and even on her wide-open eyes as she screamed continuously, her eyes wide open in terror and agonizing pain. Tentacles gripped both her arms. Other tentacles held her face in a vice-like grip as she tried to save herself.

Her husband was now in, what seemed to be, violent death throes. As helpless as his wife, his entire face, torso and both arms were also covered in tentacles, along with a gelatinous blob laying on his shoulder. Some of its tentacles were hanging down the front of him, and the others down his back as if it was using him as a rest stop. The angry, red-black track marks being left all over him were ugly and marked the areas where the powerful neurotoxin venom was being injected into.

The white mass now surrounded the couple completely and the lifeguard quickly backed out of the water before they came any closer to him. Right now there was nothing he could do to get them out of there without being attacked himself. He ran back to the chair where he left his radio and called for immediate emergency help, stating the nature of the emergency. All available lifeguard, EMTs, and paramedics were called to the scene.

The lifeguard was frantic. When another lifeguard arrived, he helped him get the boat into the water and get out to the couple who were now still and unmoving in the water. Sirens were heard in the distance. The beach personnel had called for ambulances to the scene. Police were also on the way. For them and for the elderly couple in the water, it would be too late.

The white mass was now filling the entire swimming areas. Evacuation procedures were immediately launched on all the other beach areas. Sightings of large white masses were seen in all the other areas of the entire beach as far as the eye could. There were other victims further down the beach and more ambulances and medic personnel were called also. In the blink of an eye, the entire five mile long beach had become a disaster area, with five fatalities-including the elderly couple-and nine injured victims still alive and struggling.

CHAPTER 13

Miami, Florida, August 5

The *Argonaut* had departed the dock a few minutes late because of a glitch in the crane hydraulics. The crane was necessary, not only for research and scientific purposes, but also because it was used to lower the lifeboat in the case of a catastrophic emergency. The ship was never allowed to go out unless *all* the necessary equipment was functioning properly. Fortunately it turned out that only a minor adjustment was necessary to bring it on track again. Once it was deemed normal and functioning again, the ship released its lines and set sail for the designated area.

On board were Rebecca, James, and Julie as the scientists. The ship's crew included: Captain Bill Jensen, who had had years of experience as a tugboat and then fishing captain before taking over the running of the *Argonaut*, his first mate Dexter Rinehart who had some years of experience in handling boats of various sizes up to seventy five feet in length, and then the two deckhands, one of which was a female who happened to have good experience in sailing and working on fishing boats. She knew how to handle lines and tie knots just as well as her deck mate, if not better. All had their various jobs at the Institute when not sailing. Loretta was spared from the Institute's cafeteria kitchen to be the cook on board. Only Rebecca, James, and Julie were affiliated with the Science and Research Studies Department.

It was a typical Florida day with its bright sunshine and rain showers that stopped as suddenly as they started; the seas were a little choppy and the warm breezes filled the air with the scent of the sea. It was pleasant enough for anyone to want to take deep breaths and enjoy the various sensations of the open ocean and freedoms that sailing on it permitted.

Some called the oceans and seas the final frontiers. Many scientists throughout the world considered them much lesser known than outer space. It is a world filled with areas that are little known or not known at all, likely harboring hundreds of species of creatures that have yet to be discovered.

The ship, not surprisingly, was valued in the millions. It had state of the art equipment, most which the scientists wouldn't need on this particular mission. The equipment that *would* or *might* be needed would be the sonar, depth sounders, VHF communications radio, the side-arm davit and winch system which can handle a load up to two thousand pounds, a small mechanical vehicle with a camera that's lowered into the water and remotely controlled from the ship for underwater picture taking, and a DGPS chart plotter system for navigation. The radar is used only when needed and is usually kept on anyway the entire time the ship is underway.

Various small laboratory equipment items are usually kept on the ship, although scientists can bring others they would need that aren't kept on the ship. By the time they got underway, they would have everything they needed. In addition, enough food and water for at least a week was kept on board, stored in the mess deck, which had a small kitchen for cooking meals and a good sized refrigerator for keeping perishable items edible.

It's basically very well maintained by the Institute, not only because of its tremendous value and necessity for the Institute, but also because it's a huge, financial asset. Because of that, the Institute also employs special mechanics and engineers to keep it in top shape, and lesser skilled employees to keep it clean and help minimize any deterioration by the salt water. All equipment is checked at least monthly, including the remote-operated vehicle, to maintain proper operating status.

"How long before we get to our area, Bill?" asked Rebecca. The bridge was not very large, but enough to accommodate all the required electronic equipment and navigational tools.

"Oh, I'd say about thirty or forty minutes. The water is a little choppy, so I'm doing about fifteen knots right now. Might bring it up to twenty if the choppiness smoothed out."

"Ok." She left the bridge and went down to the outside deck where James was standing at the rails on the port side, looking out.

The day was a beautiful one, when the brief showers didn't interrupt the sunshine. All in all, he thought it was a pretty nice day for this sailing mission.

"We should arrive at the scene about-" she looked at her watch-"seven forty five or eight. But we should keep an eye out for anything before we get there."

"Julie can help with that also," he said. "There's enough binocs for all of us here. Every so often I've been looking out there. Not seen anything yet."

Rebecca, as well as James, knew that if they spotted any jellyfish, they'd have to slow down or stop the ship immediately and check them out. There's a lot of different species out there, some near the surface, others deeper. They were looking for only two kinds and no other that they had to be concerned about.

In addition, they had to note their global position of where they first spotted the boxes or Irukandji. It wouldn't mean that was where their invasion began. It only meant one global position in which they were located at that specific time. It might be a small or large swarm, a separated part of a still larger swarm or the beginning of an unimaginably-sized one that would be a serious threat to anyone or anything in the water, except for sharks. Their skin would be too tough for tentacle nematocysts to penetrate.

Julie was on the other side scouting out the water with her binoculars. One of the deckhands also volunteered to scan the water, with the last set of binoculars on board. Together, areas of water all around the boat from forward to aft were checked out for anything suspicious. So far there was nothing. As they got closer to the designated area, however, their scanning became more intense and focused. Chances are, the jellyfish that had been there would be long gone and they might find nothing. So Rebecca decided on a strategy, which she would first mention to James, and then proposed to the Captain.

James thought it was appropriate and a good idea. Because of the time that had elapsed between the naval incident out there and now, it stood to reason that because the jellyfish would have moved, the question remained, to where? Did they flow with the current, or did they swim? These species could, of course do either. How far would they be from the area was another question which could be calculated within a reasonable distance of travel.

Based on his recent research of the box jellyfish, James knew that they tended to swim more than just rely on the current. In other words, they seemed to prefer to have control over their own motions and travel ability. Their swimming ability was superior to many other species. They had been known to swim up to four knots, or four point six miles per hour, which was phenomenal for a jellyfish. Considering both of those facts, it was not beyond any reasonable assumption that the reported swarm could be miles away from the site by now, and likely were. The real mystery was, in which direction?

There was no way that any boat, or even a large ship, could cover hundreds of square miles of open ocean within any reasonable time and expect to find what they were looking for. The ocean is so huge and vast that looking for even a large swarm would be the equivalent of looking for a needle in a haystack.

So in consultation with James, she decided on the best plan of attack. She went to the bridge and conferred with Captain Bill and first mate. Their course had been plotted for the site, and they had the global coordinates. All that had to be done now was slow down to a reasonable pace some time before they reached the area.

"So you want to stop and search before we reach the site?" asked Bill.

"Yes. Those things won't be there. They'll have moved, and fairly quickly. We don't know which direction, but I would guess as a safe bet, to consider them moving in the direction of land. Do you know which area of land is closest to the designated area?"

"Um, not sure. Let me take a look at the chart. Dex, take over here, will ya?" Dexter moved to take the helm as Bill moved to the other side to check the chart, site coordinates, and nearest land.

With the scientist and captain both looking at the chart, Bill pointed out where they were now, and where the designated area was. Then he moved his finger to what appeared to be the nearest point of land to the designated area.

"Now these guys," he said, "from what I gathered from the news, started out in Key Largo. That's pretty much as far north in the keys as you can get. But based on where they were for the event, they were in an area considerably northeast of that, although still not that far away considering the amount of ocean there is. But where they were is closer to somewhere else than Key Largo." He ran his finger to what appeared to be the closest area, then took a navigation instrument to calculate distance based on the chart's distance scale. First he checked with the distance from site to Key Largo, then from site to nearest point of land that appeared on the chart. He found it. It was a difference of twenty miles and less than from Key Largo.

He raised himself up. "There you go, Becky. There's your nearest point of land. I can't tell you if these things drifted toward there because I don't have instruments here to read currents."

Rebecca looked down at where his finger was pointing. "Doesn't matter that much anyway," she replied. "They're more likely to have swam rather than drifted."

"Well, whichever the case, we better hope that they neither drifted nor swam toward this point of land."

Now she raised herself up and looked at him. She had a strong hunch of what was coming. The chart wasn't clear to here where that point was because it was used mostly for navigation and not as a regular atlas or road map. The only thing she could decipher was that his finger pointed to somewhere in south Florida on the east coast. And there were plenty of towns on that entire coast.

"Oh? And where exactly is that?" She had to pose the question, despite the dreaded anticipation of it being a populated area. His answer certainly confirmed that.

"Fort Lauderdale."

****

Already other groups had come in from other directions and, after finding where the main swarm was, joined it. All of them, millions, sensed the warmer waters but knew nothing of the global climate changes that brought about their population explosion. They knew nothing of the fact that humans were the primary contributor toward climate changes, and that these changes not only affected global temperatures, but also global weather, water temperatures, and even the ocean currents.

All they knew, if one could call it that since they had no brains, was there were a lot more of them in a very short span of time. They felt the instinctive urge to move and migrate. Despite the fact that they are not social creatures, something kept them staying together.

For reasons unknown, as a large swarm, they swam in unison in a northward, slightly northeast direction. They felt no need for that. They just swam together. As small fish in their paths tried to avoid them, the tentacles would reach out like strings, barely touch them and within seconds the fish was being brought up to the underside of the bell where a trunk-like structure was located. At the end of this structure was the creature's mouth. Slowly the fish is pulled into the mouth and through the trunk-like structure where it's final destination is inside of the transparent bell. This is where the creature begins to digest it.

Hundreds, perhaps thousands of small fish, were caught in the deadly web of countless   tentacles. For those entering the web, there was no escape. Complete avoidance of the entire swarm was the only chance to escape certain death.

And so as a unified force, it journeyed slowly toward its unknown destination. The thousands of bells pulsed as the creatures aggressively swam. Neither currents nor waves swayed them from their journey.

****

Aboard the Argonaut, August 5

With their predetermined and planned search pattern, the ship slowly began its search just outside the perimeter of the designated area. Just as Rebecca had believed, there were no signs of any jellyfish there. Therefore there was no need to enter the area.

Based on their navigation plot set by the first mate, the ship slowly searched a pattern a half mile to the right and to the left of the directional route toward Ft. Lauderdale. This meant going back and forth in a zigzag pattern, only with each turn they would be a little closer to land than before.

The idea was that because they didn't believe the jellyfish would swim in a perfectly straight line toward the city, they had to account for deviations from a direct route-thus the back and forth search. It wasn't exactly a military type search, but then they weren't military. They weren't here to look for and rescue someone. They were here to find the creatures that were causing death and havoc on Florida's southeast coast cities and towns, and find a way to put a stop to them before they spread further north.

While they all looked out over the water, Rebecca was called up to the bridge.

"Becky, you have a phone call," Captain Bill informed her. Dexter handed her the ship's phone. She couldn't imagine who or why they'd be calling her now.

"This is Rebecca Wares."

She listened as the receptionist at the Institute said that she was told by Dan Worthington to call her with the news. There was nothing she could do with it except know what she was about to find out and how it related to their current mission. It was another nightmare on what seemed to be a string of them one after the other.

"Oh my God," she said softly but not enough for the captain and first mate to not hear her. They looked at her almost simultaneously, knowing the news was not good. "Ok, thank you, Maureen. Tell Dan we'll be after it and we'll inform when we know where it's headed." She hung up and looked at the two men, the shocked look on her face telling them there was another attack and maybe somebody else got killed. That's what Bill figured, and he was right.

"You were right, Bill. It hit Lauderdale. Five people killed. Nine other injuries. All beaches there and in towns on either side of it are closed. This is turning into a major disaster. Where the hell are they all coming from and why?"

From behind her, James answered the question as he stepped into the wheelhouse. "They're coming from the Pacific, most of them. But it's also highly likely that some of them were born near these shores as well."

Rebecca turned to look at him.

"So you think these brainless creatures have formed a large coordinated attack against our shores? Tell me that's not what you think?"

"No, I don't think that's it. The question as to why they came *here*, to *us* is a big mystery. I don't think anyone will figure that out. Don't forget, they weren't all over in Australia. They may have originated out there. But if *people* can move all over the world, then why not *them?* There's really nothing to stop them. We know that global climate change definitely has something to do with this."

She looked at no one and nothing in particular on the bridge. Her mind was trying to find all kinds of rational explanations for what was going on. Then she told him what happened in Fort Lauderdale.

"We better find them and see where they're headed. We find that out and we can warn all beach towns in their path to evacuate their waters."

"Good idea, Jim. Captain Bill, we still on course in the direction of Lauderdale?"

"Yes ma'am we are."

"Can you get us there the closest safe distance you can? We'll need to check it out and then I'll have to make a decision as to which direction we troll from there, either north or south."

"Ok. Heading there now. I'll let you know when we're the closest we can get, then I'll stop the ship pending your decision."

"You probably won't have to stop, I'll likely decide while we're on the way."

"Becky, how are you going to decide which direction to take?" asked James curiously.

She looked at him with a sheepish grin. That suggested to him that it would be a decision she made based on logic and chance.

"James, my friend, I don't have the slightest idea. But one thing is for sure. I'll likely take us north to look for them. Know why I'll choose north?"

The ship pitched down a little more than expected, and the two almost lost their balance. Fortunately, the wave motions left as quickly as they came.

"Sorry about that, folks," said Captain Bill. "I was coming about to head toward land. Had to hit the wave a little bit off to make the right heading."

"That's ok, Cap," replied James. "We're good." He turned his face back to hers. "Now you were going to tell me why north?"

"Because, my friend, there are a lot more people north of Lauderdale than there are south. Not the most scientific explanation, but when you think about it, it makes sense. Don't you think?"

She looked up at him and he was smiling back at her. Little did she realize how attractive he found her. Maybe when this was all over….coffee, tea, dinner? He was thinking about that until she interrupted his thoughts.

"Why the hell are you looking at me like that, Mr. James?" She was subtly smiling.

He shook his head as if to rattle those brief thoughts out of him. "Well, I was, uh..." Then he cleared his throat. His sudden look of shyness clued her in to what he may have been thinking about. If she read him right, then maybe she'd play hard-to-get. She did find that brief   look of shyness very attractive. For now, back to the moment.

"Ok, what do you think?" He found turning himself back into a professional instantaneous from a regular guy filled with pleasant thoughts of Rebecca and seeing her as more than just a friend. It was not the easiest thing in the world to do. But he somehow managed.

"Oh, uh, yea. I agree. Makes sense," he nodded a little too eagerly. *God, she smells nice!*

She looked at him and tilted her head to the side. "You alright?" she asked, her smile never wavering.

"Absolute, Becky. I'm fine. Really."

"Absolute Becky? Hey, fella, don't get gorky on me now, ok? Get your mind out of the gutter, Mr. Smarty. We pull this mission off and get rid of these things eventually, and maybe I'll treat you to dinner for helping me on this." Somehow her woman's intuition told her what was on his mind. The fact that he knew that she suspected was what brought him back to Mr. Professional from Mr. Smarty.

"Hey, that'd be great!" He realized suddenly he sounded a little too eager-almost overjoyed-to hear that. But he wanted to treat *her*. Nevertheless, it was a start. Instantly he returned himself once again back to the present without erasing his smile.

"That makes the most sense. Besides, most of them came from the south, stands to reason they'd still be heading northward." His facial expression didn't quite seem to match the seriousness of his words, and seemed to be saying something different. In fact, to her he looked like he'd just been caught with his hand in the cookie jar.

She looked at him looking at her, trying to repress what she tried to keep as a smile. But the silliness of the moment caught up with her quickly. Her control bubble suddenly burst, triggered by his comical expression, in an explosion of laughter.

For the first time, she was seeing him in a different light and she liked what she saw. For now, though, she too had to repress thoughts other than professional ones. There would be time for some recreation perhaps, after this was all over. Slowly, she was forced to return them both back to business. It was fun, she had to admit. And necessary to help keep them from going crazy with all that was going on. A little levity to help maintain sanity was always a good thing, she believed.

"C'mon, big guy. Let's grab some coffee down below. We can talk strategy there." He followed her down.

CHAPTER 14

August 6

The helicopter, owned by Suncoast Flight Tours, Inc. flew twice daily Mondays through Saturdays year round. Although tourists to Florida bombarded the state primarily September through March, there would always be tourists during the rest of the year. Many of them had never flown on helicopters before, letting their curiosities take hold of them; while others liked flying as a recreational activity and seeing the world from above. It was mutually beneficial as well as prosperous for Suncoast.

During a weekday in mid-August, the chopper was flying three tourists over the waters which stretched from just north of Miami to between Coral Springs and West Palm Beach. It was a bright sunny day. Very few flights from Suncoast took to the skies on cloudy days because Florida rainstorms or thunderstorms had a bad habit of appearing quickly, sometimes with little to no warning. The company considered cloudiness as the only warning signs it would get; thus, the no-fly rule on such days.

The winds at the chopper's altitude were west-northwest with speeds ranging from five to ten knots. The company used the AS 365N Dauphin 2 helo type because it could carry up to fourteen people, which included the pilot, co-pilot and up to twelve passenger tourists. With twin engines, it could fly up to two hundred mph. They were considered pretty reliable, even when the winds picked up. As with all machines however, they had their limitations as well.

Today the co-pilot was talking to the tourists in the back through headphone-connected radio transmissions from the cockpit. Helicopter engines are notoriously loud and even those with the best hearing can barely hear a sound coming from someone who is shouting inside one of these flying machines. Hence the earphones for everyone on board.

Down below, they could see the clear green waters of the Atlantic Ocean on Florida's southeast coast. The view was stunning, seeing the waters meet with the coast lined with some of the state's most fabulous beaches. For the first time flyer, or for anyone else for that matter, it was literally breathtaking.

As the three passengers took in the view and listened to the droning of the co-pilot talking the talk of a tour guide, one of them pointed downward and verbalized something. Of course no one, not even himself, could hear him because of the combination of the earphones on the ears, the one way transmission of the earphones (which were in the process of being changed to, but not yet replaced with, a two-way communications system between passengers and pilots), the co-pilot talking, and the helicopter noises.

As this particular passenger gestured to the others of what he was looking at, the others focused through their windows of what was brought to their attention. They didn't know what they were looking at but it certainly didn't look natural to them. In fact, it appeared to be some kind of unnatural phenomenon in the waters below that interrupted the beauty of the water. The passengers all looked at each other, wanting to speak their thoughts but realized it would be futile.

One of them pulled out a pen and pad of paper and wrote, "Algae or fungus?" The other read it, then looked down at the leviathan-sized white mass, then back to him and then at each other. One shrugged, then shook his head. The other agreed and shook his head also. They wished they could speak to the pilots about that.

While the passengers were viewing it, unknown to them the pilots also were.

"Gary, what do you make of that?" asked the pilot, as he turned the chopper slightly to give his partner a better look.

The co-pilot looked down at it, raising his eyebrows. "What the hell is that?"

The pilot, Tony, formally known as Capt. Anthony Carberry, shook his head.

"Man, I thought I've seen everything, but I sure as hell never saw anything like this. I don't have a clue what that is. Why don't you let our customers know what's happening?"

Gary, the co-pilot, got on the speaker and informed the passengers what they were doing and their brief attempts to investigate the phenomenon. He, too, wished they already had the two-ways, but it would be another three or four weeks before the switch and installations were started. In the meantime, they had to make do with what they had and do the best they could.

Tony was starting to seriously consider reporting this to the ground authorities. But he wanted to get a closer look to see if he could find out anything more about this mass. From this altitude, they couldn't tell if it was moving or not. They also didn't know if it was an animal, some kind of vegetation, or something else.

"Ok, Gary, I'm going to request descent to the lowest permitted altitude. Fort Lauderdale Tower 15, this is Skyhawk five-niner on fourteen, over." The response came a few seconds later.

"One-five, Skyhawk five-niner. We are observing a large unusual phenomenon in the waters near or just north of Coral Springs. Would like to descend briefly to try and make out what it is. Request permission to descend to one thousand and would report this, over."

Seconds ticked by as the pilot waited for his answer.

"Uh Skyhawk, describe the phenomenon."

The pilot could not legally descend until it got the ok from the tower, with good reason. Other aircraft could be in the same area and priority was always given to safety. To get that answer, he had to answer their request. So he described it as accurately as he could, also mentioning that they couldn't tell if it was moving or not.

More seconds ticked by as again they waited. Tony figured the ATC was consulting with his supervisor regarding his request. This was not something that controllers heard on a regular basis.

"Tower one-five to Skyhawk, over."

"This is Skyhawk, go."

"Permission is granted for you to descend to a thousand, just over the area of the sighting. Report what else you see of it and then ascend back to your current altitude. This is now being reported to USCG, over."

"Roger, Tower one five, I copy. Thank you. Will contact you again shortly. Out."

"Ok, Bill. You heard. Let's take a look."

As the chopper descended, Bill let the passengers know as they might want to take a closer look also. In the cabin, all three had their eyes glued to the window trying to see as best they could while the water steadily came a little closer to them, as well as the phenomenon.

Little by little, coastal and marine details became clearer and larger. The white mass looked even larger from a thousand feet. But from a thousand feet, there was another difference. At their original height of eight thousand feet, the pilots and passengers saw only a continuous white sheet. From a thousand feet, they saw a few individual characteristics and water in between them.

"Bill, take over for a minute, will ya?"

"Sure." Bill took the controls and formally let Captain Tony know he had them. Tony then pulled out his binoculars and looked down. He wasn't a scientist by any means, but he was no dummy either. He did do well in biology in school. That helped, because he could tell the individuals down there weren't plants. They were moving, and looked as if they were swimming, although even with binoculars, he couldn't tell for sure. But he knew it had to be reported. He didn't know what they were, but he would assume they weren't good until proven otherwise.

"How about I hover over them for a bit?"

"Sure. Go ahead. Might be easier to determine what they might be."

As Gary maintained the altitude, he wished they could descend lower, but they had to stick with the approved altitude. This was a highly populated area, and they were relatively close to the shore. "This good?" he asked the pilot.

"Fine. Just stay there for a second. Damn, I wish we could get lower."

As the chopper hovered, an image started forming in Tony's mind. It was one he didn't like. Staring through the binoculars at the creatures in the water, he used the strongest power the lenses had. Then he stiffened. *Holy Mother of God!*

Taking the binoculars away from his eyes for a moment, he looked straight ahead to the shoreline, then back to the leading edge of the mass, then northward. He wasn't ready to say anything yet.

"Turn her tail a bit to starboard." Gary moved the controls.

As the tail turned, that brought his view more southward. "Stop," he ordered.

He looked out bare-eyed, then used the binoculars. The mass extended as far as the naked eye could see. Then he looked to his right. The leading edge seemed to be moving. *Toward the coastline!*

Right now it was still about a quarter of a mile away from the perimeter of the swimming areas, from what it looked like. But if it was moving toward the coast, as it seemed to be, those people could be in danger. He decided to alert the tower. He had a pretty good idea from his intensive view of the creatures what they were.

What he *didn't* know included three things: the species, the fact that they weren't typical for this area, and their lethality.

"Take us back up, Gary. I've seen enough."

The co-pilot took them out of hover position and started ascending, while Tony notified the tower they were returning back to their original height.

"Well?" asked the co-pilot. "Figure out what they are?"

Tony looked at him with an expression that alarmed the co-pilot.

"Yea. I believe I have. Jellies."

"Jellies? Are you shitting me? Holy Toledo!"

Tony grabbed the mic and notified the tower and notified them of his exact position, and the results of his assessment.

"Did you say, jellyfish?" the ATC asked to confirm.

"Roger, that's affirmative. Hundreds, maybe millions. From my observations, it looks like they're moving toward land. Toward the swimming areas. Recommend you notify the ground authorities from Lauderdale to Coral Springs. I would give a heads up also to West Palm Beach. The creatures seem to be heading northward but spreading toward the coast as well."

There was silence on the radio for a moment. "Copy that, Skyhawk. Notifying. Thank you for the report. You are clear at your altitude currently."

Tony then took back the controls and let Bill inform their three passengers in the back of what they had seen. Their tour, although coming to an end, had been most enlightening and one they'd never forget. They wished they could communicate with each other because they were eager to talk about it. But until they got back on the ground, they could only remain silent and wonder. One of them pointed down and then mimicked taking a drink. The other two seemed to understand, nodding their heads and smiling. Yes it did call for a drink when it was all over.

CHAPTER 15

The Coast Guard wasted no time in sending a couple of their vessels to check out the area. They already knew about the Fort Lauderdale incidents and casualties. The fact that the jellyfish species had been confirmed by local marine experts expedited all movements by them that might ordinarily have taken considerably longer because of service protocols and the chains of command. The situation had apparently been given high priority and the district commander, an admiral, was kept apprised of the situation.

Enroute to the area from the base at Miami were two vessels. One was a one hundred twenty five foot patrol ship called the Coast Guard cutter *Jackson,* and the other was an eighty two foot patrol boat often used for search and rescue, as well as conducting port security operations when needed. It would take them approximately two hours to arrive at the scene traveling at a speed of fifteen knots. On board the larger vessel was a marine biologist from the Miami Institute, who knew that her colleague, Rebecca Wares, was at sea onboard the *Argonaut.* Her mission was the same but in a different area.

****

Aboard the Argonaut, August 6
After a coffee and some discussion of a more serious nature and that of issues at hand, the two scientists had come to a tentative conclusion that there could be a remedy to this problem. But first, they had to assess the entire problem; that is, they needed to find out if the migrating jellyfish problem was isolated to southeastern US shores or was occurring throughout the world.

They knew that these species, both the box jellyfish and its miniature cousin the Irukandji, were prevalent in mostly warm tropical or subtropical waters, although they had been found as far north in the Atlantic as the British Isles. Up there they were far and few between and posed little concern to humans. Although they could survive in any waters, cold or otherwise, they stuck to mostly the warmer waters where they seemed to thrive better.

"So the plan is simple. We hit the Fort Lauderdale area and take an eyeball measure of the swarm, assuming they did go there." Suddenly her face became one grim expression as if a light switch had been flicked off, from the happy to the unhappy, then she went to sit down.

"What's the matter, Becky?" Now James reflected the same expression, except that it was out of concern for her. Something was wrong. He joined her at the table.

She put her head down on the table for a moment, then lifted it, rubbed her hands over her face then rested it on her closed hands. Her expression hadn't changed.

"I feel so damn shitty about before, James." Her eyes expressed a sadness that put her on the edge of tears.

"Becky. Becky what's wrong?" Now he was *really* concerned.

They ignored the constant mild rolling and pitching of the ship. James knew he really needed to get to the heart of the matter regarding what had hit her so emotionally hard all of a sudden.

She looked at him after deciding he deserved to know what was bothering her.

"We, um, were having a little silliness up there," she said rolling her eyes upward. "I had temporarily forgotten that an elderly couple, probably ones as nice as my mom and dad, had died from these creatures and numerous other people were seriously hurt. And here we are, joking and laughing. That's what hit me all of a sudden." One tear from her left eye rolled down. She didn't wipe it. James took his thumb and gently wiped the tear from her cheek. He felt her soft skin for the first time.

"Hey, listen," he said softly. "We are going to tackle this and beat this thing. That little bit of humor up there, when you think about it, was necessary. It not only helped break all the tension that I know we were all feeling, but it also helped get us back on track, this time with a determination that can never be broken. We're going to win with that determination. We are."

She looked at him and subtly nodded. Her eyes didn't leave his, as if waiting for more encouraging words.

"So don't blame yourself for that. I feel bad, too, about those people. But there's nothing we can do to save them. All we can do is get on this thing, get control of it, and get rid of it. Save more people from being hurt. Know what I mean?"

She nodded, still looking at him. "Yea, you're right."

"Besides, I didn't regret one bit what you said up there or what I said. I happen to be very attracted to you, but I was afraid to say it. And it probably wouldn't have been the best time for me to come out with it anyway."

She looked at him with a smile that seemed to say it all. *You're a nice man, Mr. Smarty. Thank you for that and for being there for me.*

She took his hands in hers and held them tightly, keeping his eyes glued to hers. She had the most beautiful green eyes he'd ever seen, he decided.

He responded by holding hers firmly as well.

"Thank you," she said very softly, squeezing his hands. "I, um, have to admit, that I'm attracted to you too. I really liked the brief appearance of the little boy in you upstairs." She giggled at the thought. He chuckled at that.

"Well," he started to say. "I have always tended to be a little shy with pretty women. That's just the way I am." He gently rubbed the soft skin of her hands, then cleared his throat. He decided he better stop now before they really lost track of what they were supposed to be doing. He deliberately and suddenly changed the tone of the moment, mainly for himself but also for her as well. There would be better times for them to casually enjoy each other's company. "Shall we see what's happening topside?"

She stood up smiling. "My my, you truly are Mr. Smarty. Where did you learn that term?"

"My dad was a sailor in the navy during World War Two. He told me war stories when I was a boy. I used to love that. Some of the terms he used I remembered. That's one of them."

"Ok, then. Let's go topside and find out when we might arrive at the scene." He followed her up the steps to the bridge to get an update on their status.

"What timing," said Captain Bill. "I was just about to call you up here. Got another call for you Becky. Somebody named Marge this time. Said it was very urgent."

"Really?" She turned to briefly glance at James, then turned back and took the phone from the captain.

"Rebecca here. Marge, that you?"

Marge was one of the other scientists from the Institute who sometimes worked with her, but was mostly researching and studying more details on the lifestyles of crustaceans and their role in the various ecosystems of the oceans. This time she was working on something far different. In fact, she told Rebecca right off the bat where she was.

"A *Coast* Guard boat? Why? What's going on?"

Marge then filled her in on what was happening. It turned out, surprisingly to Rebecca, that they were actually working on the same thing, but from different angles. Now the helicopter report made this whole thing much more sinister and apparently more threatening than she had originally thought.

"You alone on this?" she asked Marge.

"Yea, basically. Right now this ship is heading to the same area off the beaches near Coral Springs. The area around Lauderdale is inundated with these jellyfish. Fortunately, everyone got out of the water right after the ones who got stung, so no one else was affected. For now, all the beaches there have been closed until further notice. This is a disaster, let me tell you, Rebecca. I'm no jellyfish expert and neither is Bob. But you're out there and they needed someone with marine biology expertise. To help me out, Bob volunteered."

Rebecca then realized they would need a little help in identifying the jellies, just to be sure.

"Ok, so are you familiar with the box jellyfish?"

"For the most part I am. I don't know all the intricate details, but I do know where they originate and how they get about, in addition to their ability to really hurt people and kill."

"Alright. We're on the way toward Fort Lauderdale but since you've seen it already, can you tell me where the back edge of the swarm was first spotted?"

"Sure. We first saw it right when we entered the Lauderdale coast area. It seems to go on forever. I've told the Coast Guard people what we have and right now they are patrolling around the area and warning boaters to stay clear of the area. There's so many of these things that they can get trapped or wrapped around boat props and really screw them up, no pun intended."

Rebecca reminded her to tell the Coasties not to touch them in any way. She informed Marge of the four sets of eye clusters on the top of the bell, and the long, nearly ten foot tentacles that trail behind them. Even the Coast Guard boat, which was lucky so far in not getting any of them entangled in their props, could suffer engine failure if that happened. They, too were to stay clear of the swarm. She then told Marge they would start to head northwest to find the leading edge. When she finished talking, Marge informed her that she had pictures of the jellies with her that she would show the boat personnel so they'd recognize them when they saw them in the water.

Once it was established that they would be coordinating their evaluation of the situation with Marge and Bob and the assistance of the Coast Guard, the game was on and all the stops were pulled.

First, on the advice of the marine specialists and the Miami Marine Institute playing an active role, the Coast Guard issued an unprecedented venomous jellyfish warning to all beaches ranging from Boca Raton to West Palm Beach; and then further northward a venomous jellyfish watch was issued from Jupiter to Vero Beach. The scientists emphasized the necessity of the word "venomous" to be included in these reports and broadcasts. Most native jellyfish in the area were not deadly or seriously harmful to humans. Their stings just hurt for a while but, for the   most part, were not life-threatening.

It was important that the public took these warnings and watches seriously and not be complacent about them. Their lives were dependent on that. Of course, there would always be the skeptics who chose to either ignore the warnings, or decided that the authorities were nothing but a bunch of alarmists.

Whatever the case, both the state and the feds were now involved, along with the Miami Institute. Rebecca went to Captain Bill to update him on the situation, while James looked out the windows of the bridge. The ocean was beautiful, he thought, but held countless deadly secrets hidden from view above the surface. When it was angry, as in choppy or wavy seas, it could be deadly. When it was calm and serene-looking, it was just as deadly. If looks could be deceiving, calm seas were a perfect example of that.

"Bill, I have a request based on the facts of what's happening on the shore. Can you plot a course toward West Palm Beach?"

"West Palm Beach?" he echoed as a question. "Don't tell me they've been spotted up there too?"

Rebecca shook her head.

"No, not yet. I think they're heading northward, though. I want to find a spot that is potentially ahead of them and then backtrack to find the leading edge of the swarm. We need to get a bead on their track and approximately how fast they're moving, with or without the current. They can swim relatively fast for their species so we need to get there as soon as we can."

Captain Bill turned toward his mate as he steered the helm.

"Dexter, plot us a course for West Palm. See what you come up with for an ETA for running at eighteen knots."

"I'm on it, Cap." The first mate then turned and went to the other side of the bridge where the plotting table was located. With their GPS, he marked down their present position on the chart, then with the navigational compass and Paralock plotting ruler, he painstakingly calculated various EPs or estimated positions along a magnetic bearing of 275 degrees. He noted the current time which was five pm and calculated their present distance from West Palm as one hundred fifty nautical miles. With these figures, they would be arriving when it was dark.

Dexter put his tools down, and turned toward the captain.

"Bill, got the time. We'd be arriving there at dark. About one am to be more exact."

"Ok. Becky, hear that? Want to do a search in the dark?"

"Not particularly. Let me think for a minute."

Searching for jellies in the dark was not a good idea because even with strong lighting, they still wouldn't be easy to see. The reflections of the light against the surface plus the dark of the water below the surface would make an accurate assessment much more difficult than during the daylight, even with a cloudy day. She looked at her expert.

"James, what do you think?"

He inhaled deeply and let it out. "Well, I would suggest that we head to the area anyway. We probably should get some rest en route. When we get there, even if it's dark, we can still look around in case we *do* spot something. Hang around there and when it gets light we can go full speed on looking for them. If we don't see them by daylight, then it's likely they just haven't arrived yet."

Rebecca nodded. "I agree. Shall we eat in the meantime? I'm getting hungry."

"Yea, me too. I can go for something right now."

She turned to the captain. "Ok, Bill, let's go for it. After we eat, I'll probably lie down for a while and rest until we get there. Want to join us?"

"Naw, I'll let Dexter go first."

"No, Bill, I'm good. You go first, I can wait."

"You sure?"

"Positive. Go ahead."

"Alright. I'll send Ronny up to assist. Then I'll come back and relieve you."

"Don't worry about it. You've been on this thing for several hours now. You need the break. Just relieve me later to eat and then I'll come back to it."

With that plan mutually agreed on, the three went down to the mess area. Loretta's cooking fragranced the dining area with the delicious smells of pot roast, mashed potatoes, and specially prepared green beans in a cream sauce. For dessert was homemade apple pie. It was a combination that a starving person would never be able to get enough of. As soon as they entered the area, their stomachs seemed to scream for it.

Before long, they were filling their mouths. For now, it took their minds off the task which lay ahead of them. Added to that was the fresh coffee that seemed to relax them, rather than stimulate them. This was a time of pleasure, brief though it would be, that they would not be deprived of.

CHAPTER 16

Boca Raton, Florida, August 6

It had been a long but fun-filled day for the Ringston family. They were here for their two week vacation from Winston, Massachusetts-a suburb not far from the city known for its historical tea party from the eighteenth century. Boston was a city of many characteristics, including numerous road circles. If you didn't know your way around or have at least a GPS, you could easily get lost.

It was here that Howard Ringston worked in his marine bio-engineering firm. He had earned more than enough leave time to take his family somewhere beautiful and nice where they could spend good quality fun time together and still have plenty of time for each of them to enjoy their own favorite activities. He'd always heard how nice it was down in Boca Raton, Florida. Though quite pricy and known for its well-to-do residents, he was making enough of an income to easily afford a trip there for his family of five. And so after mutual agreements that Boca Raton and its beautiful beaches would be the place to go, off they went.

Their hotel was right on the beach area. The beach itself included, in both directions, miles of creamy white sands dotted every so often with leaning palm trees offering shade for those who liked the shade. The beaches were nearly totally free of trash and debris, giving it the beautiful, well-maintained appearance that they were known for. It looked like a vacationer's paradise. To those who were fortunate enough to be able to go there and enjoy it, it was.

Overlooking the beach and then the miles long boardwalk, their hotel also had an outdoor swimming pool and Jacuzzi. Often, guests would go from one to the other, then take a dip in the ocean and go back to the Jacuzzi or pool again. They had the choice to do it all as long as they wanted. This is what Howard wanted for his family to enjoy.

Late that afternoon after a day of sunbathing and swimming, they came in to clean up a bit in preparation for going out to dinner. Although Howard and his wife Jill had a separate room from their two teenage sons, Eric and Mark, the rooms were next to each other, which allowed for access from one to the other by way of a door between the two rooms themselves.

Howard wanted this arrangement. Although his sons were basically responsible and good kids, still they were teenagers. He and Jill need to keep an eye on them and at least know that they were fine.

Howard turned on the TV while Jill was in the bathroom, taking a shower to wash off the salt water and sand. With the remote, he turned to a channel that was showing news and then relaxed for a bit in the chair. His shower would be after Jill was finished in the bathroom. He didn't mind the wait at all, as he listened and watched the TV, not really paying much attention as the anchors talked about the political report and then some local robberies that police were investigating. After that, talk about local events and the beaches and then a commercial.

"Honey, can you bring me the bath towel? I don't know why but I left it in there for some reason." Jill's voice brought him to his feet. "Sure. Coming." He saw it on the bed and brought it to her. When he returned to the room, the commercial was still on and he sat down in his now-dry bathing suit looking at the TV.

The screen then showed in big bold letters "Breaking News". Then back to the anchors.

"And now this just in. A warning has just been issued by the Coast Guard and the Marine Institute in Miami about a swarm of jellyfish moving up the east coast. They were first spotted in the Miami area and seem to be migrating northward. Marine scientists have warned that this particular species may be dangerous and the public is warned to stay out of the water at the local beaches until the area is cleared of them. News Channel Five received reports that a couple of weeks ago swimmers were stung in the Fort Lauderdale and Pompano Beach areas. Eight people were reported to have died from the stings, and numerous other people were injured and had to receive immediate treatment in local hospitals. David Wright has the story."

Howard immediately stiffened and sat straight up, gluing his eyes to the TV screen. He turned up the volume.

The field reporter, David Wright, was already talking.

"Scientists say these are not the common typical jellyfish that most people in this area encounter from time to time. These are box jellyfish, which are known to have originated in Australian waters and appear also off the shores of Hawaii. Unlike the common, non-life threatening jellyfish that most people know about, these are dangerously venomous, can swim up to speeds of about four miles per hour and are the only species that are believed to have sight as well." Then he went into the report of their tentacles and symptoms of having been stung.

"Right now, warnings have been issued from Miami to West Palm Beach and then watches from points north of there up to Vero Beach. Swimmers and those on the beaches are strongly advised to heed the warning signs posted on the beaches. If they say no swimming and why, obey them.

"If you're stung and don't get immediate treatment, you can die. If you're within the warning or watch areas, either stay out of the water or stay very close to shore if signs have not been posted, and listen to beach authorities for ongoing advisories. David Wright, Fox News, Miami."

Howard was stunned. He didn't know how long he sat there but it must have been a few minutes before her voice broke the shock.

"Ok, hon. The bathroom is yours." Jill was brushing her now dried hair as she stepped out of the bathroom. Her smile faded as she saw the surprised look on her husband's face. "Hey, what's wrong?"

He told her everything he'd just heard on TV.

"Are you serious?" Her eyes quickly went to the TV but the report was over.

"Maybe I better contact them?"

Jill quickly jumped on that. "No, no, no. Absolutely not. Are you *kidding?* This is our vacation and we're not even from around here. You get involved in this and *poof!* There goes our fun times in the winds of paradise. No, I can't let you do that."

"Wait a sec. Just hear me out. Just for a sec."

She looked at him with the beginnings of a scowl but didn't say anything. He took advantage of the moment.

"I can give them a quick briefing on the company and what I do. Would be good for the business and the company. *And,* it could help this entire region out. This is right up our alley. Sometimes you have to grab the opportunity when you can, otherwise you lose it forever. Besides, it isn't just that. It could save lives and that's the best part of all. Saving lives. Human lives. This could prevent others from getting hurt or killed."

She couldn't argue that point, she admitted to herself because she felt the same way about saving lives. Being a registered nurse involved that from the very beginning.

There was silence for a few moments as her mind was going full speed and he could sense that. He let her think about it as he sat and looked at her.

"Well can you at least wait until tomorrow to call them? We need to get ready for dinner now."

He smiled, although guardedly. This was not something he would ever have anticipated, nor desired on a vacation.

"Ok. That, I can do. I'll call them in the morning. Let me hop in the shower and wash this salt funk off me."

As he jumped in the shower, she opened the inter-room door and checked on the boys. They hadn't showered yet, having gotten involved in a video game.

"Hey, will you guys hurry up? Get going in the shower. We'd like to leave for dinner sometime before tomorrow."

"Ok, Mom," they both said. One of them ran into the bathroom after grabbing clean underwear while the other got his clean clothes ready for going out. She sighed and closed the doors. Reminding teenage boys nowadays of the necessities seemed to be a regular thing. At least with *their* teenage boys that seemed to be the case.

****

Aboard the USCGC Jackson, August 6

Marge was a veteran of boating and sailing on the seas being the marine biologist she was. This was her *first*, however, on a Coast Guard boat. The one hundred twenty five footer was rigged differently than the ones she was used to sailing on and seeing a bunch of crewman in navy blue work uniforms and wearing baseball caps didn't seem to quite fit the scientific   expeditions she had become accustomed to. She had to remind herself occasionally that this was a military boat, not a science one.

"Ma'am, the captain is requesting your presence on the bridge." She was a young twenty two year old seaman whose presence seemed to be somewhat refreshing from a formerly all male crew.

"I take it that means he'd like to see me?" she said pleasantly and with a smile.

"Yes ma'am."

"Ok, young lady." She looked at her name tag. It was her last name-Hagelworth.   "What's   your   first   name,   Seaman Hagelworth?"

"Sarah."

"Ok, Sarah. Lead on." The girl turned with Marge following close behind. The forty nine year old scientist wished she was that young again. Two minutes later she was on the bridge, greeted pleasantly by the Lieutenant who was the captain of the boat. He was wearing officer's khaki's and a baseball cap as well.

"Ms. Holbrook, welcome aboard. I'm sorry I didn't greet you right away but I had to take care of protocol for getting underway."

"That's OK, Captain. I understand."

"I'm Lieutenant Holloway, captain on board. I'm pleased to meet you."

He was young and handsome, considerably younger than her. *Oh, if I were only twenty five years younger,* she thought again. He looked like he'd be a good catch.

They shook hands. "Pleased to meet you too, Captain. Tell me, why are you called captain when you are a lieutenant? Sounds confusing to me."

He laughed then explained. "Perfectly understandable. It can be confusing. The lieutenant part is my actual rank. The captain part is my role on the ship. The confusing part is that an officer with the actual rank of captain can also be a captain on the ship. But not every captain is a captain on a ship or a base."

"I see," she nodded her head. "Well in that case, I'm glad I'm just a civilian. No one can confuse my role with any other. Makes things a little easier that way, know what I mean?"

He laughed again. "In that respect, I envy you. Anyway, I want to go over where you want to search, and about what you're looking for. We might need your advice regarding public safety regarding these animals."

"Sure. I can give you that information, but I have it below. Can we meet somewhere where there's less radio racket? I need to show you some materials so you'll have a better idea, and I don't want voice competition."

"Sure. We can meet in the boardroom downstairs. Just a moment."

He turned to his officer colleague. "Bob, I'll be below in the officer's mess. Take over here, will you?"

His subordinate, Ensign Tom Branson, responded with a salute.

"Aye, Captain." Then he loudly announced, "Captain departed the bridge. The OOD has the con."

Holloway led Marge downstairs to the officer's mess, which was right down the hall from her quarters. "I'll be right back, Captain. Have to get my materials."

"Ok. Have coffee in here if you want some?"

"That would be wonderful." She left to get her things and returned within a minute.

Both sat down at the officer's dining table as Marge pulled out some papers and some pictures she had downloaded and printed back at the institute. Ruffling through some of the papers, she separated them from the papers and placed them on the table in front of the captain.

"Now these," she pointed at them, "are what we are looking for. Look at them good, Captain."

He picked up one of the pictures which showed several of the box jellyfish. These were the first pictures he'd ever seen of them, except on TV. He recognized the squarish bell and the long, sinister-looking tentacles.

"I remember seeing these on a TV documentary one time. What are these dots on the front of the bell?"

"Those are eye clusters. Apparently they can see."

He raised his eyebrows. "Really? I thought they're supposed to have no brains?"

"They don't. It's still a mystery to scientists why they can see with no brain, but then again they're not built like anything else on the planet."

He looked at some of the other pictures which were views from different angles, and a few close-ups.

"Incredible how these things can be so deadly."

"Captain, each one of these can kill at least sixty humans. That's a lot of venom power in each one. And they have a smaller cousin of the same species that are almost as deadly. They're a hell of a lot smaller, much harder to see, and can put someone in the hospital in the blink of an eye."

"Oh yes. I think I've heard of them, again on TV." He struggled a bit to think of the name. "Arakandi, or something like that?"

"Irukandji," she corrected him. "But you were close. Very good."

He immediately recognized the name and nodded his head. "Right. That's it. Ok. So...what's your plan?" he asked, brushing off the compliment.

Marge rested her head on her hand as she looked down at the pictures, her mind now thinking ahead.

"Well my associate is on the *Argonaut*, our Institute research vessel. Because we saw the back edge of the swarm near Lauderdale, the *Argonaut* is going to try and keep ahead of them by swinging up to West Palm Beach and backtracking to meet up with the front edge. That way we can get an idea of just about how large this swarm really is, how far out it stretches from its edge closest to land, and how fast it's moving northward. What we need to do here is monitor its movement. I do know that something is in the works to deal more aggressively with this, but that's being looked into by the Institute."

The captain nodded. "In the meantime, we'll continue to warn off boaters approaching the swarm from seaward."

"Also, it might be a good idea to show these pictures to your crew," Marge suggested. They need to be aware of what they look like and the dangers they pose. They should be warned not to pick them out of the water."

"Oh, absolutely," Holloway agreed immediately. He got up. "Can I take these with me now? I'll have one of my crew show them around after I brief the bridge people."

Marge started to rise. "No no, please," he said with his hand gesturing toward her seat. "Enjoy your coffee, Ms. Bickford. We'll be having our supper meal at 17:30 here. You're our honored guest and you can eat with the officers here. There's three of us on board, including me. When you're ready, you can come back to the bridge or feel free to roam the ship. I only suggest that you avoid the engine room. Can get a little hot and oily down there."

Marge nodded and said she'd be up shortly as she took another sip. Believe it or not, she liked the coffee. Not too many civilians could say that about military coffee. Her mind soon returned back to the environmental and health threats at hand. She also wondered what was up with the Institute regarding a possible solution to this spreading problem. They said they'd eventually get back to her, and so all she could do was wait.

CHAPTER 17

Boca Raton, August 7

After making several calls, Howard Ringston finally was directed to the appropriate people to discuss what he needed to talk about. He had something to offer which could help the situation down here. The fact that he was initially passed from one agency to another and from one person to another didn't frustrate him to the point of giving up. In fact, it had the opposite effect which meant he was more determined than ever to talk to the right people. It turned out that the right people were in the Miami Marine Institute which, as he had found out in his numerous calls, was the agency which started the investigation of this whole situation.

"Miami Marine Institute, may I help you?"

Howard expected and got a receptionist to begin with. After he had explained who he was and why he was calling, the receptionist connected him with the assistant director of marine operations, Susan Bysendorf, who had a PhD in oceanography. She questioned him after he went through the explanation again and said she had heard of the products he was working with although she didn't know for sure if they were actually operational yet in this country. He said it was just beginning, but that this could be something that should be considered, especially if it could prevent further injuries or deaths of people. She agreed and asked him to hold while she consulted with her boss, Dan Worthington.

****

Two miles off the coast of West Palm Beach, August 7

They'd been here for several hours now but had yet to see the leading edge of the swarm. Rebecca picked up the ship's phone and called the Coast Guard vessel that Marge was on. It was fortunate that she'd had the presence of mind to get the number when Marge had called her the day before.

The phone was answered by the radio communications officer, who then patched the call up to the bridge.

"This is Lieutenant Moxley. Can I help you?"

Rebecca identified herself and asked to speak to Marge.

"Sure. Stand by, ma'am."

Rebecca heard small phone noises as he moved it in his hands. She heard him calling to someone on the bridge to get a hold of Marge for a phone call.

"She'll be here in one, ma'am. Stand by."

Be here in one? she thought. She assumed it meant one minute. She was right.

Very quickly after first hearing her voice on the bridge, she was on the phone.

"Hi Becky. Hey, girl, what's going on where you are?"

The two women quickly briefed each other of their status and location. Both had been advised to keep the comms length to a minimum in case an emergency came up. Even on a mission such as this, the vessel was obligated to immediately respond to any marine emergency in its area.

"They *are* moving north, Becky and fairly quickly. When we first arrived, a few hours ago, they were at the southern end of Fort Lauderdale waters. Now they are beyond the northernmost waters, just leaving the Pompano Beach area and approaching Boca Raton."

That was what Rebecca had feared. It sounded like they were either swimming at their maximum speed, or were swimming at a lesser speed but had a current to help them along. Whichever it was, it was not a good situation.

"Marge, how far are you out from shore? Give me the most exact calculation you have."

"Just a minute, Beck. Let me find out."

Rebecca waited as she heard her colleague ask the bridge officer for the distance, who then asked the navigator. In about thirty seconds she had her answer.

"We're about a thousand feet from the shore max, maybe a little less. Can't get much closer because of the shallows. We needed to get a bead on how close the swarm was to land."

Rebecca stiffened, afraid to ask the next question yet knowing what the answer most likely would be. She had to confirm for the record what she knew based on what Marge had just told her.

"So, you're on the outside edge of the swarm?"

"Yes. We are. Going north it extends as far as the eye can see."

"What about the inside edge? Can you see it from where you are?"

"Hold on, let me check."

Rebecca could hear her telling the bridge officer of the urgency of this call and she needed to keep Rebecca on the line for another minute while she checked on the status of the swarm. She heard Marge's voice in the distance. "Sir, can I borrow your binoculars for a minute?" Then nothing but radio noises and male voices.

In about two minutes, Marge came back on.

"Becky, I'm afraid I can't see the inside edge from where we are. Looks like it's pretty close to the shore."

"Can you use binoculars and tell me for sure?"

For a few seconds, Marge was silent. "I *did* use binoculars."

This time Marge was met with silence. Then a voice on the other end of the *Argonaut* bridge making an announcement. "Hold on for just a second, Marge."

One of the deckhands stated he had just spotted with his binoculars a whitish mass floating in the distance south of them. He stated it looked pretty wide and the inside of it was close to shore, while the outside edge of it extended beyond a reasonable swimming area.

"Lend me your specs for a minute please."

As he gave it to her, she quickly took them, ran out to the outside of the bridge and looked in the southward direction. *There it was. Oh my God!* She had known it would be huge, but not this big. It was heading directly in the ship's path. This was bad, very bad news and not just for the southeast coast of Florida but for the entire east coast of the state. Not to mention for the ship as well.

Handing the binoculars back to the deckhand, she had seen enough.

"Captain Bill, get us out of here. Further out as much as possible while keeping the swarm in sight. We don't want them entangled in the ship's props or engine intakes."

"You got it, Becky. Dexter, increase speed to ten knots, turn to bearing one three zero for about three minutes, then decrease speed to five knots and come around to two two zero. Let me know when we're at that position."

"Aye, Cap."

While Dexter handled the helm, Captain Bill checked the navigation chart to confirm their position in relation to the land. Rebecca was already back on the phone.

"Marge, ask the Coast Guard to send a message asking the ground authorities to have the jellyfish watches for those indicated areas to warnings. That means from West Palm Beach to Vero Beach. Ask that watches be extended from Vero to Daytona at the very least. Best recommendation is to extend the watches all the way up the coast of Florida. We have a more serious threat to the east coast than we thought."

"Wow. Ok, I'll tell them. I better get off this thing and let them know. Talk to ya later."

After hanging up, she saw the ship maneuvering to a safe position further out to sea but still close enough to continuously monitor the moving swarm. They couldn't see the opposite end of it. She realized that it could be miles long.

"We reached your position, Captain."

"Okay. Bring her to all stop."

"All stop, aye."

The seas were relatively calm which allowed for the stop position. It allowed them to get a better handle on the movement of the mass in the water, but they would not be able to stay stopped for too long, due to the current and tides affecting their position.

****

Miami Marine Institute, August 7

Dan was on the phone with a Howard Ringston who intrigued him with what he was starting to say. When Sue had told him of the existing device, he was interested in learning more. It was all too obvious that catching all these things in the water would not only be impractical, but impossible as well. What Ringston had to offer as a way to deal with the problem seemed to be a godsend if it was true and really worked.

"So Mr. Ringston, what company is this that you work for?"

"It's called Marine Bioengineering Solutions, up in Boston. It's been in business for about   ten years now. I'm a marine engineer with them. What they started producing included robotic vehicle cameras for research vessels like I assume you have. Then we started getting involved in the more lucrative but much more complicated transport submersibles for research. We've decreased production on those, however, due to a lesser demand for them. But occasionally we get an order for one.

"Our newest project is not the first that's been created. We call it, for lack of a better term, the Robotic Jellyfish Sweeper. We made a contract to buy a number of these from the Koreans and rent them out to government agencies or other agencies who felt a need for them in certain situations. The South Koreans call it the Jellyfish Eliminator Robotic Swarm or JEROS. They agreed to sell some to us on two conditions: one, that we didn't try to claim it as our own creation. Of course we immediately agreed to that. It would have been illegal anyway. The second condition is that we call it something else. It could be close to what they call it but not exactly the same. We agreed to that also, and thus the sweeper nomenclature."

"How many of these do you have?"

"Oh, I'm not sure of the exact number, but I believe about fifty."

"Tell me what they do."

What they did was astounding. Ringston explained that they were robots floating on the surface of the water. Using submerged nets, they sucked up jellyfish as they traveled somewhat like a vacuum cleaner. A propeller then shredded them into pieces. Traveling about four point six miles per hour, they could each remove about eight hundred eighty pounds of jellyfish per hour. Their purpose was for elimination of jellyfish where they are a serious threat to the human population as well as the area ecosystem, and assisting in controlling their breeding. In addition, they are also used in prevention of jellies from entering human swimming areas.

Dan was immediately interested. From what was happening down here, cost was not an obstacle. Here was a man offering a solution that no one else could come up with for dealing with this kind of problem. It seemed like the perfect one. How else could they get rid of these things?

"How many can we rent and how quickly can you get these down here?"

Howard knew he had done the right thing.

"You can rent as many as you want. The price is good and with a discount since you are a granted Institution and a scientific one as we are. I'll call today and we can expedite shipment. I think fastest we can get them here is three days from now. I know with what you're going through that seems to be a long time. But remember, that's a lot of machinery, very expensive to be exact. We pay for the insurance on shipment. All you have to pay for is the rental and the shipping and handling. That can be taken care of and arranged after your threat has been eliminated. We're willing and happy to work with you on this. You have to get rid of this problem, then worry about the financial issues later. Lives have to come first, right?"

"Mr. Ringston, you are a lifesaver. However, expenses should be the responsibility of the state of Florida. Because this is an operation well beyond the limitations of our institute and what we do, the state has to become involved. Let me get a hold of someone at the DEP and tell them about this. I know someone personally there. The operation, once approved and I don't see why it wouldn't be, would be entirely funded and operated by the state. I'll give them your number and the number of your company. This is something we have to get going on right away. Why don't you give me your phone number and I'll get back to you as soon as I can."

After phone numbers and information was exchanged, the ball was put into motion. It would take time to get the operation going and time was not on their side. Dan Worthington got on the horn again to make his pitch. He hoped he could convince the state that this was their only option to get rid of the swarm. Otherwise, more people would get hurt.

In the meantime, Howard had to explain to his family why they should avoid the ocean for swimming for the time being. He laid it all on the line so they'd understand. They, understandably, were not happy about the situation but realized that even if they could go in the water, they wouldn't be comfortable knowing those things were on the way. The fact that they were even in the region put a huge dampner on their beach going. Instead, they chose to go to water parks and, of course, the hotel's swimming pool and Jacuzzi.

Before they left to go anywhere, he got on the phone and contacted his boss at the company, explaining the situation and requesting ten sweepers be readied for possible immediate shipment. He informed him that shipment should be expedited pending Florida's approval and provision of the address where they would be sent to, as well as the financial information and arrangements. His boss, hearing about what was happening down there on the news, readily agreed to Howard's request, and got his number at the hotel as well as his cell number in case he needed to contact him regarding the shipment. Other information would be exchanged once the state came through with the request. Howard knew this was all a bunch of red tape, but realized this is how state governments and the feds operated.

Once his call was completed, they packed the car and set off to their first destination of the day which, of course, would be the nearest waterpark. While they would be having fun, someone else, in another area, at another beach and town, would not be.

CHAPTER 18

Jupiter, Florida, 6 PM, August 7

The beach at this time was empty. At six pm, the two teenagers knew the lifeguards were gone, which was why they chose this time. Despite the posted warning signs for no swimming and the reason, they chose to ignore it. For two days now all they had was the pool at their hotel and they were starting to get a little tired of it. They came down here for the ocean from their Midwest home, not to play around in a pool which they had at home.

Steve and his brother Joe decided they would be careful. After all, it's the least they could do if they were going to ignore the no swimming signs and swim when there was no one around. Why *not* be careful? That way, if anybody asked, they could say they were. At least, that's the way they were thinking.

What they were *not* thinking of was the serious danger they placed themselves in. They looked out at the water which looked as inviting as it was calm. Gentle waves lapped up onto the shore and it sure looked like a swimmer's paradise. No one around. They had the area all to themselves.

Of course they didn't tell their parents they were going there. Instead, they told them they would just be walking around a bit and taking in some of the sights of the area around where they were staying.

The two brothers played Frisbee for a bit on the beach. Questions, how would they explain the wet bathing suits when they returned to the hotel? They had been given a curfew of eight pm and it was a little after six now. Not much time but they would use it to their advantage. They planned to sneak into their separate room from their parents without them knowing it and calling them from the room to let them know they were back. Simple and very do-able as far as they were concerned.

Taking off their shirts, they ran into the water and dived under. The water was cool and refreshing from the late summer heat and humidity. It felt so good. They took full advantage of it, careful not to yell or talk loudly yet splashing each other to enjoy the moments while they could. They neither saw nor felt anything threatening and couldn't understand the overreaction of the adults to what they *thought* was a serious issue. Man, there was nothing here but water and that's it. No sharks or anything like that. No other people to bump into. They started swimming a little further from shore, frequently diving under and coming back up for air.

They remained careful not to make too much noise so as not to attract unwanted attention. As the eighteen year old came up and started treading water, he saw a lone figure a little ways down the beach and informed his brother to stay quiet. The figure was walking slowly along the water's edge as if in a relaxed late afternoon stroll, heading toward them but not having spotted them-yet. He couldn't tell if it was a man or woman because he or she was too far away to tell. But best not to take any chances.

Quietly they continued to swim around. The sixteen year old was wearing his waterproof watch, so occasionally they checked the time so they wouldn't run overtime on their little escapade here and get back to the hotel late. Their hotel was only five minutes from here, if that much so they could be back in no time once they left here.

For the next thirty minutes, they enjoyed the freedom of being here without the restrictions that adults imposed on them, especially their parents. They didn't consider themselves bad boys for doing this—only doing something just this once during their stay here so they could say to their friends back home in Missouri that they swam in the Atlantic and had the best time of their lives. Diving and swimming, treading water, quietly splashing each other on occasion, and just enjoying the feel of the water; this is what they'd always dreamed of and now they were absolutely loving it. Overcome by their enjoyment, they were unaware of the subtle current carrying them a little further away from the spot where they had entered the water as it was starting to get darker.

Steve advised his brother that they should start heading into shore. After asking him the time, which was now seven fifteen, he decided they better start heading back. As he positioned himself to start swimming back in, something brushed against both his lower legs. Initially it was feathery light and he briefly thought it was just a piece of seaweed. Until the white-hot pain hit him like a fully ignited blow-torch. It was nothing like he ever felt in his life before and he screamed like never before either. Joe looked at him in horror and yelled, "What's wrong? Steve, what's wrong?"

He swam to his brother to help him, only to see his jaw and the rest of him stiffen. His eyes were bulging out and his mouth fully opened to emit another piercing, bloodcurdling scream that defied any logic. Joe was scared beyond understanding and tried to help Steve, who now started thrashing about and convulsing. Foam and spittle started coming out of his mouth. The thrashing about was so violent that he really couldn't get too close to him without being hit by flailing arms. The younger brother immediately screamed for help to anyone who might hear him on the beach or anywhere else on land.

He wanted to pull Steve in but had a lot of difficulty getting close to him. He didn't know CPR or even first aid. What he *did* know was that he was having some kind of seizure, which he never had in his life before. As he started to head toward shore, something feathery light brushed across his chest. His face went under water only momentarily as he positioned himself to get back to shore as fast as possible. But he had no time for that because the white-hot pain hit him like a sledge hammer across the face and chest.

He too started screaming uncontrollably. He felt his muscles spasm violently all over and progress into involuntary contractions.. He had no more control of his legs and was unable to see what was happening to his brother. Like his brother, who had now gone under the surface, his muscles were rippling violently throughout his body, followed by a series of seizures and then frothing at the mouth.

On the beach a little closer, the lone figure had stopped strolling, then stood still for a moment looking in the direction where the boys were in the water. Whoever it was thought they heard screams for a moment and was looking to see if anyone or anything was in the water. The boys never knew if the person had seen them and would never know anything else. As the venom continued to wreak its havoc on the younger boy's body and vital organs, his breathing started to fail, his muscles rippled and convulsed without working, his nervous system felt nothing but agonizing pain from head to toe, his face was on fire, and his kidneys started shutting down. In seconds, his heart stopped and he slowly descended beneath the surface, his severely scarred face and chest forever marking him as the latest casualty up to this point in time. They could not have imagined, only a half hour before, that their swimmer's paradise would become their watery grave.

****

On the Argonaut--coast of West Palm Beach, August 7
They'd been monitoring the movement of the mass pretty much all day, confirming its northward movement. Rebecca felt helpless to be able to do anything about it. Every so often she'd get in touch with Marge to confirm the movement of the back edge. She wondered why this movement. *Why the hell are they moving this way and so close to shore? Why the hell didn't they stay out in the open ocean where they could swarm and swim all they wanted?* When it came to Mother Nature and any possible acts of God, accurate explanations were pretty hard to come by. She realized that all too often. Sometimes there are things or happenings you just can't control or even predict.

****

Aboard USCGC Jackson, August 8
Marge had just gotten off the phone with Rebecca and they were both pretty much in a position to monitor the movement only. The Captain was off the bridge and one of the officers, an ensign, had taken over as Officer of the Deck, or OOD. A phone rang on the bridge.

"Stand by, please. Mr. Bennett, a call for you sir. They said it's urgent."

The OOD went and took the phone. "Ensign Bennett here."

On the other end were the authorities in Jupiter.

****

Miami Marine Institute, Miami, Florida, evening of August 8

Dan Worthington was trying to stay on top of everything but as with most top jobs, it gets to be pretty lonely up there. In addition to knowing at all times what was going on with all the current projects and who was doing what, he was also staying posted on the happenings off the east coast and the swarm monitoring by their ship and the Coast Guard's. His new mission to be added was to see how the arrangements for the sweepers were being done.

He'd already spoken to his connection at the Florida State Department of Environmental Protection and was promised that it would be given top priority. In fact, his connection had all the hopes and expectations that one could have with the state when it came to emergency and truly urgent matters that affected public health as well as the state economy. No one could expect any less under the circumstances.

But as fate would have it, there was that gnat-like annoyance of red tape; that proverbial curse of government bureaucracy that always seemed to find the right times to hold up everything that was important. Things started going a little too slowly considering the current situation, to put it mildly. When the connection started getting antsy after two days of hearing nothing from his superiors, he started making more calls and reminded his supervisor that if something wasn't decided very quickly about this sweeper issue, more people could die. Then how would the state look-more specifically, the state DEP? Lawsuits? That could happen. Negative media coverage of the DEP? That would be far worse than a lawsuit.

As it turned out, the connection got a call back the next day. Paperwork was being processed. A call was made to Boston. It was a go.

"Well it's about freakin' time!" he said to no one in particular. He got on the horn and called Dan Worthington to let him know it was getting done. Although Dan was thrilled that now something was going to help them fight this thing, he remained guarded. It would take two days to process and prepare the robot machines and another day to process the financial paperwork for the state to be billed. It would be three days before they could ship all ten down to Florida.

The good news about it was that the company would fly the machines down on a priority flight. They would deliver them to the state's docks in Miami where they would be loaded onto state research vessels with cranes to on and off load them. Their arrival time would be on the fourth day after the processing began.

The bad news was the loading time onto the ships. They would end up taking up much of the open lower deck space, but there would still be a little room to walk around. Most of the crew would be in the upper deck. Fortunately, the company, with the help of Howard Ringston, had agreed to send someone down to help with the operation of the sweepers.

Ringston's boss asked him if he would help with the mission. He knew he and his family were on vacation, so he offered a bonus without any obligation whatsoever. He could say no with a promise of no repercussions. If he chose to help, he'd be given an extra ten days' vacation and it wouldn't be taken off of his vacation time. Because it was a lot to ask of an employee on vacation, especially a good one, to work during his time away with family, he believed that compensation for the inconvenience should be well worth the temporary sacrifice. Howard considered it and discussed it with his family. The boys thought of the extra ten days down there and immediately said yes, he should take it. Jill was a little reserved about it at first, but then thought, *hey, why not?* "Go for it," she said. And he did.

CHAPTER 19

Jupiter, Florida, August 8

It took some time before the two teenager's bodies were found in the water. With the witness's help, the rescuers were able to gradually hone in on their location. From a distance the witness had spotted the two boys after they started screaming. He knew they were not playful screams and had run as fast as he could to the part of the beach closest to them. Because he was aware of the potential dangers in the water indicated by the posted NO SWIMMING signs, he was hesitant about diving into the water. He wanted badly to help them. An inner voice warned him not to go in. He could end up like them and then they'd never get the help they needed. So he dialed 911. *What the hell were they doing in the water in the first place?*

Each body was limp and rescuers noticed dark, ugly whip-like markings, which contrasted sharply with their bluish-white skin. They immediately noticed neither teenager was breathing. The four rescuers, in communications with each other, began to realize this was looking more like a recovery operation than a rescue.

As they drove the boats back toward shore and waiting ambulances and accompanying police officers, they checked for other vital signs but found none. When they got both bodies on the shore, they checked the pupils. Both pairs were fixed and dilated. There were no radial, apical, or carotid pulses in either boy. Not knowing how long they'd been in the water, they got them in the two ambulances and tried defibrillation on them as they were enroute to the hospital. They also tried rescue breathing. They were last ditch efforts to save the young boys before they called it.

On arrival at the Palm Beach Medical Center, they rushed them into the ER where they were quickly assessed by emergency personnel, including the emergency physicians. But it was too late. None of their vital signs returned and they knew by now that even if their circulation resumed, their brains would have been oxygen deprived for too long not to have catastrophic damage. Consequently, they called time of death on each of them, approximately one minute apart. They saw the horrible tentacle scars. Based on all the news reports and the beach closings, they knew what had killed them. What they didn't know, of course, was why they were in the water. That would forever be a mystery to them and their family.

It was tough, even for a veteran emergency and trauma medical crew, to deal with the death of any young persons, especially children and teenagers. For *both* of these boys to die like this under these circumstances was such a horrible tragedy that only informing the parents of these deaths would be more difficult. And that remained a question. Who were the boys? No one had a clue. There were no forms of identification on them.

Because of this, they had to inform the police. Although not forensically trained, one of the doctors had the presence of mind to check for "normal" scars or tattoos-anything that a loved one could easily connect with that person. One of the boys had a small scar on his left shin from a minor injury years back, so there was something to work with. If identification could be made on one of the bodies, it's possible they could eventually id the other one. Because there was a kind of resemblance to them, they had to consider the possibility that they were brothers.

When police came, they took notes, and advised the hospital personnel that the medical examiner's investigators were on their way to assess the bodies and then transport them to the county morgue.

An hour later, they were on their way. In the meantime, police checked to see if anyone had called in a missing persons report on two teenage boys. So far no reports. This was not good. If no one called in soon, they'd have to go to the media for help. The last thing law enforcement wanted to do was to publicize the death of anyone without first notifying the family. Because there were no ids on these boys and no one knew who they were, there'd be no choice. They'd give it an hour and then, with the chief's authorization, go public with it.

****

Aboard USCGC Jackson, August 9

Bennett notified the captain who needed to know all the latest information, especially all that was significant. He then let his scientific guest know the jellies had claimed two more victims. What he didn't know and wasn't told was that they were deceased-only that they'd been stung and were rushed to the hospital in what was believed to be a critical condition.

"Oh my God," was the only verbal reaction she could give. "Two teenagers. After all these warnings." She kept her voice low, but it noticeably indicated how upset she was. She could only look at the ensign, who returned the same anguished look. Having given out all these warnings well in advance, all parties concerned-both the Coast Guard and the scientists-had hoped for no more victims and a return to normalcy after these things left the area. There would be no accounting for the unexpected actions of those who would ignore those warnings.

"There's nothing we can do to help, Mrs. Holbrook. I suggest we continue our ops here, as per the captain's recommendation until such time as we can no longer remain."

She looked at him. "What do you mean until we can no longer remain?"

"Well that basically means that, if the District Commander believes we can no longer serve a useful purpose out here, we can suspend operations. Oh I know we are bringing you out here for scientific reasons and that's fine. However, this cannot be an indefinite mission. How long, I don't know. Just to give you a heads up, should the captain be notified at some point in the future that the district is pulling the plug on this, then we'll have no choice but to return you to where we picked you up. Be assured, though, that we'll be out here for a while longer, I expect, before that happens. You'll have plenty of time to get a full assessment on where this swarm is heading to. So I say relax for now. I just wanted to keep you informed about this."

"Well, I appreciate that, Mr. Holloway. I want this thing to come to an end also. May I call my colleague on the *Argonaut* and let her know about this?"

"Certainly." He turned around to the quartermaster of the bridge. "Petty Officer Thomson, will you patch Mrs. Holbrook through to the *Argonaut*? She'll give you the number."

"Thank you, Ensign." Marge walked over to the phone and waited for the patch to go through.

****

The media hit on it immediately as breaking news. Not only did the local media broadcast the news of the tragedy, but the networks got a hold of the story as well. This was something that would easily make a parent's worst nightmare even worse. Because there were no calls of missing teenage boys, the authorities had no choice. They had to find out who they were. The question remained as to why no missing persons reports had been called in. Where were the parents and didn't they know where their sons were?

There was no way to tell if the parents were watching the news broadcasts when they aired the report. For a while after they were aired, there were no immediate calls. Then a few started trickling in to the Boca Raton police station. All were determined not to be their parents. The scar on one of the boys had not been mentioned on the air. All callers were asked if there was anything on either of the boys that could help identify them, and if they were related or friends. No details were given out. Questions were asked that were meant to elicit particular information that only the true parents or other family members of the boys would know. If they got a hit, then they'd ask them to come in for further questioning and then id the boys at the morgue. They didn't tell the parents that because these were unnatural deaths, the legal system required an autopsy. Because no consent of the parents was required or necessary for the autopsy, it would be performed. Should the parents be identified they, of course, would be notified of the results. But they would not be allowed to see the bodies until after the procedure was fully completed.

One of the callers, a woman, sounded frantic on the phone, stating her two sons were now considered missing and she had no idea where they were.

"When was the last time you saw them?" asked the desk officer.

"Several hours ago," she replied. "They told me they were going to go walking around the area. I assumed the area around our hotel."

"What's your name, ma'am?"

"Emma. Emma Thomas. My two boys are Steven and Joseph."

"Describe them for me, please."

She described them, including their ages. The officer noted their ages seemed to approximately fit those of the victims.

"What were they wearing?"

She described their clothing.

"Any identifying marks on them, scars, tattoos, birthmarks?"

"Yes," she said. "There's a small scar on the left shin of the older boy. That would be Steven that has the scar."

The officer's eyes looked up and straight ahead. This could be her.

"Just a minute ma'am." He covered the mouthpiece of the phone with his hand and told the detective who was nearby that he had a possible hit on the parent of those boys.

"Ask her to come in. No, wait! Get her address. I'll come to her. Last thing we need is to cause her more distress. It's bad enough that her boys are missing."

The officer took down her address and phone number at the hotel and gave it to the detective. He left right away to speak to her. This was not one of those cases that could be put on the backburner.

****

Office of Palm Beach County Medical Examiner, August 9

The autopsies were performed simultaneously. One by the chief medical examiner of Palm Beach County, Dr. Michael Glassman, and the other by the assistant CME, Dr. Kendra

Billington. Both were well-experienced forensic pathologists and reputable in their fields. Between them they had performed as many as five thousand autopsies.

Each would have similar findings from the bodies. Cause of deaths in both boys were venom toxicity which overwhelmed both the nervous and circulatory systems in their bodies, and drowning which was caused by the effects of the venom on their nervous systems. The effects of the neurotoxins were enough to seal their fates. Respiratory arrest would have been caused by the venom neurotoxins attacking the part of the brain which controlled breathing. The attack on the brain by the venom also caused seizures, in which they likely would have lost consciousness. Because the pathologists found water in their lungs, drowning was consistent as a primary cause of death. The mechanism of death on each boy was listed in detail on the death findings and-eventually the certificate- of the numerous destructive effects on the body by the venom which, in turn, contributed toward the drowning events.

Toxicology tests were consistent with venom poisoning by the box jellyfish. It was clear that without immediate medical help, they had stood very little chance of making it. The amount of venom each had received was enough to kill sixty people.

The medical examiner's office then notified the police of their findings and the word soon spread that Jupiter was hit. When it hit the news on all the media, including the newspapers, tourism seemed to take a sudden nosedive. Suddenly, a lot of people-mostly tourists- were packing up and leaving the state entirely. A few chose to go to the Gulf side, but not enough to make much of a dent in the tourist numbers.

The bodies were kept in the coolers, awaiting the family's arrival for identification and disposition of the bodies. The doctors had made sure they were appropriately readied for that and for the subsequent funeral. It would be up to the funeral directors whether they could make the face of the boy who'd been scarred there presentable enough for a viewing.

****

The swarm was continuing to move northward. From what Rebecca and the others could see, Port St. Lucie would be next. Rebecca decided that they couldn't stay out here forever either. Was anything being done on the home front, or could anything be done to stop this northward migration? She decided to consult with Dan and call him. Maybe there was something he could think of that hadn't been thought of before. At the same time, she had to also deal with the tragedies at Jupiter. These creatures were causing many more fatalities within a month's time than shark attacks in the past five years. Something had to be done and fast.

"This is Dan. I'm not at my desk right now but if you….."

"Oh crap!" mouthed Rebecca. "Where the hell are you, Dan?"

….. number after the beep, I'll get back to you as soon as I can and have a nice day."

"Dan, this is me. Call me as soon as you hear this. I need to know if anything's in the works right now about this swarm. More fatalities in Jupiter, and this mass is heading right now toward Port St. Lucie. Call me please!"

Frustrated, she headed back downstairs where James was snacking on something.

"Well? Find out anything? I know you were going to call about what to do here."

Rebecca brushed her long hair back and sighed. "I called him. That is, I called his voice mail. Left a message for him to call me back asap. Jupiter's been hit. Two more fatalities. They're beyond us now, James. I told Captain Bill to slowly head us northward. I'm going to take a look outside to see what I can see."

"I'll go with ya. Let me get the binocs!"

Outside, they looked out the port side as they slowly made their way north, following the coast. Scanning the water, they didn't see any signs of the swarm at first. James scanned the waters closer to the shoreline as far as his binoculars would allow him to see. Slowly he panned the lens from north to south and then froze in place as he stared at one area of water.

"Whoa, baby. Hey, I think I spot something."

That caught Rebecca's attention immediately and she fixed her eyes on James.

"What? What do you see?" Her voice was tense because she felt it.

"Here, take a look. From your position, look straight out there to about your one o'clock position. Tell me what you see." He handed her the binoculars.

Carefully she took aim with the lens and focused on that area pointed out by James. There. There it was. That had to be it. The leading edge of the swarm. The white mass just below the surface of the clear, green water. Had the water not been clear, it would not have been easy to spot, if it could be seen at all. They were lucky in this respect.

"I'll be a son of a bitch. That's it. That's it, James!" She looked toward the shoreline, trying to estimate the possible distance from the swarm to the beach. It was hard to tell from this angle and distance, but they dared not get too close. They had to think of the props. She handed the binocs back to James. "Keep an eye on them. I'll be back."

Running up to the bridge, she went directly to Dexter, who was back on navigation. Captain Bill was back on the helm.

"Dexter, can you tell me what town on the shore we're closest to right now?"

"Sure. Let's go over to the chart table over there."

At the table, he bent over and spread out the chart until the area could be clearly delineated. He pointed to where they were.

"Now here's where we are right now, according to my dead reckoning calculations." He dragged his finger over to the nearest point of land from their location. "This spot is, um, let's see..."

He then looked at a map which was very similar to the chart as to the area they were in. Although both the chart and map showed their location, only the map showed the town they were closest to. His finger landed on it.

"Looks like we're smack between Hobe Sound and Stuart. These things are moving fast."

This was not good. In fact, it was worse than she thought. "Yea, you're right, Dexter. They're moving much too fast."

The fact that it was getting close to Stuart meant it was approaching Port St. Lucie. Fort Pierce would be next after that.

A phone rang on the bridge and a deckhand who was up there answered it.

"Ms. Wares, it's for you. It's Dan."

She nearly ran across the bridge. "Thank God," she replied to no one in particular, except maybe God Himself.

CHAPTER 20

She barely had the phone in her hands when she started talking.

"Dan, I'm glad you got my message."

"Yea, Rebecca, I had planned to call you. Things have been kind of hectic on this end."

"Oh? What's going on?"

"Might have a way of getting rid of these things."

"What? Are you kidding me? Is this for real?"

"I'm not kidding, Becky. I've been in touch with a guy who works for a company that engineers and makes jellyfish vacuum cleaners."

"I've heard of such things. Didn't they start those things over in Korea, or China?"

"South Korea. His company was able to borrow their idea, under contract that they would not claim it as their own. Fat chance of that. They're patented. But they have to call it something other than what *they* call it. Anyway, he's arranged to have a bunch of them flown down here from Boston, where the company is."

"What *do* they call them here?"

"Robotic Jellyfish Sweepers."

Rebecca burst out laughing. Captain Bill and Dexter looked at her, thinking that maybe the guy was telling her a good joke.

She was laughing so much *they* started to laugh. It's hard to ignore contagious laughter.

"That's the funniest thing I've ever heard."

"Hey listen, Becky, the name might sound funny to you but if this guy is right in what he claims about what these things can do, our swarm will be swept off the face of the earth. Literally."

She wiped the tears from her eyes, but not the smile. As funny as it sounded, it was very promising news. These things could be the miracle they needed.

"Ok. Sorry. Um. So, when are these things supposed to get here? You know the swarm is moving fast northward? Just left Jupiter with two fatalities. Now they are nearing Stuart and points north. The current must be helping them along."

"Yea. Sounds that way. It looks like at least two or three days. They're expediting the order. Will be brought out there in three days. They're flying them down to Miami, hopefully by day after tomorrow. We're already arranging for transport of these things by Naval and Coast Guard oceangoing tugs to where the swarm is. You need to keep me updated at least once per day as to its location."

"Sounds reasonable. Ok. That means they won't get here at this location until the twelfth. What I'll do is give you the latest location daily of the leading edge. Marge, over on the Coast Guard boat, can give you the trailing edge location. How fast do these things work?"

He told her, and she was far more impressed with their speed and efficiency than their name. After promising her next update, she hung up and passed the word about it to the bridge personnel, then went down below to let James know the good news.

James was on the skeptical side about the robots. Sounded too good to be true, to him, and he let her know about that.

"I don't know, Becky. I've heard about these things but never seen them in action. There has to be a glitch somehow about these things. Sounds like a true dream-come-true for all those who are anti-jellyfish. Did he give any listing of their down side?"

Rebecca shrugged and admitted that Dan hadn't mentioned anything about their   disadvantages. "The only thing is that they are bulky and time consuming to load and unload. Otherwise, they are reputed to be pretty reliable and efficient. If they can chop them up and spew them out as fast as the company claims, it might be the only thing that gets rid of them. Then the only thing everybody here has to worry about is the animal activists that might scream the "cruelty to animals" spiel when they hear about this. They always seem to forget about the people that have been killed or seriously hurt by the very animals we are trying to control in some way."

****

Four hours later, approaching Stuart, Florida

Each member of the mass was swimming, helped along by the strong northeast current that seemed to double their speed. It was as if each member was a conscious part of one large unit, on a unified mission to travel somewhere, anywhere. Their direction and speed was controlled by the current and to a certain extent, by their swimming. They neither could not nor would not intentionally avoid anything in their path. Humans meant nothing to them. Anything they ran into on their journey would immediately be stung and eaten if it was part of their regular menu.

Just to the north side of Stuart, a lone boat was anchored about a quarter mile offshore. It was still daylight, but the sun would be setting in about an hour and the light would gradually fade. The man on the boat was monitoring while his partner was scuba diving below taking pictures of the colorful reef and some of the small creatures that inhabited it. A line was tied to the boat's stern that connected the boat to the diver. Any trouble and the man onboard would signal with three tugs on the line.

According to their chart, the water here was about seventy five feet deep. The diver would need to respond to the tugs immediately with two tugs and then head for the surface. It had been an agreed-upon arrangement made before the trip so communications could be maintained in some way.

Although the man on the boat was aware of the jellyfish situation reported in the news, the diver hadn't indicated he knew about it. Because the problem wasn't in their area, he hadn't shown or verbalized too much concern about it. His friend, who was not a diver, felt quite guarded about it. And he was a little of the nervous type. Keeping a close eye on the time, he knew that both dusk and dawn were the most dangerous times to be in the water. It was during those darkened hours that sharks prowled around and hunted for their next meals. And now this jellyfish problem only added to the danger. The man didn't like it at all.

He then decided to give his friend another fifteen minutes and then tug the line for him to return to the surface. If these jellies were on the move, as the news reported, he didn't want to be here when they arrived. And he didn't want his friend to be in the water when they did, not to mention when the sharks arrived also.

****

Aboard the USCGC Jackson

Marge couldn't understand why the phone was busy so long. After trying to get through three times, there was finally a ring followed by someone answering.

"Hi, this is Marge over on the *Jackson*. Can I speak to Rebecca please?"

When Rebecca came on the line, Marge informed her that the trailing edge was now just north of West Palm Beach. In turn, she was informed by Rebecca that the leading edge was entering the northernmost waters near Jupiter and heading toward Stuart. This indicated the tremendous size of the swarm.

It was then that Rebecca informed her colleague of the robot plan to sweep up the jellies.

"No kidding?" Marge sounded surprised, but pleasantly so. "As far as I'm concerned, they can't get those things down here fast enough. I'm not, mind you, all for killing off sea creatures. In fact, that bothers the hell out of me. But at the same time, I sure as hell don't want any more people hurt or killed by these things, which I know they are very good at doing. And I know they can't help it because they are what they are and that's what they do to survive. On the other hand, all ecosystems that they enter suffer from their presence. So on that basis, I won't lose any sleep if this particular swarm is permanently swept into oblivion."

"I feel the same way, Marge. Anyway, I better go. Can't stay on the line too long. Anything else comes up by either one of us, we call the other."

"You got it. See ya later."

****

The diver could never be fascinated enough with the awesome and mystifying beauty of the coral seabed. Colors that rivaled the rainbow indicated a very healthy and life-supporting environment. Hundreds of small fish circled around and in and out of crevices among the coral, careful not to rub against the razor-sharp edges of the coral itself. Patches of seabed plants dotting the landscape around the reef waved gently back and forth with the motion of the water, as if beckoning one to join them in their relaxing reverie.

He snapped the shutter so many times on the camera, he thought he might run out of film sooner than he expected, so he slowed down a bit. It was far too easy to keep clicking the shutter with the awe-inspiring view down here.

He was wearing an underwater watch and occasionally glanced at it. He did now and he saw that it was getting close to seven thirty pm. Then he spotted what looked like a sea cucumber and went over to investigate. He took a picture of that and examined it in his hand. He'd seen one of these before. As simple as the creature was, he was always amazed at some of the things that lived down here.

His movements on the seabed were not indicated by the connection line.

Along the top ridge of the boat, near the stern, a small sharp metal boat piece stuck out. The man on the boat who owned it either hadn't noticed it or brushed it off as something minor that could be taken care of at a later time. He would later regret that.

The seas moved with gentle rolls. The sky was partly cloudy and the winds blew at a mild five to ten miles per hour. There was no rain forecast for that day. A storm was predicted for the following day.

With the gentle rolling of the sea, the boat had a mild pitching and rolling motion which would have little to no effect on someone with sea legs but have a significant effect on someone with balance problems.

With the movements of the boat on the water, back at the stern there was an unseen process taking place. As the boat owner looked around and made sure all was in order and continued to keep track of the time, a small area of the connection line was rubbing against the sharp metal that was sticking out. With each pitch and roll of the boat, the line first hit gently against the metal then rubbed against the sharp end. With the next pitch, it rubbed against it again. One thread of the line was torn through. Then the line moved away.

Down below, the diver continued to explore and collect small specimens by inserting them in a pouch he had strapped to his suit belt. He didn't notice the water getting slightly murkier because he was so focused on what he was doing. The water was still clear, but becoming less so.

South of where the boat was, it moved steadily along with the current. Its members had slowed down a bit on their swimming, letting the current ride them along. They were heading toward the boat, still in the distance about a quarter mile away. Their ignorance kept them completely unaware of that.

On the boat, another gentle pitch, another gentle roll. The line moved in the other direction and once again first hit and rubbed firmly against the metal piece. After several more times of doing this, another thread on the connection line tore through. This made the line considerably weaker. When the line became taut, the tension weakened the remaining threads even more. With the next pitch and roll, another thread was ripped by the metal piece. The process still remained unseen by the boat owner. With one thread to hold the line together, it was now just a matter of time.

On board, the boat owner looked down at his controls, smoked his cigar and waited patiently before he tugged the line. A few more minutes and then he'd give his diver friend the signal. As he looked up, he saw something in the water off in the distance. Not sure of what it was, it got his curiosity going. Picking up his small binoculars, he focused on the area for a better view. After focusing the lens, his eyes froze on the most peculiar sight he'd ever seen.

Another pitch, then a roll. The line hit one final time against the metal piece. As the bow went gently down and the stern up just a bit, the motion created enough tension in the line to perform its final act. The sound of it snapping was silent against the sounds of the water lapping against the sides of the boat. While the end of it on the line attached to the boat dangled lazily over the side, the end attached to the part connected to the diver floated freely on the surface   of the water. Neither man knew of the sudden disconnection. They both believed all was well.

That is until the boat owner realized he didn't like what he was looking at. Whatever it was, it appeared just below the surface and it seemed to be heading in his direction. *What the hell...?* He was seriously wondering all of a sudden if this was what was being reported on the news. Could it be way up here already in Stuart?

Based on the time of day it was, that they'd been out here for some time, and seeing this coming at them, he decided they better get the hell out of there. It was time.

Pushing his hat more firmly on his head, with cigar in mouth he headed back toward the stern. He quickly grabbed the line to tug it, only to find the cut end dangling in his hand. His cigar dropped out of his mouth as he opened it. He then looked out at the water, trying to gauge as best he could the approximate location of where his friend would be down below.

With both hands, he grabbed his head and shouted up at the sky.

"Son of a bitch!"

He wasn't a true blue curser and didn't really like doing it. This, however, was a case of helplessness and frustration that seemed to require it. He didn't know what to do. He didn't know how the line got cut. What he *did* know was that their situation was now dire. He had a diver and   friend who was down below, with whom he lost all contact with. It was getting late and the sun was now just above the horizon. Soon it would be dusk, but his friend wouldn't know that below. Predators would be emerging from the dark depths for their nightly hunting patrols. And now this thing, whatever it was, was coming at them.

Although there was nothing wrong with the boat, he couldn't leave his friend here. But he couldn't contact him either. Time was not on their side, and danger began to surround them. He quickly made his decision and grabbed the mic for the radio.

CHAPTER 21

Miami Marine Institute-, August 9

"Well, thank you Mr. Ringston. I appreciate, *we* all appreciate your help in this matter. We'll let your company know of the invaluable help you've given us.

"So we will notify the proper people and let them know to expect the robots tomorrow."

Dan was thrilled and glad that he could be a part of this solution to a potentially national or international threat. He took down Howard's current and home addresses and phone numbers on the likely chance that the Institute would send him a letter or gift of appreciation. The Institute occasionally compensated or donated with free admission tickets to an entire family with no expiration date.

After contacting his connection with the state DEP, he was informed that the transport ship company was contracted by the state of Florida to prepare the two vessels for the shipment of the robots to the designated areas and that they would arrive two days earlier than initially stated. He got on the phone to call Rebecca.

"Hey, Becky it's me. Just wanted to give you the news that the robots will be here a day earlier than expected. Tomorrow to be exact."

On hearing the news, she felt the rush of excitement. Rarely does one hear of *anything* being delivered early.

"Wonderful! When do you think they might be delivered out here?"

"Hard to say for sure. Supposed to get here very early in the morning. Then they'll have to be loaded onto the transport ship and sent to the current location of the swarm. You probably won't see them until late morning at the earliest. Here's the deal.

"Tomorrow, after I find out that they've left the dock, I'll contact you for the latest coordinates of both the leading and trail edges. I won't need to know the nearest towns for those ships, but would like to know that information for news purposes. Once you give me those coordinates, I'll contact the ship and give them that info. They'll already have given me their numbers to call them. Once they arrive there, move away from the area. Don't get close. The ships will have their own on and off-loading cranes. They'll put these things in the water. Five will be at your end, and the other will be a little further south."

"Sounds good to me, Dan. But who the hell controls these things?"

"Good question. One of the company's men happens to be in Boca Raton on vacation with his family. He's the one that called me about this and got this whole thing started. He's going to sail on the ship to start off five of the robots. Once he starts them, they'll run automatically, detecting and picking off bunches of these things. Might sound like a bunch of wood chippers, from what he tells me. After he detects with special equipment that they are no longer terminating any more jellies, he'll shut them down with a remote device and the ship will begin picking them up.

"Now I know your next question. So I'll save you from asking. The company is sending another man down from Boston to help coordinate this operation. He'll be on the second transport ship, closer to where Margaret is."

"Dan, do you really think this is going to work?"

Dan coughed on the other end. "Sorry. Got a tickle in my throat. Anyway, yea. This *has* to work. There aren't any other options for getting this thing under control or stopping it. If it doesn't work, we're screwed. But based on the successes that the South Koreans had, there's no reason to think it won't work here. That's what he told me."

Rebecca felt a bit overwhelmed, but not in a negative way. She was relieved and hopeful, to say the least. At the same time, a lot had happened and still was happening in a relatively short span of time.

"Ok. This is great news. I'm looking forward to seeing these things in action. I'll pass this on to everyone."

"Right. Do that. Don't forget and be sure you tell Margaret this. She has to let the Coast Guard people know. They'll not only have to keep boaters away from the area, but they'll have to stay out of the area themselves."

"I'll call her as soon as we hang up. She'll want to know the good news anyway."

After she hung up with Dan, she thought for a few moments and was already savoring, in her mind, the anticipated victory over this problem. This was not something she'd ever forget. She dialed the *Jackson's* phone number and waited to speak to her colleague.

****

Jupiter, Florida, August 9

The detectives had met with Emma Thomas and her ex-husband whom she had notified about this. After determining that she was telling the truth, they brought them over to the morgue to identify the bodies. As soon as the sheets uncovered their faces, they immediately broke down. The fact that their boys were dead was bad enough. But to see the terrible long angry scars over their faces and bodies as remnants of their horrific ordeals made it all the worse. The police thought the mother was going to have a nervous breakdown when she became hysterical and started crying at the same time. Only the ex-husband and father of the boys was able to keep her in check and gradually calm her down.

They were told what killed them. As for understanding *why* this happened, no one could answer that. What they knew was that if the boys hadn't lied to them but followed through with what they were *supposed* to do, then they would be alive today. No one would ever know why they deviated from their stated plan. Closure would be difficult but would be found.

****

"Mayday, Mayday, This is the diving yacht *Seawolf*, calling a Mayday on channel 81,
      over."

The boat owner named Peter released the button and waited for anyone to respond.

Only static and unintelligible sounds were his reply.

He called the Mayday again, hoping he wasn't in a communications dead area. Sometimes a boat would enter such an area without knowing it until communications was attempted. It worked on the same principle as blackout areas for cell phones on land.

He was met again with static and strange sounds. Through the static he thought he heard a response, and immediately got on it.

"This is the diving yacht *Seawolf* calling a Mayday. Have diver in the water but unable to contact him. Have dire situation. There's something in the water coming right at us and it doesn't look good. Appears diver is in serious danger. Please respond. Here is my location."

He then gave the coordinates, uncertain whether whoever sounded like they were responding actually heard him. He repeated the coordinates on the off-chance that the person on the other end received his transmission. He already knew the other channels wouldn't work. Only channel 81 on his radio functioned. It's possible that the Coast Guard heard him, but he couldn't know for sure. They monitored this channel as well as most others.

For now all he could do was wait and monitor the movement of the "thing". He looked out over the water and saw that it appeared a little closer than before. It had a whitish, translucent tinge. As he processed in his mind what he was seeing, he noticed that it had an inner and outer edge to it. In other words, it had a width, which appeared to be approximately a hundred feet. He figured if it had a width, then it had to have a length. Unfortunately, it was impossible for him to determine that.

But if it *was* the mass of jellies, then he knew as a boatman he dared not let the boat get caught in the middle of that mess. Engines and props were very expensive to repair. As a precaution and despite the fact that he hated doing it, he moved out to sea a little farther, enough to be beyond the reach of the outer edge. He looked at the spot where his diver friend should be and knew that he would have to come up soon.

The sun was just peeking over the horizon now and daylight was dimming. As it got darker up here, so it also would down below.

Suddenly he heard an engine and looked up. A small ship was approaching him. He saw someone on board waving their arms back and forth, suggesting they were signaling him. He waved back. Could this be a response to his call for help?

About ten minutes later, the ship pulled up alongside his boat. To him it looked like some sort of a fishing or research vessel. He noticed the cranes on deck and all kinds of lines everywhere. His boat was dwarfed alongside it. There was a woman on deck and two deckhands. Then he saw a man coming down from the bridge above.

"Hi. We heard your distress call. What's the trouble?" It was man who had come from the bridge.

Peter told him about his diver down below and the oncoming mass in the water.

"Yea, we know it's there. We've been monitoring it the past several days."

"Monitoring it?"

That's when Dexter identified who they were. "You can't get a hold of him down there? How much in his tank did he have when he went in?"

"He had two tanks on him, enough for about an hour and a half. No more than two. There was a line connecting him to the boat, but somehow it got cut and I can't communicate with him. I'm afraid of what that thing is and seeing as it's getting dark--well, you know sharks and all that."

"Are you ok? Is your boat running ok?"

"Yea, I'm good and the boat is fine. I'm just worried about my friend in the water."

"Ok, listen, I've got scuba experience. Let me get in gear and I'll go down there and get him. We don't have much time. This is Rebecca, she'll fill you in." With that, he ran up to the bridge to tell Captain Bill, then ran back down below decks to gear up.

Peter looked at her, and told her his name and why they were out there. "I really appreciate you answering the call. My radio came back with mostly static and I was afraid no one heard me."

"No problem. I'm glad we heard you. We weren't very far away because we've been monitoring this swarm."

"Yea, what is that? I've never seen anything like that before."

"That is a swarm of box jellyfish. Very deadly to humans. It's hit the southeast Florida coast and is heading north, mostly carried by the Gulf currents."

Dexter had come back up and readied himself on the side of the boat. He was wearing one tank and fins. After putting on his mouthpiece and mask, he quickly dived over the side and started heading underwater in the direction of the boat man's friend.

It was imperative that he find him quickly before the swarm reached their area. Already it was less than a quarter mile away which, considering what it was made up of, was far too close for comfort.

Looking around as best he could, visibility was fair but could have been better. There was some murkiness in the water, which meant he had to be careful in his search and look for the best spots where the diver might be located.

He saw the colorful reef up ahead, and a lot of small tropical fish swimming about. Darkness would soon fall and already dusk was beginning to settle in so he had to find the diver very soon. Up ahead, he saw a dark upright figure and knew it was him. Swimming quickly toward him, the boat diver noticed another diver coming at him quickly which, underwater when you didn't expect anyone, could be quite frightening. The approaching diver pointed upwards and made the football signal, T-ing his hands, for him to stop what he was doing and head to the surface. Peter's diver seemed to understand, nodded his head, and they both headed back up.

As they headed up, something in the water caught Dexter's attention. The other diver didn't seem to notice it. They were about fifteen feet below the surface. The first mate immediately recognized what had been described to him by Rebecca. The square-shaped bell and long tentacles. The bell was pulsing, which meant it was swimming and it seemed to be heading in their direction. He didn't know why but somehow it had separated itself from the rest of the swarm, perhaps as a scout to investigate what it was detecting in the water. Who knows, he thought. They had to get out of there fast.

He chose a direction and then motioned to the other diver to follow him. Dexter led him away from the swimming creature at about a ninety degree angle at what he quickly calculated was a safe distance. Then he motioned for them to surface. It was important that they get on   board their vessels as quickly as possible.

Once they surfaced and Dexter got their bearings as to their position relative to the boats, he tore off his mask and removed the mouthpiece out of his mouth. He minced no words, speaking quickly and decisively.

"Get to your boat as fast as possible and get out of the water now."

"What's happening?" asked the diver. "What's going on? Who are you?"

"Get to your boat now and once we're both on board, we'll explain everything. There are things in the water here now that can kill you if they contact you. Go. Go now!"

The boats were only about thirty feet away, but when something dangerous is coming at you, it could seem like thirty *thousand* feet. The boat diver swam as quickly as he could to his boat and Peter was waving him on frantically. He looked down to see something in the water just below the surface heading quickly toward his friend. It was catching up. He saw the long, deadly tentacles behind it. The bell was pulsing more rapidly now.

"C'mon," yelled Peter. "C'mon Fred. Swim."

Fred swam as fast as he could, but with a full load of scuba gear including two tanks, it was not easy and made for slow, cumbersome swimming.

"For Christ's sake, Fred, unload the tanks. Get rid of them. They can be easily replaced. You can't."

The bell was now about forty feet away and pulsating rapidly to narrow the distance.

Fred was now making a desperate attempt to unload his gear. On board the boat, it would not be difficult. But in the water, he found it agonizingly difficult because he had to try and keep himself afloat at the same time he was maneuvering his arms and torso to get the equipment off of him in the water.

As soon as Dexter saw the diver having difficulty, he swam over to him. Fred started feeling the burden lightening as Dexter helped get his gear off and let go of the tanks where they sank to the bottom. They were both about equidistant to both boats. Dexter didn't see the jelly coming.

"Go!" he yelled to the diver. Fred immediately started swimming to his boat, while Dexter swam off to the side toward his. He was now about fifteen feet to the boat. The bell was behind him at about eight feet.

Fred was exhausted and gasping with all the efforts that he could make. He heard Peter keep yelling at him and thought that as tired as he was, his friend's yelling voice was not going to make him swim any faster than he was. He was doing the best that he could.

Distance to the boat was now ten feet. It was now well within reaching distance. His swimming slowed a bit. His muscles were aching like never before which put a dampener on his speed, and he was taking in huge gulps of air as he fought to keep swimming and get to the boat.

The jelly was now four feet behind him. Fred hadn't a clue what was there. The only thing that seemed to stick out in his mind was that the man told him there were killer things in the water. Normally he didn't scare easily. But the sound of the man's voice and the fact that he had made a trip down there to get him and bring him back up with a great deal of urgency certainly suggested to him that the situation was pretty serious. That plus his buddy on the boat screaming at him to get on board as fast as possible was enough to help him overcome the exhaustion that he was feeling from having to swim fast with a heavy load of equipment on him earlier.

He was five feet from the boat, and Peter was sticking his arm out to reach for him. Gasping heavily for air, he put all he had into reaching that hand.

The bell was now one foot away. Fred stuck his arm out of the water. The bell was now six inches away. Fred's hand was now in Peter's. Peter pulled as hard as he could while grabbing

Fred's arm while Fred was putting all his strength into clambering onto the boat. With Peter's help, he started lifting himself out of the water. His bare legs were thrashing as he struggled to get all of himself on board. Then the sensation of a million red-hot burning needles slamming into his lower legs and feet brought the blood-curdling scream out of his open mouth.

While the crew of the *Argonaut* watched in shock and disbelief, Peter pulled the screaming diver out of the water into the boat, with an additional but unwelcome guest. Tentacles wrapped around the diver's lower legs and feet as the venom was continuously injected into him by millions of nematocysts. Now Peter started screaming for help as he witnessed the horrific sight. The bell, now still, lay flaccid along the man's left side.

The *Argonaut* immediately pulled up alongside the boat. Rebecca and the two deckhands carefully but as quickly as they could transferred themselves from the higher deck of the ship to the yacht. James ran up to quickly join them.

"Dexter, go get me that vinegar in the kitchen, quickly! And tell Captain Bill to radio the Coast Guard for help. We need a medical evacuation here as quickly as possible. Ask for a helicopter."

Seeing that jelly attached to the poor man, Dexter didn't have to think another thought. He ran up to the bridge to give the word to the captain, then ran back below deck to get the vinegar.

In the meantime, Rebecca had to figure out a way to safely detach the tentacles from the man's legs. Every second that those tentacles were attached brought him closer to death. The man continuously screamed and thrashed in pain far beyond a level that humans should have to endure.

She looked up at the boat man. "What's your name? Peter?"

"Yea, that's me. Oh man, what *is* that thing?" His look of horror plus his older age made Rebecca wonder if he would be prone to a heart attack. What he was seeing right now no one with a weak heart should see. She could only hope that he didn't have that.

"That is the deadliest jellyfish known to man. Peter, do you have some kind of long stick or short pole on board?"

"Like a yardstick or something?"

"Anything that I can use to get these tentacles off of him. And either heavy gloves or some kind of clamp. Both would work nicely."

"Yea, I got some." He ran off and down into the cabin.

"Becky, you need to let me do this. I've got lots of experience handling jellyfish." James looked at her with the determination that only someone with his kind of expertise could show. "Besides, the last thing I want is for you to get stung from this thing."

She tilted her head to the side and looked at him with her green eyes boring into his. "Why Jimmy, are you being *chivalrous* with me?" He looked at her face with its serious expression but sensing she was trying to hold back a smile. To him she never looked more beautiful.

He looked down but it was already too late. "Why James Robertson, you are blushing!"

Her face suddenly broke out in a smile.

He didn't know exactly how to respond to that. "Well, it's the only thing that makes sense right now," was all he could come up with for a reply, quickly glancing back up to see her still intensely looking at him. Was it admiration he was seeing in those passionate green eyes? Gratitude? Or something else?

At that moment, Peter came back up with a yard long metallic pole and heavy gloves and quickly handed them toward her. James quickly grabbed them and asked her to step away. He didn't know what the pole was for, but he didn't care. Right now it was a tool he needed. Almost at the same time, Dexter appeared at the side of the ship with the bottle of vinegar. Fortunately it was plastic rather than glass. He tossed it to Peter after making sure the cap was on tight enough.

James then put on the gloves and as carefully as he could, moved one of the tentacles toward the outside edge of the victim's leg. With the heavy work glove, he gingerly lifted it and inserted the pole underneath it. With the glove and the pole, he lifted the tentacle high enough to cause the others to be lifted off of his legs as well, followed by the bell, which dangled below them. Now the jellyfish was completely off of him as she held it in the air away from her body. The others watched in shocking fascination at the creature she was holding which could kill so many people with one stroke.

Peter came back with a fishing bucket anticipating that he might need it.

"Thank you Pete. You're a man after my own heart." He lowered the creature into the bucket. It was likely dying, she knew, but those tentacles would remain just as deadly, even after their owner's death. "Got a cover for it?"

"Uh, no, 'fraid not. But I have another bucket that I could insert into it, to put on top of the thing."

"That'd be great."

He turned and took the vinegar bottle on the deck near to where he and the still-screaming diver was. His thrashing now began to turn into seizures. He poured the vinegar over the ugly dark-red raised tentacle scars encircling his lower legs and feet, which forced a brief scream out of him. Then he started foaming at the mouth.

As Rebecca watched and James stayed with the suffering man, Captain Bill came out on the outside bridge wing of the ship and yelled down to Rebecca.

"Becky, the Guard is on its way with a chopper. Should be here in about ten minutes. He gonna be ok?"

She looked up at him. "I hope so Bill. The vinegar may have bought him some time. They just have to get him to the hospital pronto if he has any chance. He's having a seizure now so I don't know. But we're doing all we can for now."

"Ok. I'm going to maneuver the boat further away to give room for the chopper."

She waved at him with a final yell of okay. All she could do was reassure him that he would be ok. She joined James and provided a cloth material to place under the victim's head to protect it from injury. And all everyone there could do now was wait for the helicopter and pray that this poor victim of unfortunate circumstance would make it.

CHAPTER 22

Port Authority, Miami, Florida, August 9

The large transport ship that was contracted by the state of Florida was readying its decks for the cargo which would be arriving the next morning. There would be plenty of space for all ten. All extraneous items, things, lines, and whatever else they kept on deck that were not needed for the operation were removed and stored to keep the area as clear as possible.

At the airport, three trailer trucks with flatbeds would be waiting for a specific cargo flight and ready for on loading. Special large equipment would be on hand to pick up and put onto the trucks once they were off-loaded from the plane. It was a fairly large operation which would require special handling, but every detail of all movements had been quickly but very carefully planned and expedited. Because of the seriousness of the situation, what would normally have taken at least a week or more to process and conduct took only two days. As a result, at the end of the day before the arrival, all crews were ready and all equipment was there and ready as well.

****

Off the coast of Stuart, Florida

A Coast Guard specially trained rescue swimmer had lowered down from the hovering chopper onto the boat deck. While he tended to the victim, preparing him for the basket lift, the chopper retrieved the lowering line, then a few seconds later lowered down another line with a basket attached. The swimmer was also a hospital corpsman in his service rating, equivalent to an army medic, so with an emergency order, he was able to give an injectable pain medication that might ease off the pain level. The man, however, was barely conscious still thrashing from the pain and before the basket was lifted up into the chopper, the corpsman had to ensure he was strapped down firmly for safety reasons.

After that, he was lifted, then it was the swimmer's turn, and soon the chopper was off to the nearest trauma center which was in Miami.

It took several minutes for their minds to process all that had happened within the past half an hour. Rebecca and James leaned against the side rails of the yacht while Peter offered them a soda or beer, which they declined. He leaned against the steering wheel and then spoke up.

He explained that they left Boca Raton and headed up to this area because they heard that the coral reefs in this area were spectacular.

"Freddie and I were childhood friends. We grew up together in the same neighborhood and always supported each other when times got tough. He was always into cameras and picture taking. That's what we came up here for. God, I hope he's going to be alright. You think he'll make it?"

That Peter was upset and distressed over the injuries and suffering his friend was under-going was clear to them. Rebecca wanted to assure him that Freddie would be fine, but because his situation was more like fifty-fifty chances rather than eighty-twenty, she didn't want to give him false hopes.

"He might come out of this ok, but I don't know for sure," she told him. "There are people who do survive a box jellyfish attack if treatment is provided within an hour or two. He had some kind of treatment quickly after being stung and then airlifted to a hospital. So his chances are, I would think, better than someone waiting for help for a longer period of time."

"They would be taking him to Miami, right?"

"Miami-Dade General," replied James. "They have a great trauma center there, so his chances are even better. There's no guarantees, but there's enough reason to keep your hopes up."

"And prayers," added Rebecca. "Pray for him. If anyone can make him better, it would be God."

"Yea, absolutely," said Peter hopefully. "I'm not very religious or the praying type but if it'll help him, then I'm all for it.

And speaking of help, I want to thank you again so much for responding. You just may have saved his life." He then shook their hands, again offering them a beer. Again they declined with another thanks.

As they climbed back onto the *Argonaut*, James waved. "No problem Pete. We're just glad we happened to be in your neighborhood. Good luck to your friend. We hope he's gonna make it."

James looked out over the side rails to the swarm which was considerably closer now. Fortunately, it had not approached the ship and boat but stayed within the same proximity to the shore as before.

With Rebecca and James saying their goodbyes to Peter then watching him sail back to his dock in Boca Raton, they headed back down to the galley to grab a coffee. Beer, they chose not to have out here. Coffee was another matter.

Down in the galley, when they were facing each other, Rebecca walked up to James, grabbed his face in both hands and gave him a long firm kiss on the lips which caught him completely off guard. He succumbed nearly instantly to her bold move and sweet smell. His arms wrapped gently around her as she kissed him with a forceful determination that he'd never seen in a woman. He savored the moment, thinking that maybe this was only a one-time thing and this was just her thank you. Her kiss was considerably longer than what he expected. When she finally lifted her lips from his, she kept her face very close to his. Her large green eyes totally mesmerized him as they stared intensely into his.

"Mmm....what was *that* all about? What the heck did I do to deserve such a fantastic moment?" He spoke almost as if he was in a trance. In a way, he was entranced.

"You were wonderful out there. You helped me and you helped Peter and showed sincerity. I very much admire those qualities in a man."

He could feel himself blush, almost with embarrassment as she subtly pressed her hips against him. He was sure she could feel him down below. "Well, I, um did only what anyone else would have done, ya know?"

"I also admire humbleness in a man."

She pressed her hips tightly against him. He knew then that she could feel his erection, and was doing that deliberately. He had never thought that she was this sexual of a person--until now. But warning bells rang inside of him. There were other times and other places that would be far better for hanky panky stuff and emotional rendezvous than here and now.

"Dinner is on me when we get back," she said softly, bathing his face with her warm, sweet breath. "I won't take no for an answer. After that, we'll just have to play it by ear. Won't we?" Her smile and intense stare clearly told him that she had more than just an attraction and interest for him. Much more. The combination of her beauty, her smell, the softness of her lips, the feel of her warm breath--well, for him was initially overwhelming yet unimaginably pleasurable. He had never had a woman come on to him this strongly before. But he was glad it was her and not someone he hardly knew.

"Yea, guess we will." Right now he was emotionally taken by her that he believed he would stand on his head on the pitching deck if she asked him to. He felt the firm slimness of her waist.

"I've wanted to ask you out for quite a while," he told her. "Guess I had to build up the courage before I could do that." She kept her face close to his and he felt her fingers on his cheeks. Her voice was feathery soft. Her thumbs gently caressed his face.

"Keep this up," he said, "and I won't want to let you go. You realize you're making me fall for you hard?"

She pushed her hips forward even more, pressing herself firmly and deliberately into his erection.

"I like the way you put it," she responded.

"Hey, wait a minute. I didn't mean it *that* way," he chuckled. "Really."

"I know you didn't. But I beat you to it. And I'm glad. I've wanted to go out with you for some time also. Bet you never expected this, huh?" Her eyes seemed to go back and forth slightly as she looked at him. It was a look that was clearly much more than sexual.

He smiled, completely unable to take his eyes away from hers. "No, I sure didn't. I've wanted you so badly but I wanted just as badly never to force myself on you. I couldn't accept that in myself. I'm really really glad you didn't handle that jellyfish. If it had stung you, I never would have forgiven myself for letting that happen."

Her eyes appeared to water slightly as they softened their stare into his.

"I wanted you too," she responded, her voice now feathery soft. "When you kept me from handling that jelly, I knew the real reason why. That's when I knew I was going to have you. I *would* have you. And I wasn't going to take no for an answer."

"And now you do."

"And now I do," she repeated, nodding her head.

Then she brought her face forward and this time she kissed him with a fiery passion that could only be described as pure, emotional hunger and desire as well as sexual. Her hands held his face more firmly, and he responded by holding her tightly against him. When she finally pulled her lips away, she still held his face in her hands. He then placed one of his hands on her cheek and felt a sudden overpowering rush of overpowering emotions that could only be described as love.

She placed her hand on top of his and looked at him. Both of them could feel the powerful emotional and sexual chemistry between them. This was a side of her that he could never have known until now. But it was a side that he really loved. And he knew that he truly loved her as well.

When she pulled herself away finally, she was reluctant to do so but knew they had to stop this before someone came down here. There would be plenty of other times for this.

"You're mine now, big guy," she said to him softly. "Got that?" Her face nearly touched his.

"Yea. I'm yours all the way."

"You belong to me, lock, stock, and barrel. But, no hanky panky on the job, starting now. We better get back up to the bridge to see what's going on."

"Ok, sweetheart. You're the boss," he replied then quickly ran his hands down from her back and playfully squeezed her buttocks.

"Always remember that," she said, then kissed him hard on the lips briefly, and pulled away.

"C'mon, grab your coffee, hon. We need to get some updates here." She wasted no time in reminding him that unofficially she was still his boss.

He followed her up the stairs to the bridge, not failing to notice or admire the shapeliness of her figure or the undulating movements of her buttock cheeks under those pants as she climbed.

He shook his head and told himself to knock it off. This was not the place for thinking these things. As if she could read his mind, she stopped and looked over her shoulder down at him.

"Enjoy your sightseeing, honey, cause it's now about to end," she said with a smile. "Temporarily, of course." He looked up to her face and knew she was playing with him.

He gently slapped her behind. "C'mon, hurry up and get up there. You're not taking long enough." She giggled as she reached the top and he quickly followed her up. From this point on, it would be all business as far as everyone else was concerned. He was hers now and that was all that mattered, except for the issues going on outside. It was time for an update on the situation.

****

Port Miami, August 10

As the swarm continued its move northward along the coast, a cargo plane landed at the general aviation field adjacent to Miami-Dade International airport. Within the hour, ten large strange-looking metal objects would be off-loaded onto a large flat-bed tractor trailer to be hauled to the Port of Miami docks where they would then be loaded onto the ship that would bring them to their ultimate destination.

It was a time-consuming process, not only because of the several transfers of the ten devices that were required, but they required special handling to prevent any damage to any of them. Each one was estimated to cost approximately two hundred thousand dollars. For most agencies which required their use, renting them was the most practical way to go and the most economical.

It was already figured into the transfer process that it would take about two days for the transfer to be completed and shipped to the affected areas. The Coast Guard was closely monitoring the operation and ensuring that all federal and US maritime laws were in compliance by the cargo company which owned the ship and that the ship itself was seaworthy, per US federal regulations. It was a lot of red tape but expedited to the maximum because of the urgency of the situation.

The trucks were waiting on the airport tarmac.

****

Off the coast, the *Argonaut* had received word that the robots had landed and that it would likely be about two days before they'd see them arrive to this area. There wasn't much the scientists on board could do but continue to monitor the swarm. It was now moving just beyond the northernmost stretch of Stuart and heading toward Port Saint Lucie. It was a cloudy day but then some cloudy days in Florida didn't last all day. Pokes of sun filtered through cloud openings as if the sun were attempting to take over the sky once again, which it usually did. It was a balmy eighty seven degrees but the sea breeze made it feel slightly less humid than it really was.

On the bridge, Captain Bill was checking the charts while Dexter manned the helm. The silence was frequently broken by the sounds of radio transmissions on the channel the ship always manned when out at sea. If any distress signals came in and they were the closest to the vessel sending it, they were required by international maritime law to respond, no matter what their current mission was. This applied to all ships out at sea.

During the ten years that Bill Jensen captained the ship, he'd responded twice to distress calls. One of them was for a small boat with an engine that failed and they needed a tow into shore. The other, a few years later, was for a fifty foot yacht which had somehow caught on fire and the one fire extinguisher they had on board wasn't enough to put out the fire. The *Argonaut,* being out on a short research mission, was the closest vessel and had responded to rescue the occupants. The Coast Guard had soon after arrived to see the boat just burning away. Despite their valiant attempts to save the boat with their hoses spraying sea water over the fire, it could not be saved. The fire had consumed too much of it and rather than tow in what was left of it, they let it sink per the owner's request. With the rescue completed, the *Argonaut* left for port to return them to shore, while the Coast Guard, after receiving all the names and required

information, completed their paperwork on the incident. That was the last case of their distress response, which was about five years ago.

Out on deck, Rebecca was alone looking out over the water and at the leading edge of the swarm, while James was down below, checking his portable equipment he'd brought with him. Near the boat, she saw something small in the water which looked familiar to her. Not knowing what it was, she took no chances and grabbed a long pole with a net on its end and stuck it in the water near the object. Carefully she maneuvered the pole as the boat slightly pitched and rolled until she had it in the net, then picked it up. When she brought the net closer to her, she suddenly realized what it was. An Irukandji. More confirmation that they were here, too, along with their bigger cousins.

Somehow it separated itself from the swarm, but that wasn't surprising. With that many jellies, a few were always bound to stray from the main body. It was as inevitable as someone getting stung if too close to it. After looking at it without taking it out of the net, she flung it back into the sea. She knew that both species of box jellies were in that swarm that ever so slowly but steadily made its way northward. She knew that two days wouldn't get here fast enough.

As a marine biologist, she was an advocate for all sea creatures. But when one of them became a constant serious threat to humans and there was no way they could be controlled safely without harming them, then the only option left was extermination of those which were a threat and had already killed humans and would continue to do so. In her mind, even extermination should have its limitations. Here was an example of that. When the robots started doing their job, it would be only this swarm that would be vanquished from the sea, not everywhere on the planet. She wasn't looking for extinction, but removal of a serious threat.

"What'cha doing? See anything interesting, other than our "friends" out there?" His voice startled her and made her jump. She hadn't heard him coming.

With her hand on her heart, she took just a moment to catch her breath.

"Don't scare me like that. Wow. Didn't hear you coming."

He stroked her hair that was hanging down. "Oh, sorry, darlin'. Didn't mean to do that. I try not to be a scary guy." She cuddled herself against him briefly, then pulled back.

"Found a 'kandji. There. Out there in that swarm." She turned around and he joined her at the railing as they looked at the moving mass.

"Yea," James replied. "Who knows how many are in there?"

"Too many," said Rebecca. "Too freaking many."

James bent down and rested his elbows on the railing. "Captain says we're close to Port Saint Lucie now. He also said some weather is on the way."

"Really? What kind of weather are we talking about here?"

"Thunderstorms. Winds picking up. Sometime this afternoon."

"Just what we need, right?"

"Tell me about it. Bill suggested we secure our loose equipment. Seas might pick up a bit as well as the winds. Maybe I'll head down and stow away my loose gear." He then stood up and Rebecca pressed herself against him. She was almost as tall as he was which brought her face very close to his.

"I think we *both* better stow our loose gear," she said. His arms went around and he put his hands on her back as he hugged her to him. Her hands were flat on his upper chest.

"You drive me crazy, you know that?" he said, with a smile that betrayed his love and affection for her.

Her face pointed slightly upward. "I know," she said, gluing her eyes to his. "Let's go, big guy, before we forget why we're here." She kissed him briefly but fully and then pulled away and headed toward the doors leading down below. He followed her, knowing what they had to do now while pushing aside what he really wanted to do. He decided that their time would come when this was all over. They were an item and he was hopeful to keep it that way. Out here, work always had to come first. Work now, play later.

CHAPTER 23

Aboard the Argonaut, August 10

The thunderstorm hadn't lasted very long, but it was severe enough. The winds had picked up quickly, which had an effect on the seas. The formerly calm sea was now inundated with whitecaps everywhere. On the horizon, as seen from the *Argonaut*, a tanker ship slowly made its way toward wherever it was heading, somewhere north. It was now late afternoon and close to mealtime, although eating would be a bit precarious because of the increased pitching and rolling of the ship.

Despite that, Loretta was down in the galley preparing the evening meal for the crew anyway. She'd learned over the years that when on a ship, you had to adjust your normal routine and go with the flow, so to speak. In other words, take off your land shoes and put on your seafaring boots because everything you do on board a ship at sea screams "sailor" and that includes cooking. Not too much oil on the griddle or it'll go off onto the deck when the ship rolls. Batten down anything loose or those things will go flying as well. A cafeteria kitchen is one thing, a ship's galley is another. If you can't distinguish the two, then you shouldn't be on board,   she always believed.

Rebecca and James were down in the mess hall, along with Josh and Sarah, the two deck hands moonlighting from the Institute. Normally they worked in the museum's exhibit areas, helping tourists make their way through the displays and answering questions about particular displays or sea creatures. They weren't experts in the field but rather young persons in their late teens getting a stronger feel for marine science as preparation for studying for that degree in college. Their acceptance for duties on board the *Argonaut* away from their normal duties made their jobs all the more important toward their life careers. Based on past deckhand schooling following their jobs at the Institute and on the ship, these two were likely heading toward careers in marine science, either as biologists, or some other field having to do with the oceans.

The smell of roast pork was delicious and permeated the entire room. No doubt it was drifting up to the bridge as well. Along with that, Loretta had prepared yams, a green bean casserole, fresh dinner rolls, and two apple pies for dessert that weren't homemade but were from a local bakery in their area of Miami that was known for its exceptional pies and cakes.

As the four ate at one of the two long dining tables, the bridge deckhand came down and joined in. He normally stayed on the bridge during the day to assist the captain or first mate but would help out on deck if needed.

As the four of them were enjoying their meals, a thump was heard in the aft portion of the ship. Then a few more thumps. They all looked up, wondering what that noise was.

"Huh! Any idea was that is?" James was the first to ask. He and Rebecca looked at each other and shrugged.

"I don't, but I'd sure like to find out," Rebecca replied.

The other three had no clue, but nevertheless showed concern.

The bridge deckhand named Toby stood up. "Let me go check with the cap on that. See if he heard it." He then walked quickly toward the ladder leading up to the bridge and was up there in a flash.

Within seconds he was back down. "We have a situation here. Need someone to go out on deck right away toward the stern and see what you see in the water. Something is hitting up against the props it looks like."

They all jumped up nearly at the same time and headed as fast as they could up the side ladders to the outside deck from the mess deck. Rebecca followed James toward one side of the stern, while Josh and Sarah headed toward the other side. All of them looked down at the water and discovered the horror.

Somehow, possibly from the storm, the swarm had engulfed the ship in the middle of it. The *Argonaut* was now literally surrounded by a sea of box jellyfish and Irukandji. Any attempt to move the ship could foul the jellies and tentacles in the propellers, which could, in turn, immobilize the ship and force it to stand dead in the water. For them, other than capsizing or sinking, this was a worst-case scenario. It was now up to the captain to decide on a best course of action in this situation.

One of the deck crew members ran up to the bridge to inform Captain Bill. Bill then consulted with Dexter. The crew out on deck heard the engines come to a full stop. Captain Bill then came down on the deck and went to the stern to look over into the water. After confirming his worst fears, he conferred with his crew and the scientists.

"Ok, guys and gals, I know what you're thinking. At least I think I do. So we have a situation here, which we've tried like hell to avoid. I don't know what happened because we were far enough away from this mass. Apparently the waves or currents must have forced them our way. Whatever the reason, or however it happened, we are unfortunately kinda stuck here. Seeing as there may be only a few tentacles fouling our prop, I'm going to try to very slowly get us further out to sea and away from this mess.

"I don't know if it'll work. I don't want to fully foul these props. If these were lines and not jellyfish tentacles, I'd send a diver down to cut them. Seeing as we can't do that, our only option is to go out slowly and see if we can at least minimize the fouling while getting away from these things. Any thoughts, ideas, questions?"

"How much of these things wrapped around the props would disable them?"

"Good question, James. I don't know. I'm going to play on the safe side and say not too much. Maybe this old gal is tougher than we think but I don't want to test that. I'm only doing this to get us out of here."

"Bill, go for it. Do what you have to. Maybe we can try to sweep some of them away from the props with a couple of poles as we're going."

Captain Bill made it clear that he didn't like that idea. "Too dangerous, Becky. If the pole gets caught in the prop, that could permanently damage it. Nice thought but no."

No one else had any questions. "Ok, then, let's do it." With that, Bill went back up to the bridge and took over the helm, telling Dexter to turn on the sonar and man it while hemaneuvered the ship.

It was a risk he had to take and they all knew it. Better to be stuck out of the swarm than in it. Once they were completely out of it and at a safe distance, then they'd worry about how to remove the wrapped tentacles. Obviously they themselves couldn't do it.

Ever so slowly the ship made its way out of the swarm, turning at a ninety degree angle away from it and out to sea. For a while it was touch and go because the bridge crew could hear the props struggling to turn with wrapped tentacles around it while preventing or minimizing the chance of others from becoming entangled as well.

Finally they made it. But Captain Bill knew they weren't out of the woods yet. Even though it may be only a partial fouling rather than a full one, it still posed a risk to the engines. He knew they could not run at normal speed now. The ship could run, but at a lower speed until they got someone with a full diving suit, face covering, and mask to remove the tentacles by hand and knife. Compared to what *could* have happened, he considered themselves fortunate.

Dexter radioed in their predicament to the institute, assuring them they could make it back on their own--just at a slower rate. Ship maintenance would have to arrange for a de-fouling when the ship was in port.

****

Aboard the Argonaut, August 11

That morning, after having one of Loretta's fine breakfasts of sausage omelets, bacon, home fries and toast, Rebecca brought up her cup of coffee to the outside deck. James had overslept and after being woken, said he'd meet her either on the mess deck or outside. She wanted to wait for him in the dining area but was too anxious to see how things were outside. It'd been a while since she had checked in with Marge, but decided she would do that when she got back inside.

"Good morning, Sarah," Rebecca said. "Where's Josh?"

"He should be up shortly. Just cleaning up. Have breakfast already?"

"Yep. Was really good this morning. You?" She started looking out and was surprised by what she saw.

"Yea, It was good alright, thanks to Loretta. Hey, d'ya see that?" she pointed out toward the shoreline.

"Hmm, yea, looks like they moved northward faster now than I thought. They're pretty close to Port Saint Lucie now."

"'I'd say so."

Rebecca went to the port side looking back. The swarm was as long as her eyes could take her. *Damn, I wish those things would get here!* For what this area needed, those robots would be a Godsend. Maybe because the day was clearer or the air clearer-she wasn't sure-that she saw a boat, or ship, in the far distance. It wasn't on the horizon but looked closer to shore. She wondered if it could be the Coast Guard ship carrying Marge. The *Jackson.*

"Scuse me, Sarah. Have to go up to the bridge. Keep an eye on these things for me, will ya?"

"Sure thing, Beck."

On the bridge, Dexter was on the radio and Captain Bill was on the phone. What the hell was going on now? It seemed it had been only one thing after another out here. What else could it be but trouble somewhere with both men on the comms?

She stuck around as she listened to the conversations. Then James came up from the mess deck. Apparently he had eaten and was on his way to the outside but didn't see Rebecca there. His intuition that she was on the bridge was correct. She told him quietly that she just got there and suspected something was going on but she didn't know what yet. He nodded and looked at the men still talking on the comms equipment. His curiosity rose just as quickly as Rebecca's.

She listened to Bill talking on the ship's bridge phone.

"No, we are unable to respond. We are impaired due to a fouling. I'm really sorry. I wish we could help. Do you need us to patch you to the Coast Guard or can you get through ok?"

He nodded for a few seconds. "Ok, I'll let you go. Good luck to you....Thank you." Then he hung up.

"Well, so much for being able to answer a distress. Guess what? Some small boat up the ways there also got themselves fouled up in this damn swarm. How do ya like them apples? Swarm two, vessels zero."

"Bill did you tell them....?"

"Yea, Becky. I did tell them about the jellyfish and not to try to un-foul themselves or they'll permanently regret it. They're calling the Coast Guard now."

Frustrated, they weren't sure what they could possibly do now. In fact, they were basically now useless to the whole operation. There was no way Captain Bill would go any farther than where they were now. Home base back in Miami emphasized that they should return as soon as they could.

The *Jackson* was notified of this and was now responsible for monitoring the entire swarm, if that was possible at all. That is, until their base notified them that a small boat would be dispatched from the closest small boat station to Port Saint Lucie to monitor the leading edge. In no way was the *Argonaut* to proceed any further north.

In essence, their mission was virtually over.

"Well, this is a fine ending. I would have liked to see the work of those robots. When are they supposed to get here, tomorrow?" asked James.

"Tomorrow morning. Maybe we can convince Captain Bill to stick around, at least until they start doing their work."

Meanwhile, up on the bridge, Captain Bill had reported to the Coast Guard the location of the leading edge. That led to an immediate warning being issued to Port Saint Lucie and Fort Pierce. An immediate watch for Vero Beach was issued followed by jellyfish watches extending all the way up to Melbourne.

While James went back to his quarters to receive some research reading material, Rebecca went up to the bridge. She wanted to contact Marge and get an update on their status with the trailing edge as well as the arrival time of the robots.

Before she could make the call, the first mate told her some disturbing news. He heard over the ship's radio that someone in Port Saint Lucie apparently hadn't heard about the warnings for the town's beaches regarding the oncoming swarm. A man had been diving in the water for, who knows what. When he came up, something had stung him but he couldn't see what it was. The pain hit him immediately like a sledgehammer. Fortunately, he had a friend with him who pulled him into the boat and brought him back to shore. After calling for help, the man was brought to the hospital. No word on his condition.

"Oh, hell. That could be an Irukandji that got him. They're pretty hard to see in the water. He might make it since he got help pretty quickly. So that confirms that they're there now and what's next? Fort Pierce?"

"That's the next major town, but a number of miles north," replied Dexter. "If these robot doo-hickies arrive tomorrow, think maybe these stingers will be in Vero Beach?"

Rebecca shook her head with uncertainty. "Oh, God, Dexter I hope not. If they make it that far from now until tomorrow morning, that means they're likely swimming with an increased current speeding them along. The longer it takes for these robots to arrive, the further this mass will travel. I need to call Marge, see if she's heard anything yet about arrival time."

Rebecca grabbed the ship's phone and called the Coast Guard ship. Marge was not on the bridge. She waited while they called her up there to take the call. Within a couple of minutes, she heard the loud sounds of someone grabbing the phone receiver.

"Hi Becky. Your timing is right on, girl. I was just about to come up here and call you."

"Great minds think alike, Marge. What's up down there and what's the latest?"

"Well, for one thing the trailing edge is just north of Jupiter. Other than that, no other reports of people being stung. So that's good news. Apparently, the beaches are completely shut down for now around here. A couple of beach security people, aka lifeguards when the beaches are open, spotted a couple of jellies washed up on the beach in Jupiter. A few others were spotted on other, smaller beaches also. For that reason, they're keeping everyone off the beaches themselves. Anyone caught can be arrested by the cops. How's that for news, eh?"

"That was smart closing the beaches. Those things can still pack a deadly punch even if beached. Any word on the robots?"

"Yea, as a matter of fact. The Coasties here got word of a pushed up arrival time for the jelly whackers."

Rebecca's jaw dropped. "Excuse me? The jelly whackers?" She laughed at the pseudonym.

"Like that, huh? Sounds better than Robotic Jellyfish Sweepers. Anyway, TOA will be approximately seven am."

Rebecca felt a wave of near ecstasy sweep over her. "Wow, that's great Marge. Sounds like they're really pushing to get them here. That's what we need."

"Amen to that."

"So how they going to do that?"

"Well from what I was told by the young, good-looking captain here--don't mind me, I like to observe who I communicate with, haha--they're going to drop two of them near the trailing edge. Then they'll drop another four a little further north, then the last four just ahead of the leading edge, where they'll plow right into them and start whacking the hell out of them."

"I'm looking forward to seeing them in action. I've heard about them but never even saw one. This should be pretty interesting."

"I'll say. They work pretty fast."

"How long you think it'll take for them to, as you call it, whack them?"

"*That,* I don't know. Nothing was said about how long. But from what they said about their speed of action, I would think maybe as fast as a couple of hours with ten of them working on it. Hey, can you imagine being in the line of fire as they're spewing all these thousands of pieces of dead jellyfish into the air? All that stuff all over you?"

"Eeeuuu...that's disgusting." Rebecca chortled. "Marge, is that Coastie food getting to you--or that good looking captain?"

"Oh, I...would...say the latter, now that you're asking. But don't worry. I intend to remain as professional as I always am. Nice to fantasize now and then but don't let it take you over. Anyhow, that's the story. When they arrive here, I'll give you a call."

When they said their goodbyes, Rebecca knew that the situation would be on the downswing once the robots arrived. She really couldn't wait. This would be something that she might see only once in her lifetime and she didn't want to miss it. Turning around, she headed back down below to give James the good news after being assured by the captain that he would stick around for the event. He wanted to see it for himself as well.

CHAPTER 24

Aboard the Argonaut, August 11

The following morning turned out to be a partly cloudy but breezy one when the ship carrying valuable cargo set sail for the waters off of Jupiter. It had been dark when the robots were transferred from the truck to the ship. At four thirty in the morning, a lot of lights were required for the undertaking. By five thirty, the tenth and last one was loaded. They were odd-looking mechanical creatures that stood on two-what looked like-metal pontoons. Connected to these pontoons were legs that held a horizontal metal table-like structure onto which a pole topped by a flat disk was welded on.

The evening before down below, James had done some research on his computer regarding these devices. They operated more simply than he imagined and he was eager to share this information with his colleague and new-found love. When they got together the evening before, he had explained to her how they worked.

"Basically, they operate very much like a lawn mower," he started to tell her. "Before they're put into the water, nets are connected to their undersides. There are two propellers on the back of the devices which are activated when jellyfish enter the net. As the propellers turn, they suck up the jellyfish closer to them where they are then chewed up, sliced and diced, and spit out, much like a lawnmower does with cut grass. First you see jellies, then you see none. Up to eight hundred pounds of jellyfish per hour per robot. *That* is a lot of jellies."

"Wow. You're not kidding. No wonder they cost so much. But what's amazing is that their operation and mechanics seem to be so simple. Run the propellers which can suck anything into them, just like on a boat, and you get minced whatever. Hell, we could do that with our boat."

"Not exactly, sweetheart. Remember about the ropelike tentacles. Fouling on a boat or ship. No such issues with these robots. Even tentacles are chopped up."

James was right. If it weren't for the tentacles, any boat or ship could have just plowed right through them. Which brought it back to the fact that it was only the tentacles that caused all the problems with these creatures, not the bell. The bell was their powerhouse, while the tentacles were the defensive and offensive weapons. For them, it was only about survival and nothing else.

As they drank their coffee in the dining area, Julie was walking through and Rebecca informed her that they should all be out on deck by seven in the morning.

"Oh great. Can't wait to see those things. I'll be mighty glad when they get rid of them and this whole mess is all over with. Then we can get back to our normal business." She went to grab a soda out of the refrigerator. "What are these things called, Robot Jellyfish Killers?"

James and Rebecca chuckled. "You almost got it. They're called Robotic Jellyfish Sweepers. They act like a lawnmower in the water. Only the grass is jellyfish."

"That's really cool, ya know? Who would think of such an ingenious device?" Julie responded.

'The South Koreans, not us," Rebecca answered.

It was now about ten thirty in the evening. Lucky for them they had decaf coffee available. James yawned and Rebecca started feeling the pangs of sleepiness also. It had been a long day.

"Well, you two, I'll see you in the morning. Think I'll read in the sack for a while, then call it a night. Goodnight."

"Night, Julie. See you in the morning." They watched her disappear down to the sleeping quarters area of the ship.

"Guess I'll turn in too. I'm getting pretty tired myself." Rebecca got up and James did like-wise.

"Yea, me too. C'mon. I'll walk you down there," James responded. Together they headed down below one level.

After somewhat of a mutually prolonged goodnight kiss, they slowly parted ways and entered their respective quarters, after agreeing on a six am wakeup time. They wanted to be up and out there when the sweepers arrived. The next morning would arrive very quickly.

****

Off the coast north of Jupiter, the USCGC Jackson, August 12, 0600 hours

A call had come into the radio room from Port Miami. The message was then patched up to the bridge and Captain Holloway. The cargo ship *Orion* was underway to their location. ETA was given to be 0700 hours, which was seven am as planned for.

The captain then picked up the microphone and pressed the button for his overall broadcast to the ship's crew. After announcing the message, he started giving orders. His plan was to move further out to sea and place his ship in a monitoring position to give the *Orion* plenty of room to maneuver into its position for off-loading the robots in his area. There would be two of them. Once off-loaded into the swarm, the ship would move further north while the robots started doing their work.

"Quartermaster, plot us a position for one mile from this location further out to sea. Helm, go to bearing one four five at ten knots. Steady as she goes." The helm repeated the captain's orders back to him as required by protocol.

Slowly the ship started turning to face away from the coast. As it started heading out, the quartermaster had completed his plotting.

"Captain, at ten knots, we will reach our one mile position from here in eight minutes."

"Aye, very good. Helm, on my orders decrease speed to three knots and turn about to bearing two four five. This in eight minutes."

"Aye aye, Captain. On your orders, sir."

Eight minutes later, they were turning about and slowing their speed. From this position they would await the arrival of the *Orion*, expected now in less than an hour. The captain was cutting it close time-wise. Although he usually was prepared at least three hours in advance, their move to a different location was minimal and didn't take much time. While waiting in position, breakfast was being served in the mess hall.

The captain announced his temporary departure from the bridge, and that the XO, or the executive office had the con until he returned. Now it was a matter of waiting and watching.

With eager anticipation, the captain and crew waited for the arrival of the machines that would get rid of the swarm that was a threat to the entire east coast of Florida. They had surmised, without knowing actual facts, of the swarm's repercussions on the state's economy, especially with tourism on the east coast. For many tourists who went to the east coast at this time, it was just as easy for them to go to the Gulf coast where the waters were untouched by the box jellies. In fact, tourism had dropped significantly on the east coast since the attacks began some two weeks ago.

The news of the invasion had spread not only nationally but internationally as well. Talk shows had scientific guests on to debate or discuss issues regarding the swarm and its seemingly out-of-place "members." But the news also mentioned the robot solution to the problem. It was rare that anything affecting the public could be kept secret nowadays, and this was big news.

As seven am arrived, lookouts on the bridge spotted a cargo ship approaching their area. The captain announced to the crew of the arrival. There was nothing they would actively do, unless requested by the cargo ship's captain. Basically they were there to just monitor the event and keep all unauthorized boats out of the area. Search and rescue would be activated if necessary, as part of their overall duties.

It would be at least another hour before they dropped the two robots into the water. When they did, Captain Holloway and his crew watched with fascination, and for the first time these devices started their actual destructive operations.

As the ship moved slowly further north to their next drop off point, the crew and Marge, who was outside on the aft deck, watched the things move around by themselves. Although they were quieter than they had thought they would be, noises started punctuating the silence with slicing and chopping type sounds. It was clear to them that the robots were working and amazingly seemed to follow the current that carried the jellies along. Moving slowly northward, the slicing and chopping noises became nearly constant as hundreds and then thousands of the creatures were sucked up, ground, and spit out, tentacles and all.

Marge went up to the bridge and asked to use the phone to call the *Argonaut*. She got a hold of Rebecca fairly quickly and told her the ship was on its way to her location.

"Oh, that's great, Marge. How are the things working so far?"

"I tell you Becky, it's unbelievable. They're working fantastically. Whoever dreamed this up is a genius. It's been only about ten or fifteen minutes now and these two robots have already put a serious dent into the trailing edge. Can't really see the swarm from where we are. But we know they're killing the things by the sounds they make. When the sounds diminish, they apparently have cleared that spot and are carried with their little propellers to follow more of the swarm."

When the next four were dropped off in the middle of the swarm, the sounds were heard immediately and louder. Later the final four were dropped off into the water near the location of the *Argonaut*, where they also started working immediately.

After Rebecca hung up the phone, she got James and Julie and ran out on deck to watch the arrival of the ship, the drop-off of the four robots, and saw them go to work immediately on hitting the water. Even the captain came out on the bridge wing deck to watch the machines do their thing.

The *Orion* positioned itself about half a mile north of the northernmost part of the swarm. The robots further south would head northward in its direction and toward the other robots which would be heading southward toward them. When all was said and done and the entire swarm had been virtually destroyed, the ship would pick up the robots once it was clear they were done, and return them back to Port Miami where they would be cleaned and eventually returned back to the company.

About two hours later, all of the robots grouped together, silent as if awaiting further orders from somewhere. There were ship to ship communications between the *Argonaut* and the *Orion* advising the *Argonaut* that they would now maneuver into position for retrieving the machines. Captain Bill made sure his ship was well away and clear of the final operation.

****

Off the coast of Jupiter, the USCGC Jackson, 0845 hours

Marge had asked the captain, now that the robots had cleared the area, if they could slowly visually inspect that area.

"I think, Mrs. Holbrook, that that's a good idea. We need to be sure."

"That's *Ms.* Holbrook, captain," she replied with a smile. "And thank you for doing this. I think it would be a benefit to *all* of us that this whole operation was a success. I think I'll go out on deck and check it out."

As Marge went out on deck, the captain smiled and shrugged his shoulders. She was a nice lady and seemed to be competent enough as a marine scientist. He'd be glad to return to normal ship's operations when this was over, which would be soon enough.

"Helm, set course for two four five, increase speed to seven knots."

The helmsman repeated the orders back and adjusted the helm and engines.

****

The Argonaut, 0925 hours

The deck crew and the two scientists and their assistant watched as the *Argonaut* was checking out their area, as the *Jackson* did southward. From all observations made, the area was now free and clear of the jellies. The operation had been quick and efficient. It actually went much faster than they had thought.

In the distance, the *Orion* was heading southward further out to see heading back to Miami.

Slowly the *Argonaut* made its way southward, with those on deck viewing the approximate path that the swarm had taken, not seeing anything under the surface. Everyone was overjoyed. The crisis was over. The operation had been a complete success.

In view of others, Rebecca and James maintained their professional appearance out on deck while standing closely next to each other.

"What do you think, Jim?" she asked him. "Think they'll be back?"

He stared out over the water. "Who knows, Beck? If they did it once, they can do it again."

"Guess I'll go down and get something to drink. Want a coffee or soda?"

"Naw. Don't think so. I've still got ideas going around in my head about what triggered this whole thing. Think I'll stay out here for a while. Coming back out?"

"Yep. Be right back."

As she started heading back down to the mess deck, he called out to her.

"Hey, Beck, you still want that dinner when we get back?"

She looked over her shoulder at him. "Does a bear live in the woods?" He smiled as she disappeared down the ladder to the level below.

EPILOGUE

Miami Marine Institute, August 14

After a debriefing with Dan in his office, Rebecca was glad to be back to her normal duties. He had offered her to take more time off. But because she was saving up for her two week vacation to go visit her sister in Colorado in just over a month's time from now, she decided only one day would do, just to get her bearings back and acclimate herself once again to the usual routine. Being at sea for a week really tired her and she used that day to rest. Today, she was ready for the grind once again.

Although James had left to return back to the USF, he'd be back every chance he got. Rebecca hated to see him go, but they had each other's phone number. She also hated long distance romances. There was no doubt in her mind that she more than just liked him, and it was much more than infatuation. She believed he felt the same. When she asked if he would be willing to transfer his duties down here and work for the Institute, his answer confirmed her belief. He agreed to the suggestion, stating he wanted to be closer to her also. So it was now in the works and she didn't feel as bad that he had to go back now. She had spoken to Dan about it, emphasizing that they could certainly use a jellyfish expert here, which would make him an invaluable asset to them. He agreed and promised he would speak to the powers that be to consider bringing him on board. So now there was the future to look forward to.

Tony had returned to work fully recovered. Rebecca had fully briefed him about her mission and what was accomplished. He, in turn, had informed her that the news media went crazy over the success of the mission and all that it had accomplished. People were starting to trickle back to the east coast towns and beaches and the economy was starting to rise back to its normal levels again.

Florida's governor had publicly praised the efforts of all those involved in the successful operation, with special thanks to Howard Ringston who came up with the idea, his company Marine Bioengineering Solutions, the US Coast Guard, and last but not least, the Miami Marine Institute. All had contributed toward ending the crisis and preventing further loss of human lives.

Everyone was now happy things had gone back to--even with all things considered--normal again.

Off the coast of Stuart, Florida--the seabed floor

New lives were in the works, now that the sperm had fertilized the eggs. There were hundreds of thousands, or perhaps millions of them, which settled down onto the seafloor and attached themselves with a firm grip to solid surfaces for their continued development. For them, it was a never-ending cycle. The larval planulae would eventually become polyps. The fact that they were not in their habitat of origin was of no concern to them.

They would grow and develop, remaining forever unchecked. Their development would depend on the right circumstances. Once those circumstances arrived, the process would begin again, as it had done for millions of years.

Small fish would continue to swim by them in complete indifference. There was nothing down there that paid much attention to them. They were food to nothing and no creatures there really knew what they were. But the day would come when they would. And then...

THE END

CHECK OUT OTHER GREAT
DEEP SEA THRILLERS

PREHISTORIC BEASTS AND WHERE TO FIGHT THEM
by Hugo Navikov

IN THE DEPTHS, SOMETHING WAITS ...

Acclaimed film director Jake Bentneus pilots a custom submersible to the bottom of Challenger Deep in the Pacific, the deepest point of any ocean of Earth. But something lurks at the hot hydrothermal vents, a creature—a dinosaur—too big to exist.

Gigadon.

It not only exists, but it follows him, hungrily, back to the surface. Later, a barely living Bentneus offers a $1 billion prize to anyone who can find and kill the monster. His best bet is renowned ichthyopaleontologist Sean Muir, who had predicted adapted dinosaurs lived at the bottom of the ocean.

MEGALODON: APEX PREDATOR
by S.J. Larsson

English adventurer Sir Jeffery Mallory charters a ship for a top secret expedition to Antarctica. What starts out as a search and capture mission soon turns into a terrifying fight for survival as the crew come face to face with the fiercest ocean predator to have ever existed- Carcharodon Megalodon. Alone and with no hope of rescue the crew will need all their resources if they are to survive not only a 60 foot shark but also the harsh Antarctic conditions. Megalodon: Apex Predator is a deep-sea adventure filled with action, twists and savage prehistoric sharks.

CHECK OUT OTHER GREAT
DEEP SEA THRILLERS

HELL'S TEETH
by Paul Mannering

In the cold South Pacific waters off the coast of New Zealand, a team of divers and scientists are preparing for three days in a specially designed habitat 1300 feet below the surface.

In this alien and savage world, the mysterious great white sharks gather to hunt and to breed.

When the dive team's only link to the surface is destroyed, they find themselves in a desperate battle for survival. With the air running out, and no hope of rescue, they must use their wits to survive against sharks, each other, and a terrifying nightmare of legend.

MONSTERS IN OUR WAKE
by J.H. Moncrieff

In the idyllic waters of the South Pacific lurks a dangerous and insatiable predator; a monster whose bloodlust and greed threatens the very survival of our planet...the oil industry. Thousands of miles from the nearest human settlement, deep on the ocean floor, ancient creatures have lived peacefully for millennia. But when an oil drill bursts through their lair, Nøkken attacks, damaging the drilling ship's engine and trapping the desperate crew. The longer the humans remain in Nøkken's territory, struggling to repair their ailing ship, the more confrontations occur between the two species. When the death toll rises, the crew turns on each other, and marine geologist Flora Duchovney realizes the scariest monsters aren't below the surface.

SEVEREDPRESS

f facebook.com/severedpress
twitter.com/severedpress

CHECK OUT OTHER GREAT
DEEP SEA THRILLERS

LOCH NESS REVENGE
by Hunter Shea

Deep in the murky waters of Loch Ness, the creature known as Nessie has returned. Twins Natalie and Austin McQueen watched in horror as their parents were devoured by the world's most infamous lake monster. Two decades later, it's their turn to hunt the legend. But what lurks in the Loch is not what they expected. Nessie is devouring everything in and around the Loch, and it's not alone. Hell has come to the Scottish Highlands. In a fierce battle between man and monster, the world may never be the same. Praise for THEY RISE : "Outrageous, balls to the wall...made me yearn for 3D glasses and a tub of popcorn, extra butter!" – The Eyes of Madness "A fast-paced, gore-heavy splatter fest of sharksploitation." The Werd "A rocket paced horror story. I enjoyed the hell out of this book." Shotgun Logic Reviews

TERROR FROM THE DEEP
by Alex Laybourne

When deep sea seismic activity cracks open a world hidden for millions of years, terrifying leviathans of the deep are unleashed to rampage off the coast of Mexico. Trapped on an island resort, MMA fighter Troy Deane leads a small group of survivors in the fight of their lives against pre-historic beasts long thought extinct. The terror from the deep has awoken, and it will take everything they have to conquer it.

www.ingramcontent.com/pod-product-compliance
Lightning Source LLC
Chambersburg PA
CBHW031955170626
46807CB00006B/2502